"I'll have you ~~know,~~ ~~that~~ ~~I~~ ~~am~~ ~~an~~ extremely powerful and terrifying individual. My word
is law, and my wrath is dreadful to behold."

"Oh, yes! I daresay it is," Clarissa agreed calmly, her
expression suspiciously demure.

Trevor Whitlatch's lips twitched. "Beware! One day
you will incur my displeasure. On that day, you will
quickly learn to fear me."

"Pooh! You are all bark and no bite."

Whitlatch took her shoulders and pulled her firmly
round to face him. "If a dog barks loudly enough, he
often does not need to bite. But the teeth are still there,
Clarissa."

"Ah. I see. Your point is well taken, sir; you are a
tyrant after all."

Her face was turned up to his, rosy and laughing. His
senses were teased with a whiff of lemon verbena sachet. "And you, Clarissa, are a darling," he exclaimed,
leaning in. . . .

Fair Game

Diane Farr

A SIGNET BOOK

SIGNET
Published by New American Library, a division of
Penguin Putnam Inc., 375 Hudson Street,
New York, New York 10014, U.S.A.
Penguin Books Ltd, 27 Wrights Lane,
London W8 5TZ, England
Penguin Books Australia Ltd, Ringwood,
Victoria, Australia
Penguin Books Canada Ltd, 10 Alcorn Avenue,
Toronto, Ontario, Canada M4V 3B2
Penguin Books, (N.Z.) Ltd, 182–190 Wairau Road,
Auckland 10, New Zealand

Penguin Books Ltd, Registered Offices:
Harmondsworth, Middlesex, England

First published by Signet, an imprint of New American Library
a division of Penguin Putnam Inc.

First Printing, October 1999
10 9 8 7 6 5 4 3 2 1

To my hero,
William Earl Golling,
who touched my life and turned it to gold

Chapter 1

"**B**ut there is nothing to explain," said Trevor Whitlatch. "It is quite simple, madam. You will either compensate me for the goods you stole eleven years ago, or you will suffer the consequences."

A tense silence ensued, broken only by the soft ticking of an ormolu clock on La Gianetta's elegant mantelpiece. Mr. Whitlatch had not raised his voice, and his smile had not wavered. Nevertheless, Gianetta's admirably strong instinct for self-preservation warned her that her visitor was dangerous.

With an effort, she hid her alarm behind a smile as smooth as Mr. Whitlatch's. Her smile had bewitched many men over the years. She hoped it retained enough charm to see her through one more crisis.

On the other hand, Mr. Whitlatch was probably young enough to be her son. Her power to bewitch men in their prime had faded of late. Bah! If the smile failed, she would try tears. Surely one weapon or the other would melt the ice glittering in Mr. Whitlatch's gaze.

She swept her graceful hands in a dramatic, self-deprecating gesture, and addressed Mr. Whitlatch in the throbbing tones that had once held audiences spellbound. "Ah, *m'sieur*, you must understand! The world was a different place in 1791, was it not? I was so bewildered, so frightened—all of France in such turmoil! I was leaving my home, all my possessions behind. My life was in ruins. I hardly knew what I did. I never meant to take the rubies off your ship, *m'sieur*; it was a mistake."

"Yes, it was," he agreed. "A serious mistake." Mr. Whitlatch's swarthiness gave his grin the swift, white flash of a tiger's snarl.

He leaned back in the fragile, spindle-legged chair, jammed

his hands in his pockets, and stretched his long, booted legs across her Aubusson carpet. The effect of this rudeness was that La Gianetta's elegant receiving room seemed suddenly small and stuffy. Trevor Whitlatch was a large man. He inhabited an impressive physique, and several years at sea and abroad had darkened his already harsh features. This, together with the careless way he shrugged into his clothes, gave him an out-of-doors air that dwarfed most interiors. Gianetta fervently hoped her delicate furniture would hold him. She could ill afford to replace it. Mr. Whitlatch's unexpected demand could not have come at a more unfortunate time.

She schooled her features into a look of gentle inquiry. "May I ask what makes the collection of this old debt suddenly a matter of importance? I thought, naturally, that you forgave my little misstep. A small thing to miss, among the riches you bore on that ship alone—and you with so many more ships, so many more voyages! I daresay you would have given me the rubies, had I asked for them. Such a generous young man you were! And I so destitute! I believed if you noticed the loss at all, you considered it a charity, *m'sieur*."

His smile turned sardonic. "I prefer to choose my charities, madam, not have them forced upon me by theft."

"Then why did you not demand the jewels' return immediately? I have heard nothing from you for eleven years. Can you blame me for thinking you considered the rubies a gift?"

"Yes, I can blame you," he said affably. "I do blame you. I thought I made that clear."

"Ah, yes, today! But then? Then, *m'sieur*? I would have returned them to you at once, I swear!" La Gianetta made play with a fine pair of eyes.

Mr. Whitlatch was unmoved. "Return them to me now," he offered.

She spread her hands helplessly. "Now? I do not keep them in my house, *m'sieur*."

"No, you don't," he agreed blandly. "Because you sold the rubies immediately upon your arrival in England."

Gianetta's eyes flashed defiance. "*Alors!* Do you mock me? Yes, I sold them. Why fly from death in France, only to starve in England?"

Mr. Whitlatch's lip curled. "You could have sold in London what you had sold for years in Paris. Englishmen pay just as handsomely as Frenchmen for it. I suppose you have learned that by now."

She arched one delicately drawn eyebrow. Her voice dripped honey. "*M'sieur* flatters me! But if you know I do not have the rubies, why are you here? Is it possible you have suffered some reversal, sir, that makes it necessary for you to recover funds—even from such as I?"

Mr. Whitlatch uttered a short bark of laughter. "Unlikely!" he remarked. "No, ma'am, I am here only because your conduct has brought you to my notice once again. Can you guess how?"

She shook her head, but regarded him warily from beneath her lashes.

"No? I will tell you." But a small silence fell as Mr. Whitlatch pressed the tips of his long fingers together and frowned, unseeing, at the carpet. When he finally began speaking, his gaze returned to La Gianetta's face and watched her keenly.

"When you repaid my kindness with theft eleven years ago, I let it go. Your conduct was disgusting, but I did not propose to make myself a laughingstock by prosecuting you. You had played me for a fool. You knew it, and I knew it. I saw no need for the world to know it. So I swallowed my pride and chalked the episode up to experience. You had crossed me, but only once." His voice became silky, and Gianetta shivered. "No one, male or female, crosses Trevor Whitlatch twice."

"Twice? But I have done nothing else to you!"

"No, not to me." His eyes lit with sardonic amusement. "Never to me, in point of fact. Even the rubies were not stolen from me. Everything on that ship belonged to my uncle. In those days, I acted merely as his agent, bringing his goods safely from India to England."

She pounced on this digression. "If that is so, you do wrong to blame me. The fault is entirely your own! Your impulse to save my life was admirable, but you should not have followed it." Her hands swept dramatically to her temples. "You should have left me in Marseilles, to die at the hands of that mob!"

"I was extremely young, and . . . er . . . impressionable." Mr. Whitlatch's teeth flashed in another swift grin. "You were really very lovely."

She inclined her head stiffly, reluctantly acknowledging the compliment. His eyes twinkled. "You are still easy on the eyes, Gianetta. But in 1791 you were Beauty itself, to a boy who had been at sea entirely too long. And to have so famous a creature as La Gianetta begging for my help—to have stumbled upon Beauty in Distress, and have the means of rescuing her! Who could resist? Not I! That is why I promptly threw caution to the winds, concealed you on my uncle's ship, and brought you safely out of France to England with all the speed I could muster."

"Your conduct was noble, *m'sieur*. Noble! I have ever said so. I was deeply grateful to you."

Mr. Whitlatch's gaze hardened. "So grateful, in fact, that you stole a chest of jewels from your benefactor."

"But, no—a small box!" she demurred, clasping one white hand to her bosom in a gesture eloquent of pained protest.

"A small box of extremely valuable stones. You knew the theft would go undetected until the inventory sheets were checked, by which time you had disappeared. I was young, with a young man's vanity; you gambled that I would rather make up the difference out of my own pocket than publish to the world how La Gianetta had used me. It was a cynical gamble on your part, madam, but you won it. You then sold the stones and used the money to establish yourself here. You were quite brazen about it. You made no attempt to hide your identity."

La Gianetta's expressive eyes were raised to his face. "My identity is my fortune, Mr. Whitlatch."

"I daresay," he said dryly. "And now that famous name of yours is lending its cachet to another enterprise that seems quite profitable. You run an elegant, and very popular, gaming hell."

A demure smile curved her lips. "I hold a few private card parties, *m'sieur*."

"Is that the euphemism you prefer? Very well. Your private card parties are extremely well attended, are they not? I understand the attraction of your room is enhanced by the presence of certain young women. One hears that these women are every bit as alluring as they are . . . accommodating."

La Gianetta waved a dismissive hand. "People will say anything," she cooed. "Naturally I employ certain girls to run the faro table, the roulette wheel—"

Mr. Whitlatch sat upright, feigning surprise. "Faro and roulette? At a private card party?"

She stiffened, then eyed him with acute dislike. "As you say, *m'sieur*. I misspoke."

"Hm. Well, let that pass. At any rate, we now come to the point where your activities crossed me a second time."

"Crossed you! How?"

Mr. Whitlatch leaned forward menacingly. "You have in your employ a certain female who, I have reason to believe, makes it her business to prey upon gullible young men."

As this description could be applied to any of the young women presently in her employ, La Gianetta lifted an eyebrow but remained silent.

"This creature has done irreparable harm to a young friend of mine. My friend, in telling me his tale, extracted a promise from me. I promised that I would take no vengeance upon the girl. My hands are tied, then, as far as punishing the hussy who is the principal actor in this little drama. However, madam, I have no doubt that the notorious La Gianetta, though not appearing on the stage, directed the play."

La Gianetta, now thoroughly alarmed, hid behind a screen of indignation. "I do not know what you mean. What has happened? How am I to blame? Ah, *dieu!* I do not understand any of it!"

"Again I say, the matter is simple. I promised my friend that I would not approach your hireling. I therefore approach you." He leaned back in the fragile chair, regarding her keenly. "Your recent crime against my friend I am not at liberty to avenge. I therefore will avenge your past crime against myself—which I otherwise might never have done. Ironic, is it not? But there it is. 'The mills of God grind slowly, yet they grind exceeding small.' You may not understand the literary allusion, but I am sure you understand the rest of it well enough."

La Gianetta nervously fingered the pearls clasped around her throat. For a moment she wondered if she could offer them to Mr. Whitlatch in lieu of the rubies. How long would it be before he discovered the pearls were paste? Not long, she decided. Mr. Whitlatch was no fool.

"What do you want?" she whispered. "You are a businessman, Mr. Whitlatch. There is no profit to you in sending me to debtor's prison. What can I offer you to make amends?"

"Nothing less than the value of the rubies, as listed on my uncle's inventory sheet in 1791. And be grateful I do not charge you interest."

"What is the sum?"

He named it. La Gianetta paled beneath her rouge. She had
sold the gems for a fraction of their value, and still they had
brought her enough to establish herself in style. She had no
hope of paying him back the amount she had originally re-
received for the jewels, let alone their actual worth. Ruin stared
her in the face.

"I cannot possibly raise such a sum today. You must give me
time," she said hoarsely.

"But you will pay it?"

"Yes, yes, of course I will pay it!"

Mr. Whitlatch studied her for a moment. Her eyes dropped
beneath his level gaze. "Spoken too easily, Gianetta. Exactly
how do you propose to pay me?"

"How? Why, I will sell something, of course."

"What will you sell?" he inquired softly.

La Gianetta lifted one white shoulder in a petulant shrug.
"That is no concern of yours."

"Forgive me, but I think it is." His eyes bored into her. "In
fact, I think it might be foolish for me to leave empty-handed
this morning. Who knows? You might find yourself suddenly
called out of town. And then where would I be? Particularly if
you failed to return." He chuckled at the glare of pure hatred
she shot him. "Exactly so, ma'am! I would be wise to take away
with me whatever item you possess that you think might fetch
such a price."

The clock ticked. Motes of dust danced in the thin November sunlight pouring through the window. La Gianetta was
clearly at a loss. Mr. Whitlatch waited politely.

Slowly her look of confusion was replaced by an arrested
look; she grew thoughtful. She cast him a speculative glance.
He raised an eyebrow inquiringly. That somehow seemed to decide her. She reached out briskly and rang for a servant.

"I will show you my most valuable possession," she told him
composedly. "You will decide its worth for yourself."

Mr. Whitlatch was conscious of a feeling of surprise. What
the devil was she about? He had expected tears, begging, panic.
Instead, La Gianetta looked like a cat at a cream pot. She almost
purred.

He frowned. "I am not competent to judge the value of jewelry on sight. If you propose to send me away with some
trumpery bestowed on you by—"

He broke off, instantly suspicious. Gianetta's shoulders were shaking with silent laughter.

"You are competent to judge the value of this particular jewel, Mr. Whitlatch. All the world knows you are something of a connoisseur in this line."

A scrawny wench in a mobcap arrived, and La Gianetta entered into a soft-voiced colloquy in French. Mystified, Mr. Whitlatch watched as the servant uttered a frightened protest, which Gianetta swiftly quelled with a sharp word. The girl then withdrew, eyes big with fear, to perform whatever office her mistress had requested.

"Marie is reluctant to do my bidding, Mr. Whitlatch. You have seen her reluctance." La Gianetta's eyes blinked rapidly, but Mr. Whitlatch perceived that the eyes behind the fluttering lashes were dry. "Ah, *m'sieur*, if you only knew what this costs me! I, too, am reluctant to bring before you my precious jewel, my pearl of great price. I very much fear that you will take my treasure away with you, never again to be seen by me! But I will not blame you; no, for this prize has only to be seen to be desired. You will be amazed, Mr. Whitlatch. Very few people know of my treasure's existence. My treasure of incalculable worth!"

Mr. Whitlatch's eyes narrowed. Gianetta sounded exactly like a Calcutta street peddler who had once tried to sell him a brass ornament, swearing it was gold. "What sort of treasure, madam?"

She again made play with her eyelashes. "My only child, sir. A daughter."

With an oath, Mr. Whitlatch rose and strode to the window. "I am no slaver, madam! You may keep your daughter."

Her smile reflected in the windowpane. "You have not seen her yet," she said simply.

Mr. Whitlatch, torn between exasperation and curiosity, turned his scowling gaze back to his hostess. "I never heard that you had a daughter."

The catlike smile still curved her painted mouth. "Few know of her existence, and no one has seen her." La Gianetta's voice resumed its dramatic throb. "She is completely untouched, sir."

Mr. Whitlatch gave an inelegant snort. A likely tale! He was about to be presented with some pretty child La Gianetta had picked up, God knows where, planning to foist upon the public as her own. Rich men would vie for the privilege of deflowering any wench believed to be the daughter of the legendary Gianetta. The chit would fetch a high price. He supposed his demand for payment had upset these well-laid plans, and Gianetta now would try to fob him off with the girl instead of proper repayment. Mr. Whitlatch felt a stab of disgust. La Gianetta was a whore to the very soul.

"Let me be sure I understand you, madam. Do you propose to give me this unfortunate female in exchange for my stolen property? You would not hesitate to sell your 'daughter' to a virtual stranger?"

"You are no stranger to me, Mr. Whitlatch. It is true we did not know one another before you rescued me from France, and we have not seen each other since, but your conduct in 1791 was heroic. Heroic! There is no other word for it."

He almost yelped with derision. "I can think of several other words for it!"

She waved this aside. "Your reputation, too, is well known to me. You are an honorable man, just and fair in all your dealings."

A self-mocking grin flashed across his features. "If you believe me to be honorable where women are concerned, madam, you have been strangely misinformed."

To his surprise, La Gianetta met his eyes frankly for the first time. "You are mistaken, Mr. Whitlatch. You offer marriage to no one, so you believe yourself to be a hardened rake. But me, I have some experience of rakes, *m'sieur*! You are no rake. On the contrary, you are a romantic."

"I?" gasped Mr. Whitlatch, revolted.

She smiled serenely. "You have told me, *m'sieur*, that you found me beautiful eleven years ago. I was completely in your power for many days, and deeply grateful to you as well. I would have refused you nothing. You must have known this, yet you never touched me."

Mr. Whitlatch's frown returned. He shrugged, and leaned negligently against the window. "Only a cad would take advantage of a woman in such circumstances."

"My point precisely, sir. You are no cad. You would not take unfair advantage of a woman—even such a woman as La Gianetta." A bitter chuckle shook her. "Only a true romantic refuses to dishonor a harlot! My Clarissa, if she pleases you, will be fairly treated."

"Thank you, but I have no interest in your Clarissa—touched or untouched, seen or unseen, your daughter or someone else's! There is not a female on the planet as valuable as those rubies."

La Gianetta laughed out loud at this. "Again your reputation belies you! I am sure you have spent far more than that on any one of the incognitas you have had in your keeping. The rubies were nothing, less than nothing, compared to a certain set of diamonds—"

"Yes, well, never mind that!" interrupted Mr. Whitlatch, impatiently jamming his hands into his pockets. "Never was money more ill spent! I have no desire to repeat such folly. I'll be the first to admit I have a soft spot for a pretty face, but at the moment I am not in the market for—"

He broke off as the door opened. A girl in a pale blue gown entered noiselessly and stood beside Gianetta's chair. Mr. Whitlatch stared. His hands, as if moving of their own volition, removed themselves from his pockets and his careless slouch slowly straightened.

His first thought was that he had seldom, if ever, beheld such beauty in human form. His second was that it was extremely clever of La Gianetta to dress the girl so chastely. Her loveliness was enhanced by the simplicity of her frock, the modesty of the high neckline, and absence of frills. But this girl would be beautiful if she were wrapped in burlap, he realized. She had the unconscious, feral grace of a deer. And her features! Flawless.

Was it possible this girl was actually La Gianetta's daughter? He could not help hoping that she was. It would be a great thing, after all, to banish his earlier picture of an innocent maiden stolen from some peasant family. It would be a great thing, in fact, to forget he ever supposed this girl could be innocent. If she was truly La Gianetta's daughter, one could then entertain the thought—merely the thought, mind you—of accepting this preposterous offer.

It was possible to trace a resemblance. She had the raven's-wing hair, the soft mouth, the straight little nose. She also had a radiant, soft, pink-and-white complexion, the very look that La Gianetta aped with cosmetics. It was all the more dramatic against the darkness of the girl's hair and eyes. Or were her eyes dark?

As if hearing his thoughts, she suddenly raised her eyes to his. He was dazzled. Framed by black lashes, her eyes were a bright, cerulean blue; a blue usually reserved by the Maker for the eyes of infants and angels.

His decision was made too swiftly for reason to intervene. Oh, yes, he had a soft spot for a pretty face. And a face like this one could bring him to the point of idiocy. He knew this about himself; he was resigned. La Gianetta had judged her man well.

He would give anything, anything at all, to possess this piece of perfection.

Mr. Whitlatch sighed, and flung up a hand in surrender. "Very well, madam. Very well."

La Gianetta's eyes snapped eagerly. "You will consider my debt paid in full, Mr. Whitlatch?"

"Completely."

"*Bien*! Clarissa, my love, ask Marie to pack up your things. You will be taking a little journey, I think."

Mr. Whitlatch was too bemused to notice the nervousness with which Gianetta uttered these words; nor the gesture, half supplication, half warning, that went with them. Rapt in his contemplation of Clarissa's beauty, he saw only her graceful, submissive curtsey before she exited. He entirely missed the murderous fury in the glance she threw La Gianetta as the door closed.

Her mother's servant, with profuse apologies, was locking her in the garret again. Listening to the tumblers turning in the lock as Marie fumbled nervously with the key, Clarissa leaned against the closed door and tried to regain her composure. She was trembling with anger.

So she would be taking a "little journey," would she? In the company of that man, no doubt. Outrageous! Disgraceful! That any mother could make such an arrangement for her own daughter was incredible. But Clarissa had seen enough of her mother, and her mother's household, in the last two days to believe anything.

She closed her eyes, and furious tears stung the back of her eyelids. Since the moment of her arrival, she had vowed to escape this den of iniquity as soon as ever she could. And after she had refused to fall in with her mother's original plans for her, she had spent the past two days locked in this makeshift bedchamber. There had been plenty of time to think, and plan, and find a way out of this intolerable situation. Only no plan had occurred to her.

She had no one to turn to. No friends, no family. All the money she had in the world was knotted in a handkerchief in the bottom of her reticule. After the expense of traveling to London from the Bathurst Ladies' Academy, her resources amounted to less than seventeen guineas.

She had paced this room for many of the past forty-eight hours, vainly racking her brain to think of a way out. How could she support herself? How could she avoid the life of debauchery her mother was so eager to thrust upon her? Her situation seemed hopeless indeed. And now this man, this stranger, had appeared out of nowhere to take her away.

Doubtless it was another scheme of Gianetta's to force her unwilling daughter into her own footsteps. But perhaps Clarissa could find a way to foil her mother's plans. Perhaps the man could be reasoned with. He might even take pity on her plight. And even if he did not, surely she could find a way to escape— if only she could get out from under this roof!

Besides, there was always a chance that his intentions were perfectly honorable. She knew nothing about this man, or what he wanted. Why should she suppose the worst? For that matter, she knew very little about her mother. It was possible that Clarissa's pleas and protestations—although they had seemed to have no impact whatsoever at the time—had prevailed, once Mother had had a chance to reflect upon them. Perhaps La Gianetta had struck a bargain with this man to offer her daughter respectable employment. Anything was possible.

"And anything would be preferable to staying here—anything at all!" she whispered. Clarissa took a deep breath, opened her eyes, and resolutely began to pack.

This task did not take long. Her possessions were few, and since from the day she arrived she had desired nothing more than to depart, she had never fully unpacked her trunk. Her throat ached with unshed tears as she gathered her precious trinkets. Here was the pewter thimble Jane Peele had given her, to remember her by. And here, the farewell letter the six youngest schoolgirls had signed. She fought the memories back. She must not think of it. It did no good to think of it.

She was standing before a cracked pier glass, buttoning her redingote, when a timid knock sounded. Marie's muffled voice wafted through the keyhole.

"Mademoiselle? You wish for help with ze packing?"

"No, thank you. I am quite finished," replied Clarissa. A soft exclamation and the rattling of the key heralded the entrance of poor Marie, who sidled nervously in as if expecting to be slapped. Their eyes met in the glass, and Clarissa smiled reassuringly.

"You see?" she said, waving a hand to indicate the single trunk and two bandboxes. "That is everything."

Marie blinked. It was evident that Clarissa's past conduct had led Marie to expect fierce resistance, not this calm complaisance. In proof of this, two burly individuals now stepped through the door. Marie had brought reinforcements. One of the men Clarissa recognized as her mother's footman, but the other appeared to be a hired porter.

"Very good, mademoiselle," stammered Marie. She nodded at the men, and each took a bandbox and one end of the trunk. As they lumbered off, Marie edged toward the door.

"One moment, please!" said Clarissa, turning to face the little servant. Marie gulped and shrank back toward the wall.

"For heaven's sake, I am not going to hurt you! I only want to know the name of the man downstairs. Do you know his name?"

Marie stared. "But, mademoiselle, he is *Trevor Whitlatch*!" she breathed ecstatically.

The name meant nothing to Clarissa. She frowned. "Whitlatch?"

"La! You do not know? Mademoiselle, ze Monsieur Whitlatch, he is a man *très distingué!*"

Clarissa raised an eyebrow. "Famous, is he? For what?"

Marie clasped her hands at her thin bosom and broke into an enthusiastic, and extremely idiomatic, stream of French. Clarissa was only able to decipher about every third word, and finally interrupted her. "Thank you, Marie, but I cannot follow what you are saying! Something about India, and ships. Are you telling me this man Whitlatch is a nabob?"

"Nay-bob? I do not know zis word, mademoiselle. But you

understand ze man is rich, yes? Ver-r-r-ry rich! You will live
like ze queen, *hein*?" She rolled her eyes expressively, beaming
at Clarissa.

Clarissa's veins turned to ice, and her hands clenched involuntarily. "Dear God," she whispered. "Then it is as I feared."

Marie wrinkled her nose. "Please?"

Clarissa took a deep breath. "Marie, you must tell me what
you know about this man, and *why* he is taking me away." She
saw apprehension cross Marie's features, and smiled encouragingly. "Come, I won't blame you! I know you are only the
messenger."

Marie gulped, and began twisting her apron. "Oh, mademoiselle, I do not know all, me! But Monsieur Whitlatch, today he
is having ze contretemps with Madame, *non*? And Madame,
she gives him you. Now he is happy, and ze contretemps, it is
at an end."

Clarissa's eyes widened in horror. "She *gave* me to him?"

Marie nodded vigorously. "But yes!" she said, with a sigh of
envy. "You will go with him, and you will live like ze queen!"
She then bobbed a quick curtsey, and slipped out the door.

Marie's air of eager congratulation was the most shocking
thing of all. How could anyone find such a bargain anything but
reprehensible? Fear stole along her nerves. Given to the man!
Heaven defend her! All her life she had tried to live respectably,
had tried to banish all traces of her mother's influence, had tried
to deny, by the sheer force of her own virtue, whose daughter
she was—only to fall into her mother's clutches and be ruined!
Oh, it was dreadful! She dared not think what the stranger
might require of her.

Five years ago, when she was sixteen, the music master had
tried to kiss her. Miss Bathurst had been very angry—bless
her!—and the music master had lost his situation. But Clarissa
remembered the scene all too clearly. It had been most unpleasant. And now this man, this Trevor Whitlatch, would
doubtless try the same thing. Men enjoyed taking such liberties,
one was told. She had even heard other girls at the academy
whisper that kisses were only the beginning of what a man
could do to a girl. She had heard there were other, more dreadful, intimacies than the pressing together of two mouths. But
Clarissa's imagination failed her when she tried to think beyond

kisses. A kiss, in her experience, was invasion enough. She shuddered.

Well. There was no help for it. She could not stay locked in her mother's attic forever. A dangerous path of escape was set before her, but she would take it. At least until another path presented itself. And whatever happened, she vowed, she would never return to this house.

She firmly tied the strings of her best bonnet beneath her chin. It had a deep poke front, so if Mr. Whitlatch had any immediate intention of kissing her, it would be difficult for him to execute his plan. She began to pull on her gloves, then hesitated.

Mr. Whitlatch had appeared to be a man of some strength.

Tossing the gloves aside, she rummaged hastily through a drawer and, with a triumphant little smile, unearthed a long and wicked-looking hat pin. Standing before the mirror, she pushed the hat pin carefully through the wide satin ribbon on the top of her bonnet. She patted it to reassure herself of its exact location.

"En garde, monsieur!" Clarissa whispered to her reflection. Then she picked up her gloves and walked downstairs.

Chapter 2

Mr. Whitlatch's swarthy features were further darkened by a ferocious scowl. He prowled restlessly back and forth in La Gianetta's cramped entry hall, snarling under his breath. If he had a tail, he would have lashed it. His hostess had left him here, completely unattended, to kick his heels while Clarissa packed. And the longer he was left alone, the more certain he became that he had made a mistake.

Mr. Whitlatch had not amassed one of the world's largest personal fortunes by making bad bargains, but the brilliance of his business acumen had not, so far, extended to his personal life. In fact, quite the reverse. Few men had ever gotten the better of him. Women, however, were another matter.

Another matter? God's teeth! They had as well be another species!

He had a habit of choosing women in the same impulsive way he chose his business ventures. So far, it had not answered. He could bend most enterprises to his will, but women were wayward creatures and completely unpredictable. Farmer's daughter or rajah's daughter, peasant or princess, the differences were only on the surface. Beneath their various exteriors beat a single, alien heart.

He knew, of course, that he had few social graces. He was perfectly aware that his impatience made him unobservant of others' sensibilities, and that he was, as a result, constantly giving offense—to men as well as to women. But women, far more than men, seemed to conduct their conversations in a kind of code, a code that was all the more deceptive because it resembled ordinary English. Beneath the surface of their elliptical discourse lurked messages and meanings outside the hearing of a plainspoken man.

Trevor Whitlatch had an eye that grasped the big picture instantly, but, in his view, women inhabited—in fact, created—a "small picture" world. They invariably held him accountable for crimes he had no idea he had committed; wept and sulked and took offense where none was meant; grew angry when he failed to notice some infinitesimal change in their appearance, or "take a hint" he had no notion he had been given. Hints! Insinuations! Suggestions! Why the devil couldn't a woman say what she wanted in plain English?

Now he had the uneasy suspicion he had missed something. Again. Here in Gianetta's scented, pastel lair some silly detail had escaped him. Some hint he should have seized upon had slipped past without registering its significance.

The first misgivings struck him at Gianetta's smiling exit. He was sure he heard her laughing softly as the door closed.

Well, there's a hint, if you like! The magnitude of what he had just done suddenly hit him with full force. He had written off a set of very valuable jewels, and for what? Another pretty ladybird to coax the gingerbread out of him! He realized the girl could not possibly be as beautiful as she had first struck him. Nobody was that beautiful.

"Idiot!" he muttered savagely. He was in the suds again! The last one had cost him a fortune. Not that that mattered; it would take a dozen such convenients to make any inroad in the Whitlatch fortune. But what the devil would he tell Bates?

Mr. Whitlatch groaned inwardly, and cursed himself for a fool. He had promised to avenge his friend for the wrongs he had suffered at La Gianetta's elegant gaming tables. What a joke! To go off, breathing fire, and come tamely back with just such a girl in tow as had doubtless led Bates to his ruin!

At this point in his ruminations, two porters plodded carefully down Gianetta's stairs. Mr. Whitlatch stopped his irate pacing and fixed his scowl on the porters, causing them to touch their forelocks to him nervously. He watched, still scowling, as they carried a small trunk and two battered bandboxes out the front door. He then wandered out to the stoop and watched with a jaundiced eye as the men strapped the luggage to the back of his curricle.

Three small pieces. Was that all the wench was bringing? Very clever. His reputation had obviously preceded him. If he wasn't careful, he'd find himself playing King Cophetua to her Beggarmaid before the day was out.

But this time, he vowed, he was going to be careful. This time, he would set the rules at the beginning of the game. This time, he would never let go of the whip hand. He would ride this filly with a curb bit.

Mr. Whitlatch, anticipating the inevitable, then ordered one of the men to walk his horses awhile. He withdrew to pace the hall again, knowing from experience he must endure a lengthy wait while Mademoiselle made her toilette.

He hoped to high heaven that the result she achieved would not be too spectacular. He did not relish the thought of driving across town in an open carriage with another flashy, simpering lightskirt at his side. The knowing 'uns would spread the story all over town by sunset—Whitlatch had a new *chere amie*! People were always so confoundedly interested in matters that did not concern them! He had long ago grown accustomed to public scrutiny—the price of celebrity, he supposed—but he still found it baffling.

These musings were interrupted by a soft noise on the stairs behind him. Mr. Whitlatch turned and, to his surprise, saw Clarissa already walking composedly toward him, gloved, bonneted, and ready to depart.

Trevor Whitlatch, that connoisseur of female charms, was staggered anew. His scowl evaporated. Good Lord. He had not thought such beauty possible. And yet, against all odds, her ap-

pearance was perfectly ladylike. A modest gray redingote was
buttoned closely to her throat against the November chill. She
carried a muff in one gloved hand. And although her eyes were
cast demurely down in the shadow of a deep-brimmed bonnet,
it was easy to see she was every bit as beautiful as he had first
thought.

Mr. Whitlatch's regrets faded. If she looked this delicious
covered from head to toe, what might she look like uncovered?
He pushed the paralyzing thought out of his mind and bowed
with a flourish.

"My compliments, sweetheart," he greeted her. "You don't
dawdle, at any rate. I dislike above all things to be kept waiting."

She inclined her head, but said nothing.

Damnation. Had he offended her, complimenting her punc-
tuality instead of her appearance? "You look charming," he assured her, offering his most engaging smile. "But I sent one of
the porters to walk my horses. I thought you'd need another
quarter of an hour."

Those impossibly blue eyes regarded him levelly. She did not
return his smile. "For what?" she asked.

Nonplussed, he donned the charming smile again. "How
would I know, sweetheart? Whatever it is females do to keep
gentlemen waiting. Curling your hair, or hunting for your
gloves, or bidding your loved ones a fond farewell." He tried an
ingratiating chuckle. It had no discernible effect.

"I seldom curl my hair," she said repressively. "I never lose
my gloves. And I have no loved ones."

A stab of annoyance momentarily dislodged Mr. Whitlatch's
smile. What the deuce was the matter with her? The chit was
not assisting him in any way to smooth the awkwardness of the
moment. There was no trace of coquetry in her manner or her
voice. She might have been on her way to church. Or a funeral!
It would take a while to tire of looking at her, but if she never
smiled that would certainly speed up the process.

He ran his eyes over her again, and his cheerfulness returned.
It would definitely take a while to tire of looking at this one.

He offered his arm. "My curricle is at the gate again. Shall
we go?"

Clarissa placed one hand on his proffered arm and buried the
other in her muff. "By all means," she said.

She sounded perfectly composed, yet the hand resting lightly on his arm was trembling. Mr. Whitlatch glanced curiously down at the face beside him, but she immediately tilted her head so her hat brim obscured his view.

Well, he was not one to waste time pondering the inner workings of the female mind. Whatever he guessed would inevitably turn out to be wrong. So he shrugged, and escorted his companion to the waiting curricle.

The perch was high, and Clarissa's hands were occupied with her muff and reticule. Mr. Whitlatch seized the opportunity to catch her round the waist and lift her into the carriage.

Most enjoyable! When his hands slid round her slender waist, the last of his misgivings vanished. She felt soft and lithe and supple, and she smelled of lemon verbena. Hang the rubies, and hang his reputation, and hang Bates! This girl was going to be worth it.

Clarissa choked back an exclamation as he lifted her, and he felt her stiffen in his arms. He chuckled, delighted. She not only looked the part, she meant to play the lady, did she? Well, if it got tiresome, he would put a stop to it. For the time being, he would indulge her in her game. He remembered his concern that she would cultivate a far different appearance, and was grateful Clarissa had chosen this particular charade.

He swung himself easily up beside her and gave his horses the office to start. Clarissa sat bolt upright on the edge of the seat, staring straight ahead. Odd. Could she be nervous of him? Or was it more of the "lady game"? At least she didn't simper, or cling. He could not read her expression. That absurd hat of hers thwarted every attempt to see her face. Irritated, he turned his attention to the crowded London street.

"I put up at Grisham's whenever I'm in town," he told her, threading the curricle easily through the traffic. "They set a very tolerable table. I've bespoken a chaise already, but we'll go back and transfer your luggage to it. We're leaving London this afternoon."

At this, her face finally turned toward him. Her eyes were wide with startled dismay. "Leaving London!" she repeated.

Here it comes, thought Mr. Whitlatch. Tears, pleas, coaxing. Time to set the rules.

He flashed her a grim smile. "No town house for you, my girl. You'll be fixed in the country, where I can keep an eye on you. Did you want to cut a dash among all the highflyers? No, thank you! I've been down that road before."

She stared at him, unblinking. Then she turned her face away without a word. He hoped she wasn't going to sulk. That was worse than tears, pleas, and coaxing.

He had probably sounded harsh, he thought. He felt a stab of contrition, and sternly repressed it. After all, it was best to make clear at once who was the master. The last thing he wanted was to set Clarissa up in London! Next she would want cream-colored ponies and a high-perch phaeton, no doubt, so she could rake all over town making a name for herself. Clarissa in London would mean rivals bidding for her favors, and veiled references in the gossip columns, and the Bond Street shops offering her endless credit.

And it would mean poor Bates might catch a glimpse of her before he'd had a chance to explain his perfidy. Doubtless, Bates would have seen her at La Gianetta's, and any man who had seen Clarissa once would remember her forever. He could imagine his friend's emotions upon learning that Whitlatch had the fair Clarissa in keeping! No, Bates had to hear it from himself.

She still had not spoken. He relented a little. "I'll not take you far from town," he assured her. "My affairs frequently require attention in the City. It would be impractical to set you up at any great distance from the metropolis."

She neither replied nor looked at him. Pouting, was she? He adopted what he hoped was a firm, but kindly, tone.

"I am sure you and I will deal famously, Clarissa, but I wish to make matters perfectly plain to you at the outset. While I hold the purse strings, my dear, you will live where I choose. You won't find me unreasonable about small things; you may spend your allowance as you like. But don't plan to take the bit between your teeth, for you'll catch cold at it."

He could discern no reaction at all. Did she disbelieve him? Of course she disbelieves me, he thought sourly, remembering that she had only brought three pieces of luggage. She had doubtless been told that Trevor Whitlatch would pamper and cosset her like a pet poodle, shower her with expensive presents, indulge her every whim, and make her rich beyond the dreams of avarice!

He glanced impatiently at the rigid figure beside him. "No doubt La Gianetta has led you to expect satin sheets and diamond ear bobs. Well, the stories about me are true, for the most part, but I've a habit of learning from my mistakes! In the past I've spent money like water, trying to please women of your stamp. It is a singularly fruitless occupation, and I don't mean to try it again. The more I spend, the more you will demand. No, don't deny it! And you'll end by transferring your dubious affections to another, bidding me a fond farewell."

He stole another glace at his audience. She sat even more stiffly than before, but the edge of her bonnet was quivering a little, as if she were trembling with some strong emotion.

A pang of conscience smote Mr. Whitlatch. A lightskirt's career was necessarily short, and such females had to grab what they could, while they could. It was unfair to upbraid her. After all, he was something of an opportunist himself.

His voice softened a little. "I realize you have to make your way in the world. I won't begrudge you your due, Clarissa. You'll have a comfortable life with me, and I'll not discard you with a shilling. But you *won't* bleed me dry, and you *won't* entertain my eventual replacement at my expense, and, in short, you won't make me ridiculous."

Her small hands clenched into fists in her lap. So *that* was the emotion she was laboring under: anger! Mr. Whitlatch uttered a short laugh. "Sorry, sweetheart! When it is time for us to part, I will let you know—not the other way about. And to that end, my dear, I am taking you to Morecroft Cottage, where I hope you will be able to stay out of mischief."

Slowing the curricle, he deftly maneuvered his horses into a crowded and very noisy stable yard. A boy instantly leaped to their heads. Mr. Whitlatch tossed the boy a coin and assisted his companion to alight. She still had not spoken, and kept her face averted. He maintained a firm grip on her elbow as he guided her into the inn. If she planned to treat him to a tantrum, he had rather seclude her somewhere before she began. Fortunately, his arrangements at Grisham's included a private parlor. He escorted Clarissa to this apartment and ushered her inside. A fire had been lit, and the room had a cheerful, cozy aspect.

"Stay here and get warm," he commanded. "I will see to a few things and order us a little nuncheon. Do you prefer coffee or tea?"

At last, her eyes met his. God, she was lovely.

"Tea," she said. Her voice was completely emotionless. Perhaps she did not mean to enact a scene for his benefit after all. He smiled at her with great satisfaction.

"Tea it shall be," he promised. "I will be back directly." And he exited, closing the door behind him.

Clarissa unclenched her shaking hands and sent up a silent prayer of thanksgiving. She had been left completely alone in a room on the ground floor! Grisham's was a modern hotel, and its elegant windows were large. To her relief, the first window she tried slid open easily on well-oiled hinges. The windowsill was even clean. What luck. Gathering her skirts around her, Clarissa sat on the sill, swung her legs over, and jumped lightly into the mews.

Twenty minutes of Mr. Whitlatch's company had been quite enough.

Chapter 3

The mews behind Grisham's was dark, narrow, and extremely cold. Like most alleys, it was also ripe with unpleasant odors. Clarissa decided not to let her skirts drop until she reached the street.

Panic urged her to hurry, but she hesitated for a moment. How unfortunate that she could not reach high enough to close the window behind her! Mr. Whitlatch would instantly know which way she had gone. Well, that could not be helped. She would have a head start, at any rate.

Clarissa had seen little of London—in fact, practically nothing, since she had arrived squashed into the middle seat of a stagecoach and had been confined in her mother's house ever since—but she felt confident that if any person wished to elude another, the crowded streets of London would be an admirable place to begin. And if Mr. Whitlatch did find her there, she could scream for assistance. Surely he would not accost her in public.

Or would he? Clarissa shuddered. If anyone could be that brazen, Mr. Whitlatch was the man. She had learned more in the past half hour about the relationship between men and their

mistresses than she had ever cared to know. She was still reel-
ing from the shock. He would hold the purse strings, would he,
and force her to dance to whatever tune he cared to pipe? Horrible!

She must get away, and at once. Stepping carefully over a
small heap of refuse, Clarissa hastened to the end of the mews,
shook out her skirts, and, with her heart racing, walked sedately
out into the street.

No shrinking or looking bewildered! she admonished herself, quelling the impulse to break into a run. She had no idea
where she was. She also did not know where she was going, nor
what to do when she got there.

No sense fretting about it. She had prayed that an opportunity for escape would present itself. Well, it had, and she had
seized it. The die was cast.

Clarissa chose a direction at random, and walked at a pace
she hoped would appear brisk and purposeful, rather than hurried. She was careful to keep her head lowered. It was unusual
for women to walk unaccompanied in London, and Clarissa
wished to attract as little attention as possible. Passersby might
notice her, but at least (she hoped) they would not be able to describe her face.

She wished now she had thought of some ruse to get Mr.
Whitlatch to bring some of her luggage to her before she escaped. There hadn't been time to think of anything. But if only
she had desired one of her bandboxes to be brought to the coffee room, pretending to need a comb or some such nonsense,
she could have taken the bandbox out the window with her. If I
were carrying a bandbox, she thought wistfully, I might pass for
a milliner's assistant, and no one would notice me at all.

But she must not think about her missing luggage. The
specter of finding herself alone in a strange city without so
much as a toothbrush reared its ugly head, and she pushed it
firmly out of her mind. She was frightened enough at present;
she would go mad if she thought about that now. Besides, she
reminded herself, she had her reticule, with the guineas tied up
in her handkerchief. The reticule was hanging off her wrist. In
what she hoped was an excess of caution, she tucked it into her
muff as well.

While she was busied with this task, a shout of "Hi! Watch
where you're goin', can't yer?" caused her to jump back, star-

tled. An ostler was fighting to control a very fresh team he had obviously been obliged to halt when she walked directly into its path. Clarissa's eyes widened in fear. Dear God, the sign swinging over her head read GRISHAM'S—with her head down, she had walked directly back to the entrance of the very hotel she was trying to escape!

She stammered an incoherent apology, turned blindly, and almost ran across the street. She heard curses and the sound of more horses being pulled up short behind her, but this time she did not look to see whose progress she had impeded.

There were so many people! Horses, and carriages, and costermongers, and persons of all descriptions hurrying along the street—how did they avoid colliding with one another? Overwhelmed, Clarissa darted round the nearest corner, flattened herself against a building, and tried to get her bearings.

At least she now knew Grisham's was behind her. Somewhere. I have only to go forward, she told herself firmly. I cannot possibly return to Grisham's if I walk straight ahead.

She was annoyed to find that she was shaking. She walked forward, clutching her muff and staring at the pavement before her feet. The shifting, bustling confusion of traffic and noise all round her was bewildering. When an extremely dirty child with a large tray suddenly shouted, "Chest-*nuts*! Hot *Chest*-nuts!" right beside her, she nearly jumped out of her skin.

Clarissa reluctantly discarded the idea of hiding her face with her hat brim. It is dangerous to walk with my head lowered, she thought. I must pay attention to my surroundings. I will be safe, if only I do not look anyone in the face. I will pretend that I know exactly where I am going, and walk with an air of confidence. I will walk energetically, so as not to appear approachable. And if anyone addresses me, I shall simply pretend I do not hear.

She was forced to put this to the test before she had reached the first crossing. And for the next twenty minutes, she continued to ignore the various persons who hailed her.

Clarissa, who had lived almost all her life in a quiet rural setting, was completely unprepared for the outrageous and baffling behavior of Londoners. Did these strange men honestly believe she would stop and converse with them? Did they expect her to smile at their unsolicited compliments? It was startling, and extremely unpleasant, to hear the jocular greetings and odd invitations that followed her up the street. She dared not look, but was miserably certain that all the remarks were addressed to her. Some of the comments she did not understand, and did not want to understand.

Fear gradually quickened her step. She had thought only of the peril awaiting her at Grisham's. She had not considered that peril might follow her wherever she went. An unescorted female was apparently considered fair game for any man who cared to insult her.

Her frightened, whirling thoughts coalesced into a refrain that beat time with her stride: What shall I do? Where can I go? Her mind seemed numb with anxiety. She could not form a plan. All she could think, over and over, was: What shall I do? Where can I go?

No answer to either question presented itself. She kept walking.

It eventually occurred to her that if she did nothing but walk straight forward, Mr. Whitlatch would speedily find her. In fact, it was a wonder he had not found her already. The ostler would almost certainly recall Clarissa, and probably the direction she had taken. Despair clutched her.

She paused at a crossing and glanced about. The wind seemed to be picking up. Clarissa shivered. She began to understand what the fox felt, driven from its sanctuary and forced into headlong flight by the distant sound of baying dogs. She turned the corner and walked down a new street, now determined to turn corners at random in an effort to confuse anyone who might be following her.

Perhaps she could hide in a shop somewhere and get warm, at least, while she decided what to do. She desperately needed a period of calm reflection. Perhaps she could purchase it for the price of a dish of tea. She would search for a pastry-cook.

The scent of coffee and something frying lured her to a low door set in a side street. A cheerful hubbub of conversation accompanied the inviting smells. There was no sign above the door, which was puzzling, but Clarissa supposed it must be the back entrance of a public house. The sign would be over the front door.

Her fingers curled protectively round the reticule she had tucked in her muff. It felt so small, now that it was all she owned in the world! Bread and tea would not set her back more than a shilling, would it? Actually, she had no idea. But she longed to sit down in a warm room, drink a cup of something steaming, and think. She could not continue in this aimless way, wandering from street to street with no set purpose. She needed a plan.

She must think of a way to instantly remove from the streets to a safe place, obtain respectable employment, and secure her future. And these necessary events must take place today—before sundown, in fact. How to obtain these essentials with no references, no acquaintances, and not even a change of clothing to her name, was yet to be determined. Yes, this would certainly require some serious thought.

As she hesitated, a sharp gust of wind whistled round the corner, rattling her bonnet and whipping her redingote across her chilled ankles. There was no sense in standing in the street, she decided, shivering. Whatever this place was, she would get out of the cold and beg or buy a dish of tea.

Clarissa approached the door, which was ajar, and entered. She found herself in a low-ceilinged, firelit room redolent of savory smells and filled with a set of extremely busy persons. It was not a tavern or public house, however, for there was no dining area to be seen. She had entered what was apparently just a large, well-staffed, beautifully organized kitchen.

Confused, Clarissa halted in the doorway. A stout matron in a mobcap approached, addressing her in a sharp tone there was no mistaking. Unfortunately, she spoke in such a thick Cockney that Clarissa did not understand her remarks.

"I beg your pardon," said Clarissa in her soft, cultured voice. "I mistook this place for a public house."

The woman's martial air relaxed a little. She shooed Clarissa back out the door, but in a kindly way. "If you go round the front, miss, they'll take care of you there," she said, speaking more distinctly.

"Round the front?" repeated Clarissa.

Her benefactress jerked a helpful thumb.

"Thank you," Clarissa said politely. She turned to walk away, but was apparently facing the wrong direction; the matron clucked her tongue and called, "Now, now, miss!"—or it may have been, "No, no"—Clarissa was not sure.

"You'll never find it that way. Come on back, dearie, and I'll take you through the kitchen."

This was the first piece of disinterested kindness Clarissa had met in many days. Her smile was absurdly tremulous as she thanked the woman. Chuckling, the matron ushered her back through the kitchen and into a bewildering maze of dark hallways.

"Here you are, then," she promised, holding open a narrow wooden door. Clarissa stepped through it and found herself in a surprisingly luxurious foyer. But a foyer to what? She turned to ask the kind woman from the kitchen, but that busy individual had already vanished.

Clarissa glanced about, a trifle nervously. There was not a soul to be seen. A large counter ran along one wall, with a row of pigeonholes behind it, some of them stuffed with papers, some not. An array of keys hung on numbered pegs beside the pigeonholes. A brass bell rested on the countertop, presumably to summon whatever individual worked behind it. There was a ledger beside the bell, turned to face the customer rather than the counterworker. Several neatly sharpened quills and an inkwell were arrayed beside the ledger. The place seemed eerily familiar.

Well, naturally it did. This was obviously an hotel. She had walked through the lobby of just such an hotel not long ago, had she not? Clarissa crossed to the elegant front door and peered through the glass panes set decoratively in its center. As she expected, it gave onto a crowded, noisy stable yard, very much like the one she had seen at Grisham's.

In fact, exactly like the one she had seen at Grisham's.

Clarissa struggled against a rising tide of foreboding. For all she knew, she reminded herself firmly, every hotel in London had the same appearance! Still, she must not wait to make sure of where she was. A clerk or innkeeper would arrive at any moment. Fighting back panic, she stepped out the door and looked upward.

The swinging sign above her read GRISHAM'S.

A tiny sound escaped her. She hoped she would not faint. Part of her wanted to scream with vexation, and part of her wanted to collapse in defeat. This could only happen to her!

She turned to make a dash for the street, but before she could do so, a hand, viselike, closed on the back of her neck. The fingers felt long, strong, and inexorable. Clarissa gasped, and stopped in her tracks.

"Why, Clarissa!" said Mr. Whitlatch in a voice of honeyed steel. "How delightful to see you again."

Chapter 4

Her head held motionless in that unyielding grip, Clarissa's eyes darted frantically round the stable yard. It was full only of sniggering ostlers. Their sly, vulgar grins reminded her of a pack of salivating jackals. Male jackals. She would find no rescuer here. Helpless, she allowed herself to be propelled into the inn by the hand on the back of her neck.

Clarissa walked with as much dignity as she could muster, but her cheeks burned with shame. The steady pressure of Mr. Whitlatch's fingers compelled her to walk back through the foyer and into the very parlor from which she had escaped. The irony struck her like a fist. All her wanderings had achieved exactly nothing. She could weep from pure frustration.

The door shut behind them with a snap, and Mr. Whitlatch's grip transferred itself to her shoulders. He startled her with a rough little shake.

"If you *ever* play me such a trick again, I'll teach you a lesson you won't soon forget! When I tell you to stay somewhere, by God, you had better stay put!"

Shock drove the color from Clarissa's cheeks. Then humiliation, fear, exhaustion, and despair suddenly ignited her temper. Rage swept through her like a strong tonic. With one fierce movement, she broke from his grasp and turned on him, eyes blazing like coals in her tense, white face.

"How *dare* you use such language in my presence? How dare you raise your hand to me? Do not touch me!"

Mr. Whitlatch stared. "Do not *touch* you? What the dev—"

"And do not swear at me!" interrupted Clarissa sharply, raising one hand as if to ward him off. "Your entire manner toward me is intolerable! Your language is profane and familiar. Your attentions are insulting! And your company, sir, is *repugnant*!"

Mr. Whitlatch was conscious of a strong sense of unreality. The girl was addressing him in the ringing tones of an outraged

spinster. If he had not known better, he would think she was a
respectable female.

His eyes narrowed in suspicion. Was Gianetta capable of
serving him such a trick? Would she dare?

"Who are you?" he demanded. "I was led to believe—"

"I know what you were led to believe, thank you!" Her tone
was bitter. The anger suddenly seemed to abandon Clarissa,
leaving her limp. She sank, shaking, into a chair. "I know what
you were led to believe," she repeated quietly. "And I know
who led you to believe it. I know whom I have to thank for this
deplorable situation. You are not altogether at fault. But I
charge you, sir, by all you hold holy—"

A quick knock sounded, and the door opened. "Beg pardon,
but the chaise is ready, sir. You asked to be called immediately."

"Yes, thank you, thank you! You may go," snapped Mr.
Whitlatch. As the curious servant reluctantly withdrew, Mr.
Whitlatch looked back at Clarissa and frowned.

She appeared pale and fragile at the moment, but there was
definitely some steel in that slender spine. Why, anyone would
take her for a lady of quality.

He addressed her with his characteristic abruptness. "You
speak like a gentlewoman."

She lifted her chin at that, and replied with dignity. "I was educated at the Bathurst Ladies' Academy, sir."

Mr. Whitlatch's eyebrows shot up. "The devil you say! How
did Gianetta get her claws into you?"

Clarissa blushed, and her eyes fell. "That is a long story, sir,
and painful to me. I beg you will not ask me to relate it."

"Good God!" Mr. Whitlatch rubbed his chin, regarding
Clarissa thoughtfully. "Well, I will deal with Gianetta later.
This is not the first time she has slumguzzled me, but I promise
you it is the last. In the meantime, if I have offered you any insult today, ma'am, I heartily beg your pardon. As you surmised,
I was encouraged to think you were something you clearly are
not. I apologize."

She looked up at him, startled. Sudden civility was the last
thing Clarissa had expected. His eyes were very dark, and met
hers with a directness she found rather unsettling. She nodded,
not trusting her voice.

Her eyes flickered over Mr. Whitlatch's face for the first
time. She noticed, with a detached sort of surprise, that he was

handsome. Why had she thought him harsh-featured, swarthy and villainous? It must be because he had figured in her mind only as the scoundrel who wished to steal her virtue. Preoccupied with her troubles, she had never actually looked at the man. He was dark, to be sure, but his rugged features were more attractive than she had first thought.

She wondered if her years at school had made her overly accustomed to feminine standards of beauty. Harshness in a male face was rather pleasing, she discovered. And a large frame did not lessen a man's appeal. If anything, it enhanced it. How strange.

But Mr. Whitlatch, with one of his swift, peremptory movements, had crossed toward her and offered his hand. Bemused, she took it. Her own was at once enveloped in a strong clasp and heartily shaken. "Thank you! We will forget our earlier conversations," he said.

"Certainly," she murmured, feeling a little dazed.

He was still holding her hand. "I am leaving immediately for Morecroft Cottage," he told her. "It is near Islington Spa, but never mind that! I will take you wherever you wish to go. Where is your home?"

A *frisson* of dread shot through Clarissa. Of all the questions he might have asked, he had unerringly hit on the most unanswerable! She hesitated, at a loss, and pulled her hand back. Mr. Whitlatch's mind apparently traveled at breakneck speed; caught in that extraordinarily piercing gaze she could think of nothing to say in reply—nothing other than the truth. Hating the necessity to answer at all, she tried to speak lightly.

"I have no home."

Mr. Whitlatch's already keen gaze sharpened. "Nonsense. Everyone has a home. Where are your parents? Are you an orphan?"

Heavens, he was direct! Had the man no manners at all? She tried looking down her nose at him. "I am of age, Mr. Whitlatch," she said haughtily.

He shrugged impatiently. "Of age! What is that to the purpose? I daresay your family will still be glad to have you safely back. You are not married."

Clarissa stiffened. "Sir, you presume!"

He uttered a short bark of laughter. "No, I state the obvious!

But you must have relatives of some sort, even if your father is dead."

She was startled anew. "How did you know my father is dead?"

Mr. Whitlatch strode restlessly back across the room, tossing words over his shoulder. Movement seemed to be his natural mode.

"No man whose business it was to take care of you could let you come to such straits. Had you a father, a husband, or even, I daresay, a brother, I would not have found you under La Gianetta's roof. Come! We can't keep the horses waiting. Where do I take you?"

Clarissa clasped her hands tightly in her lap. She must convince Mr. Whitlatch that his prying was as unnecessary as it was unwelcome. With this in mind, she tried to achieve a pleasant, offhand tone. "There is nowhere to take me, so I must decline your obliging offer."

"Decline it?" He halted, frowning. "Do you expect me to leave you here?"

"Of course I do. My affairs are no concern of yours."

"Talk sense, if you please!" demanded Mr. Whitlatch. His eyes bored into hers with unnerving effect. She could no longer meet them; they made her feel utterly transparent. "I am the one who brought you here, apparently against your will! Why do you wish to be left at Grisham's? You seemed eager enough to be gone a while ago."

Eyes downcast, she tried desperately to think of an answer. She could not. Clarissa took refuge in hauteur. "I have told you already, Mr. Whitlatch, that my affairs are not your concern! I am very well able to take care of myself."

He gave an inelegant snort. "Yes, I have seen exactly how well you are able to take care of yourself! You forget. I found you in the power of the most notorious courtesan in Western Europe."

Clarissa's eyes flashed. "You needn't sneer, Mr. Whitlatch!"

"You needn't pitch gammon, Clarissa!"

"I do not know what 'pitching gammon' means, but it sounds excessively vulgar. And I have *not* given you leave to call me by my Christian name!"

"Pitching gammon, my good girl, means you are trying to hoodwink me. You won't succeed, so you may stop trying! And

I call you by your Christian name because I do not know your surname."

Clarissa, much agitated, rose and crossed to the fireplace. She wished her knees did not tremble so.

Mr. Whitlatch's voice sounded behind her, now edged with suspicion. "Well? I ask you again—who are you? La Gianetta told me you were her daughter."

Her back to Mr. Whitlatch, she leaned against the mantel for support. If she did not have to watch his face while she said it, it was easier to say. Clarissa stared into the fire and whispered, almost inaudibly, the shameful secret she had spent her life trying to escape.

"It is true. I am her daughter."

A brief silence fell. Behind her, she could almost palpably feel incredulity and wrath struggling within Mr. Whitlatch. She could even sense the moment when wrath won. His chair scraped against the floor as he rose.

Then his voice came, dangerously quiet. "Do not try my patience further. We are going to Morecroft Cottage. We are going now. You will walk quietly out to the carriage, and you will get in. And you will enact me no more of this charade."

Clarissa turned defiantly to face him, opened her mouth to speak—and saw his expression. She closed her mouth. This was not the face of a man with whom one could reason. Mr. Whitlatch was very angry. It was clear that he believed she had been trifling with him, and it was equally clear he was not a man to be trifled with.

He opened the door and held it for her. "Go."

He was more than capable of compelling her if she defied him. Better to obey now and argue later. She walked stiffly out without a word.

As they exited the inn, a boy sprang to attention, let down the step and flung open the door of an elegant post chaise. Clarissa gathered her skirts and hesitated on the step, peering in.

Thank God, it had two wide benches, one facing forward and one facing backward. They need not sit side by side. But if she chose the forward-facing seat, he would certainly sit beside her. She chose the rear-facing seat.

Mr. Whitlatch, entering behind her, noted this maneuver and instantly comprehended its purpose. His mouth twisted in a sardonic grin. They would look like prime idiots, both sitting backward, but it would serve her right. The motion wouldn't bother him a bit after years at sea. She'd be sick as a horse before they reached Marylebone. So he sat beside her, tossing his hat onto the cushions in the corner. She immediately got up and seated herself in the *center* of the forward-facing bench.

Before he could counter this move, the boy who had been holding the door reached in. He deftly tucked a lap rug round Clarissa, slipped a hot brick under her feet, touched his cap to her, and shut the door. Clarissa's look of amazement widened Mr. Whitlatch's grin.

"You haven't traveled much, I see."

"Only on a stagecoach," Clarissa admitted, wiggling her toes appreciatively against the hot brick.

She noted with relief that his voice had suddenly sounded almost friendly. Perhaps the muted light and cozy confines of the coach's interior would have a mellowing effect on Mr. Whitlatch's temper. She had never seen, never imagined, such a richly appointed carriage. The walls were paneled in what appeared to be oak, the squabs were of dark blue velvet, and the windows were curtained in matching velvet.

"I had no idea such a degree of comfort could be had in a private carriage," she remarked. "Do you always travel in such style?"

"Always." Mr. Whitlatch leaned lazily back against the squabs, crossing his powerful arms across his chest. "Are you engaging me in polite conversation?"

She regarded him nervously. "If you please."

"Well, I think I had rather not," he said softly. The carriage gave a gentle lurch and their journey began. "In fact, I am almost sure I had rather not. I find I am not in the mood for conversation."

She stared at him, nonplussed. "But I must explain my circumstances. I know it must appear strange to you—"

"I am not interested in your circumstances. Besides, they have just changed. Hadn't you noticed?"

She blinked. "Changed?"

"For the better, I hope, now that you are under my protection."

Clarissa stiffened. "Your protection! That's a fine word for it. Just what will you protect me from, sir?"

He chuckled. "From the predatory designs, unwelcome attentions, and physical advances of other men."

"And who will protect me from yours?" she demanded.

His eyes gleamed in the dimness. "No one, and nothing, can protect you from mine," he said affably.

Clarissa swallowed her rising fear and spoke reasonably. "Mr. Whitlatch, you are laboring under a misapprehension. You must let me explain—"

"I told you I was not in the mood for conversation. Are you going to take off that ridiculous bonnet, or shall I?"

Clarissa's hands flew to her bonnet. "Pray do not!" she gasped, clutching it protectively.

"No?" he murmured. He reached easily across the space between them and slowly ran one finger along the edge of the satin riband, just touching her cheek. "It will be very much in the way."

Clarissa's heart seemed to jump into her throat. She could feel her pulse beating there, high and fast and terrified. The touch of his hand to her face sent shivers of fear down her spine. Fear and . . . something else, something confusing. Something odd. What was happening? Her face tingled where he had touched it; it was almost as if his finger burned.

"Don't," she whispered. To her astonishment, it was suddenly difficult to speak. A strange, suffocating intimacy seemed to be pulling them toward one another in the dim light. Her eyes searched his, spellbound. But she did not find her reflection in them. His eyes held only a hot, dreamy haze.

Why, he wasn't seeing her at all! He saw nothing but his own desire.

This realization hit her like a dash of cold water. Her brows snapped together. "Don't!" she repeated, more firmly. But before she knew what he intended, he had untied her bonnet with one swift, strategic yank. Mr. Whitlatch laughed softly as the wide satin ribbons tumbled down across her chest.

The bonnet, however, remained anchored to her head. Clarissa suddenly remembered the hat pin. Her courage returned. She could wipe that hazy look off his face if it became necessary.

Mr. Whitlatch was leaning slowly toward her, his eyes still hot and unfocused. Clarissa placed her small, determined hands

against his shoulders and pushed. The time for plain speaking
had obviously arrived.

"You must listen to me!" she said, her voice sharp with desperation. "I am not interested in becoming your mistress!"

At that moment, the carriage simultaneously bounced into a
rut and turned a corner. Clarissa pitched helplessly forward into
Mr. Whitlatch's waiting arms.

He did not appear to have heard her last statement at all. Instead of responding like a sensible man, he caught her fast and
held her against him while the coach gently rocked and swayed.
If anything, his eyes burned hotter than ever. "So beautiful," he
whispered.

His words seemed to travel deliciously down her spine and
out her toes. What on earth was the matter with her? Clarissa
discovered that she was clinging to his shoulders. If she let go,
she would fall to the floor of the coach. This did not strike her
as a good strategy for discouraging Mr. Whitlatch. She continued to hold on to him—for the time being. Heavens, he was
strong!

"Mr. Whitlatch, you must let me go at once," she said, as
firmly as she could.

"Must I?" he murmered teasingly.

To Clarissa's dismay, he leaned down and began playfully
nudging the bonnet as if to push it off. Still anchored by the pin,
it refused to budge. But—what in the world was he doing to her
neck? It was making her hair stand on end. Was that his *mouth*
she was feeling? Outrageous! Shocking! She gasped with terrified pleasure.

"Mr. Whitlatch, pray stop! This is not seemly."

To her annoyance, her voice sounded breathless and shaky.
Even in her own ears, she did not sound as if she meant what
she was saying. Small wonder that Mr. Whitlatch paid no heed.

Struggling, still bound by the lap rug, she managed to get her
knees onto the floor of the coach and tried pushing against his
shoulders once again. He finally lifted his face, but his arms
tightened around her. He slid off the bench, and joined her on
the floor. She realized he now meant to push her onto her back.

The bewildering pleasure she had been feeling was instantly
banished. Real panic welled within Clarissa. How could she get
through to this man?

"Mr. Whitlatch! *Sir!* I appeal to your sense of honor—I appeal to your chivalry—"

His warm breath stirred against her cheek as he chuckled. "You appeal to me in every way, Clarissa."

His mouth was seeking hers. She squirmed and twisted frantically to avoid his kiss. Heaven help her, she had no other choice—! Clarissa struggled to get one hand to her bonnet, then tugged desperately at the hat pin. Success! Her bonnet tumbled off the back of her head just as the lap rug slipped to the floor between them, freeing her limbs.

Mr. Whitlatch's eyes refocused a little at the sight of a thin band of steel flickering before his face. "What the deuce—?" he began, but Clarissa fought her way free of him with one desperate shove and pressed herself against the far wall of the coach, brandishing her hat pin.

She hoped she looked more dangerous than she felt, braced on the narrow floor between the two benches, the velvet curtains swaying gently above her head. Now that she had actually pulled out her trump card, she felt remarkably foolish. She pointed her pin toward her assailant and tried to look fierce.

Mr. Whitlatch crouched before her with the blankest amazement writ large across his face.

"What is that?" he demanded, eyeing the wavering point of the hat pin.

"If you come near me again, I shall pierce you through!" warned Clarissa.

"Yes, I daresay, but with what?"

"It is my hat pin."

Mr. Whitlatch choked. "A hat pin!"

Clarissa lifted her chin at him. "Do not laugh! It is ten inches long, and excessively sharp!"

"Ah." Mr. Whitlatch settled himself gracefully on the floor as if it were perfectly natural to choose to sit there. He leaned against the opposite door of the coach. Amusement lit his eyes.

"You are a resourceful little puss. Would you really offer me violence, do you think?"

"Yes, I would," declared Clarissa, deciding to pass over his characterization of her.

His eyes raked her. "Let's put that to the test, shall we?"

She gritted her teeth. "If you make me do it, I will hurt you," she promised. "But I hope you do not make me!" she added hastily, seeing the speculative gleam in his eyes.

"You do this very well," he congratulated her. "I almost believe you." He leaned forward and slipped one hand around her ankle, caressing it.

With a shocked exclamation, Clarissa jumped back and tucked her feet beneath her. "What are you doing? I told you not to touch me!"

"So you did," agreed Mr. Whitlatch. "Shall we stop this game for a while? I am growing weary of it." He picked himself up off the floor, seated himself on the forward-facing bench, and with one smooth movement pulled Clarissa up beside him as though she weighed nothing at all.

Clarissa took a deep breath, closed her eyes, and jabbed. She felt the pin skitter along the surface of something and then push home. She could not help crying "Oh!" as she felt the sickening sensation.

Her cry of distress was lost, however, in the crashing oath that issued from Mr. Whitlatch.

Chapter 5

With great presence of mind, Clarissa seized the end of her hat pin and drew it back out. After all, she might need it again. Only then did she open her eyes.

Mr. Whitlatch had one hand clapped to his left forearm. Fury glittered in his eyes. It was all too clear he was fighting to control his temper. She hastily removed herself as far as possible, which was not very far. She made herself as small as she could against the wall of the coach.

Why did he not speak? He looked murderous. It was terrifying. She prayed fervently that he would not strike her. But she had deliberately injured another human being! It was all very dreadful.

"I beg your pardon," she whispered, frightened tears welling in her eyes. "But you would not listen to me."

He kept his voice level, but anger crackled through it alarmingly. "I did not think you were serious."

"No, I saw you did not. That is why I—" She swallowed. "That is why I pricked you."

"You did not *prick* me," he said through his teeth. "You stabbed me. Vixen."

That brought her head up. "I daresay you will recover from your wounds!" she said, with exquisite sarcasm. "In the meantime, I hope your manners will recover as well! A lady should not have to resort to such measures to ensure that she is treated with respect."

"Now, *there* we come to the crux of the matter," he said. He enunciated each word contemptuously until it cracked like a whip. "Pray explain to me—if you can!—how a doxy's daughter can fancy herself a *lady*."

With a low, indescribable cry, Clarissa turned to him. Her lovely face was suffused with emotion. "My mother's daughter!" she cried. "Is that all I am? Must I suffer all my life for my mother's sins?"

Tears still sparkled, forgotten, in her eyes. She looked magnificent. Mr. Whitlatch found it difficult to concentrate while sitting so close to her. It was impossible to stay angry while facing this overwhelming abundance of anguished beauty. But she had already turned away, dashing the tears from her eyes with a shaking hand.

"You need not answer that," she told him, her voice subdued. "Miss Bathurst must have read me the verses a dozen times."

"What verses?"

"In the Bible, of course." Her face, turned back to his, was woebegone. "The sins of the fathers are visited upon the children."

"Ah. Yes." Every time his eyes met hers, his wits went begging. He carefully removed himself to the opposite bench, and faced her like an opponent.

"And who is Miss Bathurst?"

Her expression became even bleaker. "She was my teacher. My friend."

"Was?"

Clarissa's eyes filled again. "She died," Clarissa whispered.

His brows snapped together. "I am sorry."

She bowed her head. "Thank you."

Mr. Whitlatch studied the girl who sat across from him, head bowed, feet pressed modestly together, hands clasped lightly in her lap. Nothing in her dress or her demeanor indicated whose daughter she was. Had he met her under different circumstances, he would have assumed she was a lady of quality, not a bird of paradise. He shook his head in bemused wonder.

"How the deuce did Gianetta manage to rear a daughter so different from herself?"

Clarissa's nostrils flared with delicate disdain. "She! La Gianetta did not rear me. My father removed me from her poisonous household at a very early age, and sent me to the Bathurst Ladies' Academy. He kept me there, at his expense, until my seventeenth birthday."

"And what became of you after your seventeenth birthday? Surely that date is somewhat behind you."

As soon as the words were spoken, he regretted them. Damnation! he thought. One never speaks of a woman's age! Why could he not bear in mind the simplest social conventions?

But Clarissa did not take offense at his plain speaking. She did not even seem to notice it. "By that time, Miss Bathurst had honored me with her friendship," she explained. "It is really she who reared me, sir. Miss Bathurst had the molding of my mind and opinions; hers was the only parental influence I have ever felt. I worked hard under her tutelage and did well in my studies. When I became too old for school, she allowed me to stay on at the academy and teach some of the younger girls."

Clarissa looked down at her hands again. She spoke so softly, he had to lean forward to catch her words. "If she had not employed me, I do not know what I would have done. By then, my father was afflicted with what would prove to be his final illness. When he fell ill, my allowance stopped. I believe no one else in his household knew of my existence."

"Who was your father?"

"A nobleman."

"Which nobleman?"

Clarissa drew herself up with great dignity. "I will not tell you."

He grinned at this hairsplitting. "Why not?"

"My father was a well-respected man, meticulous in matters of reputation. I owe him my existence, my education, the very

clothes on my back. I will not disgrace his memory by di-
vulging his identity."

Mr. Whitlatch reflected that if curiosity got the better of him,
a few discreet inquiries would easily bring him the name of
whoever was Gianetta's protector twenty-odd years ago. He
could afford to respect Clarissa's reticence.

"Then, I take it, you do not bear his name."

She inclined her head sadly. "It was not available to me, sir.
I have my mother's surname."

Mr. Whitlatch searched his memory for La Gianetta's surname, and came up blank. "Do you know," he said slowly, "I
don't believe I ever heard your mother's last name. She has always been 'La Gianetta.' "

Clarissa's eyes suddenly gleamed with something that might
have been mischief. "Her name is Feeney," she said calmly.

Mr. Whitlatch was thunderstruck. "*Feeney?* Impossible! Or,
wait—I see. F-I-N-I. Gianetta Fini."

Clarissa shook her head, and spelled the common Irish surname with great relish. "F-E-E-N-E-Y. Whatever airs my
mother chooses to affect, she was born plain Jane Feeney."

Clarissa's look of mischief increased as she saw his jaw
slacken. "I fancy that is not generally known," she added
kindly.

"Good God, no!" Mr. Whitlatch was aware of an absurd feeling of disillusionment.

Then a reluctant grin spread across his features. "Very
clever," he said appreciatively. "She picked her own name, a
name to suit her image, eh? Jane Feeney! No, it doesn't have
the same ring. But what is her accent? She speaks both French
and English with the loveliest lilt. I always thought she was
Italian."

"I daresay," said Clarissa scornfully. "Had you been Italian,
you would have assumed she was Portuguese. And so on."

This stroke of marketing genius made Mr. Whitlatch shake
his head in amazement. "Extraordinary. One can't help but admire her."

With an exclamation of annoyance, Clarissa picked the lap
rug up off the floor and began tucking it round her again. "Yes,
one can!" she snapped. "My mother is a shameless charlatan.
She has spent her life deceiving and manipulating others. Do
you admire that?"

"Your mother has lived by her wits, my girl, and carved a name for herself out of nothing. I admire that in anyone."

A crease appeared between Clarissa's brows as she struggled with the idea of admiring her mother. "I suppose she is, in many ways, a remarkable woman," she said at last. "But frankly, sir, her reputation is a cross I have been forced to bear all my life. I would fain have had a less . . . remarkable parent."

Yes, he supposed anonymity would have been more to Clarissa's liking. She seemed a sober little thing. He placed the tips of his fingers together. "So. Here we have Miss Feeney—a name which, by the by, suits you no more than it does your mother—on the horns of a dilemma. An adored father you cannot acknowledge, and a despised mother you cannot deny."

"Very succinctly put, sir."

"I have that knack," acknowledged Mr. Whitlatch. "And as a result, you were buried alive at a female academy. That must have been a hellish existence for a young and lovely girl."

But the eyes she raised to his were puzzled. "No, sir. It was a life I loved."

His brows rose. "Really? Most young people dislike school, you know. They had much rather be home."

To his discomfiture, Clarissa's face crumpled. She looked away. "I was home," she whispered. Her voice became suspended in tears; she shook her head and swallowed, fighting to control herself.

Mr. Whitlatch sat quietly for a moment, respecting her struggle for composure. His voice was unusually gentle when he finally asked, "Then why did you leave?"

Clarissa's gloved hands clenched tightly in her lap. "As I told you, sir, Miss Bathurst died." An unhappy little laugh escaped her. "You must think it odd that I would mourn a mere teacher so violently."

"Not at all. It is clear she was like a mother to you. And you had no father. I daresay it was like losing both parents at a blow."

She nodded. "Very much like that," she whispered. "Thank you for understanding."

Understanding! He was ready to disclaim, when he suddenly realized she was right. The novelty of it fairly knocked him acock. He, Trevor Whitlatch, was empathizing with another human being. He fancied most of his acquaintance would never believe it.

But Clarissa was addressing him again. "That isn't the whole," she said. Her voice was strained. "I would have gladly stayed on, even without Miss Bathurst. I enjoyed teaching, and the little girls had become dear to me."

"Well, then?"

Clarissa hesitated. "I am sure, if she had thought of it, Miss Bathurst might have made some provision that would have . . . would have ensured . . ." She swallowed, then went on. "But her death was sudden, and she had never made a will. Ten days after her death, her next of kin arrived. Cousins of some kind, I fancy. At any rate, Miss Bathurst had built her school into a profitable establishment, and they were anxious to claim it. One cannot blame them."

Clarissa shrugged, in a futile attempt to appear unaffected. "When they learned whose daughter I was, they dismissed me."

Ah, God. This empathy business was uncomfortable. Mr. Whitlatch felt his throat constrict with pity.

"Until last week, sir, I had not seen my mother for over fifteen years. But I found myself with nowhere else to go."

"I see." He absently rubbed his injured forearm. "Declared persona non grata at the academy, through no fault of your own, you were forced to turn to the very person whose notoriety was responsible for your situation. That must have been painful."

She nodded. "Intolerable," she said quietly. "But I had no choice."

He cocked his head at her. "You say you arrived there only last week?"

She nodded again. "Although it certainly seemed longer, to me. My stay there was . . . unpleasant. I am sure you can imagine."

Yes, he could. It was easy to picture the treatment Clarissa would receive at her mother's hands. La Gianetta would obviously have had plans for Clarissa, plans that involved making the maximum amount of money off her highly marketable daughter. No wonder Gianetta had laughed when he accepted Clarissa in exchange for those rubies. In one stroke, she had punished Clarissa for her defiance, and cheated Trevor Whitlatch. What a very good joke it must have seemed.

He thought for a moment, fitting the pieces of the puzzle together in the new light shed by these revelations. Righteous anger began to build within him. Anger at the pious nincompoops who had dismissed a dedicated teacher because she happened to be born on the wrong side of the blanket. And probably, he thought, because she was so startlingly beautiful. One of those sins she might have been forgiven, but not both. He also felt anger at Gianetta, who had cold-bloodedly tried to sell an innocent girl into prostitution. Her own daughter! Gianetta's sins against himself, and against poor Bates, were nothing compared to this.

Oh, he entered into Clarissa's feelings, all right. He understood them perfectly. And for a moment wished that he could lay his hands on the dolts and villains who had misused her. His hands clenched into purposeful fists as he thought longingly of that lovely prospect.

Good God, he had almost abused her himself. That thought made him angrier than ever. Gianetta had tipped him a doubler. She, at least, would pay. There was probably nothing he could do to get Clarissa her position back at the Bathurst Ladies' Academy, but La Gianetta he could certainly put to rout.

He glanced over at Clarissa and saw that she was watching him, eyes wide with alarm. He uttered a short laugh, and she relaxed a little.

"You looked ready to murder someone," she said.

"I wouldn't mind ridding the world of a certain Jane Feeney," he admitted. That seemed to please her, he noted with amusement.

"I am sorry I stabbed you," she said handsomely. "You are not at all what I supposed you were."

As if to prove her good faith, she picked up her bonnet and neatly tucked her weapon through its brim.

He grinned. "I could say the same of you. But you are in the devil of a scrape, you know."

Clarissa looked up from her task, a touch of anxiety in her face. "I realize I should never have consented to ride in a closed carriage with a gentleman who is not related to me."

He waved that aside impatiently. "You did not consent. You had no choice. That is not what I meant."

"What did you mean?"

"I meant, my dear Miss Feeney, what is to become of you? And what's more to the purpose—since you are, in fact, riding in a closed carriage with me—what am I supposed to do with you?"

She leaned forward anxiously. "You said I was under your protection. Could you . . . would you consider employing me?" Her voice was timid. She looked eager, embarrassed, and pitiful.

He stared at her. "Employ you? As what?"

A blush was mounting in her cheeks, but she did not drop her eyes. "Well . . . I had hoped, one day, to be a governess. I was educated to that end. I am a rather gifted teacher, in fact. Do you have children?"

Mr. Whitlatch struggled for words.

"I sincerely hope not!" he finally managed. "I am not married! Why the devil would I offer to set you up at Morecroft Cottage if I had a wife?"

Her blush deepened. "I beg your pardon!" she stammered. "But I thought . . . that is, one hears that many married men . . . well, my own father . . ." She stopped, covered with confusion.

"I see," he said grimly. "But I am not among those who wink at that sort of arrangement. I don't pledge my word lightly, and I don't make vows I mean to break. The day I take a wife is the day I have done with mistresses."

"Oh, I *do* beg your pardon!" she gasped, scarlet with distress.

"Besides," he went on, stretching his long legs across the coach, "I don't expect I shall regret marrying. Unlike most people, I can afford to marry for love. That's one of the advantages of wealth."

"Yes, I—I suppose it would be," agreed Clarissa, edging a little away from the booted feet he had propped on the cushion beside her.

Mr. Whitlatch settled back against the squabs with great satisfaction. "This year, in fact, I'm not going back to sea. I'm staying in the City. Once the Season starts, I intend to look around a little."

She eyed him dubiously. "The Season? I thought you were a merchant."

A grin flashed white in his sun-darkened face. "Do you think the fashionable hostesses won't let me near their well-bred daughters? You underrate me, my dear."

Clarissa sat very straight, her brows knitting. "Believe me, sir, this is a subject on which I am something of an expert.

Without the advantages of birth and breeding, you cannot enter that world."

His eyes lit with cynical amusement. "All doors open for Trevor Whitlatch, sweetheart. That's another of the advantages of wealth. I can look for a bride wherever I choose. I intend to marry for love, but I also intend to marry wisely. Noble connections are all I lack. My wife can supply them."

"Oh. A titled lady, no less?"

"I hope so."

"Most titled ladies are not born titled, you know! They have only their husband's titles."

He yawned. "I'll marry a titled widow, then."

"Well, I hope she arrives with a quiverful of children!" Clarissa said tartly.

"Excellent! That would solve your problem, too, wouldn't it? My wife could then employ you as a governess." He laughed, his eyes raking her again. "Unfortunate Miss Feeney! No bride in her right mind would let you past the door, let alone set you up in her household. My titled lady will have to be blind as well as widowed."

He expected her to utter some conventional disclaimer in response to his backhanded compliment. But Clarissa was not so easily distracted. She did not blush, or bridle, or deny her beauty. Instead, her frown deepened.

"Mr. Whitlatch, pray be serious for a moment! My situation is urgent. I must find immediate employment."

"Must you?"

"Yes! And if you are single, it is ridiculous to discuss ways I could, or could not, be useful to your wife. We must find a way I can be useful to *you*."

Some of the heat returned to Mr. Whitlatch's gaze. "You tempt me, Miss Feeney."

"I asked you to be serious!" she scolded, flushing a little.

A slow smile lit his face. "I am serious."

She ignored this lapse of decorum. "Well? How can I be useful to you? Do you require a housekeeper? I am very neat, and excessively thrifty."

The picture of Clarissa in a cap, with a ring of keys in her apron pocket, was ludicrous. Still, he hated to quench the hope flickering in her eyes. "I maintain several establishments, but each of them is run by a respectable, middle-aged housekeeper. With years of experience, I might add."

"Oh." She mulled this over for a moment, tapping one gloved finger meditatively. "I suppose it isn't reasonable for me to expect that kind of position at any time of life. I've no real experience, after all. But I am sure I could learn."

"Housekeeping is not a profession that accepts apprentices."

"No." She looked a bit crestfallen. "But where does one begin? Would one of your housekeepers employ me as a house-maid, do you think?"

"A housemaid?" Exasperation straightened Mr. Whitlatch's spine and returned his feet to the floor. "By all means! There's a nice life for you! Or would you rather I recommend you for a scullery maid? You may take your pick—on your knees all day with a rag and a bucket, or up to your elbows in grease and scalding suds. Which occupation would you prefer, Miss Feeney?"

She swallowed. "Well, I . . . I haven't thought much about it one way or the other," she said.

Now she looked utterly forlorn. An impatient exclamation escaped him. "You haven't thought at all. Take off your gloves," he said roughly.

Her eyes widened. "What?"

"Take off your gloves. Let me see your hands."

His tone was peremptory rather than loverlike. She hesitatingly obeyed. He then took her small white hands in his large brown ones and held them up for examination.

"Look at your hands," he commanded her. "What do you see?"

She eyed them warily. "Two hands. Ten fingers. Nothing remarkable."

"Nothing? I see two hands of a quite remarkable *softness,* Miss Feeney! I see ten fingers that have never done a hard day's work in the whole course of their existence."

The blue eyes flashed. "Well? What of it?" she said hotly. "Just because I have never done such work does not mean I *could* not!"

He tossed her pretty hands back in her lap. "But why should you?" he asked simply. Mr. Whitlatch leaned back against the squabs again, crossing his arms across his chest. He watched her from under hooded lids.

Clarissa blinked at him. Her forehead puckered. "Why should I?" she repeated. "What do you mean?"

"I mean what I say. Why should you? Why waste your life toiling in a menial occupation?"

She lifted her hands in a hopeless little gesture. "What choice do I have?" she asked.

A short bark of laughter escaped Mr. Whitlatch. "Some women would have no choice," he agreed. "But you are not among them."

Clarissa bit her lip. "I understand you," she said in a low tone. "But we will not speak of that option, if you please."

"Why not? You would be a thundering success among the muslin company."

Her nostrils flared with disdain. "Thank you, I do not aspire to a life of harlotry—successful or otherwise! I will take whatever respectable post you have available. Or—" Her eyes brightened, and she leaned forward eagerly. "Sir, do you have some friend, or relative, perhaps, with children? Could you recommend me to a household other than your own? If the children are young, perhaps they need a nursemaid."

Another flight of fancy. He kept his face carefully bland. "What happened to your governess idea?" he inquired politely.

"Oh, that would be better yet!" she exclaimed.

"Would it?"

"Of course it would. I enjoy teaching." But now she appeared thoughtful. She glanced speculatively at Mr. Whitlatch.

"I daresay you think I am too beautiful," she said.

Mr. Whitlatch, startled by Clarissa's prosaic reference to her own charms, waited for the self-deprecating giggle, the disclaimer, or the explanation that should follow such a remark. None was forthcoming.

His lips twitched. "I do, actually," he admitted, instantly joining in her spirit of frankness. "I'm afraid you are completely unemployable in a private residence. No woman wishes her sons—or her husband—to form a *tendre* for the governess. Or the nursemaid, for that matter."

Clarissa's hands clasped anxiously in her lap. "But do you not think, sir, that if I dressed very simply, and always did my hair in a knot—"

He shook his head. "No good," he told her firmly. "You are

dressed simply now, and I promise you I was not fooled for an instant."

"Then what am I to do?" she demanded, spreading her hands helplessly. "I had hoped to teach at the academy until I was old enough to seek employment as a governess. No one will hire me now. I am too young."

"Oh, no! Just too beautiful," he corrected her, his voice quivering.

She did not seem to notice his amusement. The worried frown still puckered her pretty forehead, and the blue eyes were anxious. "But I do not wish to be a scullery maid, after all. What should I do?"

He pretended to ponder her question seriously. "I think you should grow a beard."

She stared at him. "What?"

"If you wish to be a governess, grow a beard," he said calmly. "I am sure it would answer."

"But I cannot grow a beard!"

"How about a mustache?" he suggested. "I have seen the loveliest of females rendered hideous by a mustache."

Hiding his enjoyment, he watched the emotions chasing across her face. Her baffled expression melted into one of horror. She was plainly wondering if he were mad. Next came an arrested look, as she noticed the devils dancing in the back of his eyes. And then a wondrous thing happened—answering laughter lit Clarissa's eyes, and she smiled.

He had not yet seen Clarissa smile. It took his breath away. Dear God. He had to remind his suddenly slack jaw to stay put. He felt a schoolboy's silly grin split his face. Such beauty could deprive a man of his senses. Even his hearing, it seemed. She was speaking again, and he hadn't heard a word.

"I beg your pardon?" he managed.

The smile still illuminated her perfect features, but it had turned a trifle shy. "I had no brothers, you know, and being at school so long—I am accustomed only to the company of females. And the curate, a little. But he never joked with us."

"Ah?"

"That is why I did not perfectly understand you, when you were funning," she explained.

"Ah." He gave himself a mental shake. "I take it Miss Bathurst was not an exhilarating companion."

"Oh, she was the best of women!" Clarissa said quickly. "But not—well, not precisely hilarious. She did not approve of levity."

"You poor child!"

"A goose got into the parlor once," offered Clarissa. "That was droll."

"Miss Bathurst did not mind your laughing at the goose?"

Clarissa dimpled enchantingly. "No, because I was careful not to ridicule the goose, or shame her in any way."

He broke into laughter. God, she was irresistible. He must find some way to lure this delicious creature into his bed. If it took him all winter, he silently vowed, he would win her acquiescence.

A pity, of course, that he had to win her acquiescence, but that could not be helped. It was unthinkable to take advantage of her now that he was convinced of her innocence. He had always despised men who forced or bullied women. No, she must come to him of her own free will. But he would use every means within his power—as a gentleman—to convince Clarissa that the life La Gianetta had planned for her was far superior to the life she had chosen for herself. A governess! God grant him patience! What a shocking waste of so much loveliness.

But Clarissa's laughter had dissolved, and fear was dilating her eyes. Their speed had slackened. She grasped the strap as the coach turned into a lane. "Where are we?" she asked nervously, lifting the curtain beside her to peer out.

Mr. Whitlatch glanced briefly at the passing trees. "Morecroft Cottage, I imagine. Allow me to hand you your bonnet."

He placed it in her hands, but she made no move to put it on. She had paled again, and had the tense, hunted look of a trapped fawn.

"Pray do not make me go in," she gasped. "I cannot. Oh, I cannot!"

His eyebrows shot up. "My good girl, I will not *make* you do anything," he said, with some asperity. "You may sit in the coach all night, if you prefer. But since that sounds like a dashed uncomfortable proposition to your humble servant, I hope you will forgive me if I remove to the cottage."

He placed his own hat on his head as he spoke. She still sat, clutching her bonnet in an agony of indecision. He felt a stab of pity for her. She was really in an impossible position, the poor little innocent. And she had really done nothing to put herself there.

The coach slowed to a stop. They could hear the horses blowing and stamping. There was a rocking motion as the driver began to clamber down from his perch. The door would open at any moment. Tears of fright were gathering in Clarissa's eyes.

Mr. Whitlatch reached out swiftly to cover one of her small, cold hands with his own.

"You have nothing to fear," he said quietly. "I am no ravisher of virtuous females. Put on your bonnet and come in the house like a good girl. We will decide in the morning what is best to be done."

She stared helplessly at him. Then, without a word, she placed her bonnet on her head and began to tie the ribbons. Her demeanor was as tragic as if she were going to the scaffold, and he noticed her hands were shaking. He smiled encouragingly at her. As if in a trance, she stuffed her gloves into her reticule and picked up her muff.

Then the cold light of a November afternoon flooded the carriage as the door was opened for them, and Miss Feeney and Mr. Whitlatch were handed down.

Chapter 6

Clarissa, stepping from the carriage, found herself on a neat, graveled drive. She was facing the loveliest house she had ever seen.

Indignation stirred within her. Had she been deliberately misled, or was Morecroft Cottage named in a spirit of irony? Despite its mullioned windows, climbing ivy and picturesque appearance, this was no cottage! This was the residence of a gentleman, not a peasant. It was several stories high, large, beautiful, and extremely well kept.

Any hope she had unconsciously cherished of being taken to an obscure hovel, where their arrival might pass unremarked, perished.

She had known Mr. Whitlatch was wealthy—after all, he talked about it with appalling frankness—but she had not thought, during the trials of the past few hours, what Mr. Whitlatch's wealth might mean. She had had no way of knowing the extent of his prosperity. She now realized he must be very rich indeed. Her heart sank.

Clarissa knew rural life. She was standing before what must certainly be one of the principal homes in the neighborhood. Morecroft Cottage's comings and goings would be of interest for miles around. Her presence here would inevitably become known, and merely by stepping over the threshold she would furnish fodder for village gossip.

She clutched her muff tightly and tried to still the trembling of her hands. Mr. Whitlatch towered beside her, increasing her sensation of being overwhelmed. Even with her bonnet on, the top of her head was barely level with his earlobe.

She seized on this, trying to calm her racing thoughts. Of all things to distress her, Mr. Whitlatch's height was surely the least of her worries! There are many tall men in the world, she scolded herself. Still, the agitating sensations remained. Power seemed to emanate from this particular tall man in a very unnerving way. She was uncomfortably aware of his closeness, and felt relieved when he left her side to stride up to the house.

"Where the deuce is Simmons?" shouted Mr. Whitlatch, addressing this question to the ambient air. He tried the latch, swore under his breath, and rapped smartly on the wide wooden door. Then he backed off the doorstep and examined the windows with narrowed eyes.

Clarissa, following his gaze, saw that curtains were neatly drawn across all the windows. They appeared securely latched, and no smoke issued from the chimneys. It seemed likely that Mr. Whitlatch's summons would go unanswered.

She cast about for a soothing remark. "Perhaps they did not receive your message," she suggested.

Mr. Whitlatch turned his frown on Clarissa. "What message?"

She opened her eyes at him. "Did you not send word for your staff to expect you?"

"I pay my staff to expect me!" snapped Mr. Whitlatch.

Just as his aspect was becoming dangerous, a weather-beaten laborer came puffing round the corner of the house, clucking and exclaiming under his breath, and hobbling as fast as his stiffened joints would let him. His gnarled hands were caked with earth, as were the knees of his gaiters. One hand vaguely waved a towel.

"Lord bless us and save us!" ejaculated this individual. "If it isn't himself!"

A reluctant smile twitched at the corners of Mr. Whitlatch's mouth. "How are you, Hogan? Widening the scope of your duties, I see."

Hogan peered uncertainly at his employer. "Eh? How's that, sir?"

Mr. Whitlatch indicated the waiting coach. "When last I saw you, greeting arrivals was not your responsibility. You mustn't let Simmons impose upon you, Hogan. If he asks you to welcome the master, it's only right that he help you dig the turnips."

A cackle of mirth escaped Hogan. "He never! Bless you, sir, if I stuck me nose in where 'twasn't wanted, Mr. Simmons would ask for me notice. I've only come round to tell you, sir, that the Simmonses are on holiday—in a manner o'speaking, that is. You'll be wanting the house key, no doubt?"

"No doubt," said Mr. Whitlatch grimly. "And I'd like to know in *what* manner of speaking the Simmonses are on holiday."

Hogan scratched his head and cast a bashful glance at Clarissa. His voice hoarsened conspiratorially. "Well now, sir, 'tis their daughter. They've only the one child, and not likely to have another at their time o'life. They fair dote on her, sir. The daughter married Fenwick's eldest boy at Candlemas, and she's by way of having her lying-in this very day. And seeing as how we never expected you nowise, sir, and seeing as 'tis their first grandchild, and mayhap their only grandchild, they've gone to be present at the lying-in, sir, saving your presence."

Wrath was gathering in Mr. Whitlatch's face. Hogan cleared his throat apologetically. "They've gone only as far as the village, sir. Will you be wanting to send the groom's lad to fetch them back?"

"Immediately! And you can unlock this blasted door on your way to the stables."

"Bless you, sir, *I* haven't a key!" uttered Hogan, blinking with mild surprise. "Though I'm thinkin' there's one i' the stables, sir."

Mr. Whitlatch bit back an oath. "Then find it! You may send it back with Dawson's boy."

As the gardener scuttled off to do his bidding, Mr. Whitlatch suddenly remembered his guest. He turned ruefully to Clarissa. She stood motionless on the path, her hands buried in her muff, regarding him gravely from beneath the brim of her bonnet.

"Not a well-organized welcome, I am afraid," he said, with what he hoped was an apologetic grin. "You'll think me an inconsiderate host."

She studied him for a moment. "I certainly think you are an inconsiderate employer."

The grin vanished as his brows snapped together. "An inconsiderate *employer*? In what way?"

"Do you really intend to summon your unfortunate butler from the birth of his grandchild?"

Mr. Whitlatch, exasperated, resorted to sarcasm. "Not only my unfortunate butler, but his wife as well! Since Mrs. Simmons happens to be my unfortunate housekeeper—oh, *and* my unfortunate cook! Without them, my dear Miss Feeney, we will have neither fresh sheets nor a meal."

"I daresay you could manage on your own for one evening," said Miss Feeney calmly. "Have you no other servants?"

Mr. Whitlatch felt an impulse to tear his hair out. He quelled it.

"I think neither the grooms nor the groundskeepers will prove very useful to us, Miss Feeney."

She stared at him blankly. "You have no housemaids here? No footmen?"

He uttered a mirthless laugh. "That is the price one pays for maintaining this sort of establishment! Mrs. Simmons has dailies who come in from the village, but despite the exorbitant wages I am forced to pay everyone who crosses the threshold of Morecroft Cottage, only the Simmonses will consent to dwell beneath its roof. A respectable married couple, you know! The scandalous goings-on here cannot taint them."

A blush was creeping across Clarissa's cheeks, but she spoke with tolerable composure. "I fear I am not an accomplished cook, but I will own myself surprised if we find there is nothing edible in your larder. And I am certainly capable of putting sheets on a bed. Two beds!" she added hastily, as Mr. Whitlatch's eyebrows climbed mockingly.

Illogic irritated Mr. Whitlatch. "What of your cherished respectability?" he demanded, striding back across the gravel toward her. "Do you mean to stay here with no companion other than myself? Even such dubious chaperonage as Mrs. Simmons might provide is better than none."

Clarissa lifted her chin, and her eyes met his squarely. "I do not need a chaperone to keep me safe," she said quietly. "I have your word."

Trevor Whitlatch stared into the fearless blue eyes gazing serenely into his. Time spun out while he stood rooted to the spot, knocked as completely off balance as a man could be.

His word? She relied solely on his *word* to keep her safe?

Damnation. Her trust caught him off guard, and, perversely, the very action that would destroy it struck him as the only natural response to it. He was conscious of an overpowering urge to kiss her. He forced himself to tear his eyes away from hers.

"You honor me, Miss Feeney," he said, hoping she would not notice the sudden unsteadiness of his voice. It would be an excellent notion, he thought, to add a touch of formality to what had become an oddly intimate moment. He lifted one of Clarissa's hands briefly to his lips. The chaste salute should have restored his equilibrium, but somehow it did not. Her hand was warm from the muff. So small, so soft. He let go of it quickly.

Dawson's boy came pelting up from the stables, very much out of breath. "Here's the key, sir!" he piped. "Shall I go now, sir?"

With an effort, Mr. Whitlatch focused his attention on the stable boy's eager face. "Go where?"

The boy touched his forelock respectfully. "To fetch Mr. Simmons, sir."

Mr. Whitlatch glanced at Miss Feeney, then back at the stable boy. He passed his hand over his forehead as if waking from a dream. "No. No, that won't be necessary."

He was rewarded with a tiny nod of approval from Clarissa. It was ridiculous for her to approve of an action on his part that would surely blacken her character, but it was not his business to protect her reputation. Quite the opposite. He gladly turned his attention away from Miss Feeney's disturbing presence, and busied himself with paying the driver, opening the house, and ordering the unloading of the chaise.

During the commotion attendant upon these tasks, Clarissa gathered her courage and approached the entrance of Morecroft Cottage. Its exterior was as genteel as it was pretty, but she did not know what to expect from the interior. Doubtless the same lavish vulgarity La Gianetta's home had sported. Clarissa slipped quietly into the hall and took stock of her surroundings, blinking a little in the dimness.

Warmth and silence greeted her. A faint scent of lemon and beeswax spiced the air. As she gazed around the quiet hall, a clock chimed softly in the stillness.

Oh, what a lovely house. What a lovely, perfect house. Her homeless heart contracted with longing.

Every surface gleamed with cleanliness and care, from the mellow warmth of the wooden wainscoting to the shining brass candlesticks on the hall table. Mr. Whitlatch had referred to 'scandalous goings-on,' but there was no hint of tawdriness in this peaceful, ordered atmosphere. She was standing in what was unmistakably a home, albeit a rich one. Its inviting interior combined coziness with quiet elegance.

Perhaps she had misunderstood. Was this not where Mr. Whitlatch lodged his convenients? Her only experience of a demimondaine's residence was vastly different. Morecroft Cottage was anything but gaudy. In fact, there seemed to be few reminders of the century just past. Almost everything she saw was either newer than that, or older. Wooden beams, not gilded scrollwork, bisected the plaster walls, and instead of fleurs-de-lis or smirking cherubs adorning every surface, an elegant austerity prevailed.

Acrimonious voices in the yard caught her attention. Clarissa turned from her wistful contemplation of the house's charms and saw, to her surprise, the flustered stable boy and Mr. Whitlatch himself carrying the luggage up the step and into the hall behind her. Mr. Whitlatch grinned when he caught sight of her bewildered expression, and tossed her trunk onto the floor as easily as he had carried it.

"The driver from London is a fastidious soul," Mr. Whitlatch explained. "He tells me he was not hired to enact the rôle of porter."

Clarissa gasped. "Do you mean he refuses to unload the chaise? It is certainly not *your* place to do so!"

Mr. Whitlatch shrugged. "No more is it his," he said easily, and strolled back out to the coach. The stable boy raced to catch up with his employer's long strides.

She stood in the doorway, watching in amazement as Mr. Whitlatch lifted another armload of bags and parcels, leaving the lighter-weight bandboxes for Dawson's boy. The driver's expression of shocked disapproval, as he watched the master of the house sully his hands with manual labor, was almost comical.

There was nothing shameful in a rich man waiting on himself. It was unorthodox, certainly. Undignified, perhaps. But as she watched, a smile tugged at the corners of her mouth. Carrying his own luggage might impair the dignity of a lesser man, but it only increased the aura of power that surrounded Trevor Whitlatch. One had to admire the ease with which he performed the task, and his complete indifference to the opinions of either the outraged driver or the worshipful stable boy.

As Mr. Whitlatch headed toward the house again, the stable boy struggling in his wake, she stepped aside to let them pass. They started up the stairs with their burdens. Clarissa closed the door against the chill air, and for the first time noticed one of the rooms adjoining the hall. Even with the curtains drawn, there was enough light to see that it was a richly furnished and well-stocked library. With a soft exclamation of delight, Clarissa stepped in to peer at the titles stamped on the spines.

She was still engaged in this absorbing task when Mr. Whitlatch sauntered in behind her with a branch of candles. She immediately turned round, an apology on her lips, but her host did not seem to notice anything rude about her uninvited inspection of his library. He scarcely glanced at her. Instead, he set the candles down and flexed his powerful arms with every appearance of enjoyment.

"It feels good to use the strength God gave you!" he exclaimed with simple satisfaction. "A man should do a few things for himself from time to time."

Clarissa stared. There was nothing one could say in the face of such extraordinary behavior. Her host had walked in without greeting or preamble, stretched like a dog on a hearth rug, and cheerfully expressed an opinion that should be anathema to any man of breeding.

And yet, however taken aback she was, somehow she was not offended. There was so much unself-conscious delight in his stretch. It was charming, in the way of a cat unconcernedly washing its face, or the toothless grin of a baby. What an unaccountable man he was! She knew she ought to disapprove of such unconventional manners. Miss Bathurst certainly would. She was guiltily aware, however, that Mr. Whitlatch's unabashed informality attracted, rather than repelled, her.

"Is there anything worth reading?" he asked, showing that her occupation when he entered had not escaped his notice after all. "The books are mostly window dressing, I am afraid."

Clarissa was glad to turn her mind to a safe subject. "I am not familiar with many of the titles," she admitted. "Some of them seem to be in German, and some in Italian. You do have a *Complete Works*, of course, and several books on horticulture that might prove instructive."

"Horticulture!" A deep chuckle shook him. "I count myself fortunate that you did not come across the *Kama Sutra*."

She lifted an eyebrow frostily. "Indeed! So do I."

Mr. Whitlatch grinned. "Would you know the *Kama Sutra* if you saw it, Miss Feeney?" he asked, with an air of great interest. "You told me you were an educated woman. I did not realize your studies had been so comprehensive."

Nonplussed, Clarissa attempted to stare him down. "I have, naturally, heard of such a work. I have never seen it," she said repressively.

"I stand corrected." His grin flashed again. "Disappointed, but corrected."

From the hall came the unmistakable sound of the front door closing. Dawson's boy was gone. She was completely alone in a strange house with Trevor Whitlatch. Suddenly, Clarissa's hands and feet turned to ice. Her throat felt very dry. Mr. Whitlatch did not seem to perceive her trepidation, however, which was comforting. She was half expecting him to make some lewd or flippant remark, and was deeply relieved when he did not. She swallowed, and tried valiantly to match his air of unconcern.

"I am glad you believe men should do things for themselves from time to time, for if there are no servants at our disposal this evening, you will have any number of opportunities to do so," she observed lightly. "What is first on the agenda, sir?"

He cocked an eye at her. "Dinner," he said firmly.

She could not help laughing a little. "Am I to cook dinner in my bonnet?"

"Good God! What a Philistine I am," he remarked, picking up the branch of candles. "I appreciate Simmons as never before. By all means, Miss Feeney, allow me to show you to your room."

She followed him, albeit a little nervously. He led her up the wide wooden stairway that curved up from the hall to the landing above. When he reached the landing, however, he stopped so abruptly that she nearly ran into him. He glanced at her sideways, for all the world like a guilty schoolboy.

"What on earth is the matter?" she asked, astonished.

Mr. Whitlatch appeared at a loss for words. He gestured vaguely at the door before them, and cleared his throat. "Well, you see, Miss Feeney . . . it occurs to me that . . ." He rubbed his chin, regarding her fixedly. "It won't do," he said finally.

"What won't do?"

"The bedchamber."

"Oh, is that all!" she said, relieved. "Pray do not disturb yourself, Mr. Whitlatch. I know you were not expecting a guest. I will put sheets on the bed, and even dust the room if it needs it. Whatever its current state, the room will do very well once a fire is burning in the grate and things are put to rights."

Before he could stop her, Clarissa stepped forward, turned the knob and stepped into the bedchamber. But she stopped dead on the threshold, her hand traveling involuntarily to her throat.

"Merciful heavens!" she exclaimed faintly.

It was as if she had stepped into a completely different house. Here were the smirking cherubs and gilded fleur-de-lis she had half expected to see belowstairs. A garish sea of rose-pink met her affronted gaze. The late afternoon sunlight, filtered through pink gauze curtains, illuminated a lavish expanse of thick Chinese carpet where pink roses as big as cabbages marched across the floor to a window seat. The window seat was upholstered in rose-pink velvet, with tasseled velvet bolsters positioned to display pink silk roses embroidered upon their surfaces. The whole was bracketed by pink velvet draperies tied back with garlands of imitation pink roses. French silk wallpaper covered the walls, floor to ceiling, in a pattern depicting more garlands of pink roses festooned across a background of vertical pink stripes. Her own trunk and band-boxes, looking incredibly prosaic and shabby, were propped neatly against a gilded dressing table adorned with a repeating pattern of roses, edged in pink satin, and supporting a large mirror and a vast array of crystal vials, pink puffs and rose-enameled boxes. The focal point of the room was an enormous feather bed completely covered in pink satin, including pink satin pillow slips. Gilt bedposts supported curtains of rose-pink silk tied back with more imitation rose garlands.

And suspended over the bed was not a canopy, but an enormous mirror.

Dumbfounded, Clarissa turned her dazzled gaze back to Mr. Whitlatch. His expression was so sheepish that she had to bite her lip to keep her countenance.

"I see you have put me in the Tudor Room," she remarked.

To her delight, Mr. Whitlatch immediately understood her reference to the Tudor rose. He threw back his head and shouted with laughter, while Clarissa turned almost as pink as her surroundings. She had never before made someone laugh so heartily—at least not on purpose. It was surprisingly pleasant to bestow that gift on a fellow human being.

Chapter 7

Clarissa stood before a cheval glass and gravely regarded her reflection. It would have to do. She deftly tucked the end of one glossy black braid under the edge of another, and observed the result critically. A little severe, perhaps, but tidy. And the crown of braids helped mask the fact that her hair was unfashionably long.

She heard the clock chime again in the distance. Oh, dear. It was time to meet Mr. Whitlatch in the library. She was embarrassed by her attire, but it simply couldn't be helped. She did not own a single gown appropriate for dining at a rich man's country house. After all, she had never expected to dine at a rich man's country house! She was a schoolteacher, not a society miss.

She had put on her best muslin—white, with puffed sleeves and eyelet trim—but it was hardly an evening dress. The neckline was modest. The sleeves, which puffed prettily at her shoulders, should have ended there. Correct evening attire would leave her arms bare. Instead, the sleeves continued after the puff, wrapping closely and extending to her wrists. The effect was sweet and chaste rather than fashionable. Wrong as the dress was, it was her nicest. She fervently hoped she would not soil it.

She thought fleetingly of the enormous, gilded wardrobe she had glimpsed in the "Tudor Room," and sighed. Being someone's mistress obviously had its rewards. How lovely, to have a closet full of clothes! She wondered if the wardrobe in the pink room stood empty. If it contained clothes, what would they be like? For a moment she itched to explore that wardrobe. Then she bit her lip, ashamed of herself for entertaining such thoughts.

She was glad Mr. Whitlatch had not insisted upon housing her in that opulent, decadent bedchamber. She wouldn't have slept a wink.

Instead, he had graciously moved her belongings to this room, which was much smaller and farther down the passage. To Clarissa's mind these features were advantages rather than drawbacks. A small room stayed warmer. And the farther from Mr. Whitlatch she lay, the sounder she would sleep. She had moved to a bedchamber that was clearly designed to house visiting gentlemen, but she didn't mind. It was plain, neat, and comfortable. And spotlessly clean. Once a fire had been lit, there was nothing else needed to ready the room for instant habitation. Mr. Whitlatch's statement that he paid his staff to expect him was obviously no figure of speech.

Well, it was high time to leave the warmth of the bedchamber and proceed downstairs. Clarissa hesitated outside her door. It swung softly shut behind her. The sun was beginning to set, and the interior passage was quite cold and nearly dark. She was suddenly overwhelmingly aware of how large this house was, and how empty. A lightening of the darkness ahead disclosed where the stairs were; daylight still faintly illuminated the top of the landing. She hurried forward, grasped the handrail, and leaned over, peering anxiously into the gloom at the foot of the stairs.

"Mr. Whitlatch?" she called quaveringly.

A door opened below, and lamplight spilled onto the hall carpet. Mr. Whitlatch's tall form appeared in the doorway.

"Thank goodness!" cried Clarissa, running lightly down the stairs. "Am I late?"

"Only just," he replied, holding the door open for her. His eyes studied her keenly. "Is anything amiss?"

"Oh, no!" she said airily. Then she blushed. "I am not used to so much grandeur, I suppose. It makes me stupidly nervous."

His eyebrows arched in amusement as he closed the door behind her. "This house is not considered particularly grand, Miss Feeney. We must hope you are never invited to Castle Howard. You would be terrified out of your wits."

She laughed. "Fortunately, I do not expect to be invited to Castle Howard—during this lifetime!"

"Oh, I don't know. Stranger things have happened." His eyes traveled over her, gleaming with appreciation. "You look charming this evening, by the way."

Clarissa dropped a small curtsey. She was uncertain whether it was proper for him to remark on her appearance, but since he had, she was glad he had said something pleasant. She was certainly not going to tell him what she thought of his appearance. He looked splendid. He had changed out of his riding clothes, but, to her relief, had chosen morning dress rather than formal attire. She need not apologize for her long-sleeved muslin after all. The cut of his coat reminded her of gorgeous gentlemen she had seen in London. Mr. Whitlatch, however, looked much nicer in the close-fitting clothes than the other gentlemen had.

With his characteristic directness, he lost no time in proposing an immediate raid upon the larder. She readily agreed. If she had not been so nervous, she fancied, she would be uncomfortably hungry by now. Clarissa followed as Mr. Whitlatch wended a crooked path through several rooms that opened into one another, then down a short flight of steps to the kitchens at the back of the house.

The kitchens were immaculate and completely free of clutter. Clarissa halted in the doorway, clucking her tongue in amazement. Here at the western end of the house, the last light of day poured through high-set windows and illuminated surfaces of gleaming steel and copper, polished enamel, and well-scrubbed wood.

"Your Mrs. Simmons is a treasure!" exclaimed Clarissa. "Did you say she is your cook as well as your housekeeper?"

"Yes, but she employs several village girls as dailies."

"Well!" Clarissa gazed round the room in admiration. "She must be a very exacting supervisor."

Mr. Whitlatch hopped casually up to sit on a countertop. "She may be. I certainly am."

Clarissa stared at her host, perched on the countertop as if it were perfectly natural for a grown man to sit there. She had never before encountered such shameless informality! It was extremely unsettling. But his voice continued prosaically, taking no notice of his companion's perplexity.

"I can afford to hire the best, and I generally do. It makes life simpler. A staff that cannot perform its tasks flawlessly puts one to a great deal of inconvenience. I dislike wasting my valuable time repeating tasks that should have been done right in the first place, and by someone else."

"I daresay," murmured Clarissa, thinking of the luggage.

"I am very fond of having things just so," he explained.

This, from a man seated on a countertop! She bit back a smile. "Yes, I can see that," she said politely.

"I don't mind paying high wages for excellent work. It is well worth it, I think, to hire a staff that follows one's instructions to the letter. I treat my people well, I pay my people well, and as a result I have a loyal staff that doesn't need to be told more than once how I like a thing to be done."

"Another of the advantages of wealth, I suppose," remarked Clarissa. "One can afford to be a despot."

Another chuckle shook Mr. Whitlatch. "Are you certain you wish to join the ranks of my staff, Miss Feeney?"

Oh, heavens, she had forgotten that! This was no casual conversation. She was being interviewed by a prospective employer! It was difficult to keep in mind, somehow, while addressing a man seated on a kitchen countertop. She hurriedly snatched up an apron.

"I beg your pardon," she said, with dignity. "You are right to chide me, sir. I will adopt a more respectful tone."

"Chide you! Heaven forbid," said Mr. Whitlatch. "But if you

adopt a respectful tone, I will spank you soundly." Ignoring Clarissa's gasp, he picked up a spoon and pointed it at her. "Spare me your propriety, Miss Prim! I can think of no worse fate than to be confined in a cottage with a servile woman."

Now thoroughly ruffled, she rounded on him and spat out the first words that rose to her lips. "I can think of no worse fate than to be confined in a cottage with a mannerless yahoo!"

Horrified by her own rudeness, Clarissa clapped her hands over her mouth. But Mr. Whitlatch roared with laughter. "Bravissima!" he cheered, saluting her with the spoon. "It's always best to say exactly what you think."

"But it's not what I think!" cried Clarissa, distressed. "I beg your pardon, sir. I must be very tired and hungry. I don't know what made me say such a thing to you, after all your kindness."

"Kindness?" The frown returned to Mr. Whitlatch's features. He set down the spoon and hopped off the countertop. "What kindness have I shown you? Don't talk fustian, Clarissa."

"It isn't fustian," she said indignantly. She decided to pass over his use of her Christian name. "You have done me a great kindness, and I am exceedingly grateful to you. This morning I was a prisoner in my mother's house. I had no hope of escape short of a miracle. I must tell you, Mr. Whitlatch, that I spent many hours earnestly praying that God would send me such a miracle." She busied herself in tying the apron behind her. "And He sent you."

She marched over to the pantry and began examining the contents of its shelves. "Are you fond of pepper, Mr. Whitlatch?" she asked, holding up a small box for his inspection.

When he did not immediately reply, she glanced inquiringly at him. He had a very queer expression on his face, she thought. "It isn't red pepper, you know," she said uncertainly. "It's black."

Mr. Whitlatch looked at her. Just looked at her. A slender, aproned girl, clad all in white, with her head cocked inquiringly to one side, holding up a pepper box. The fading sunlight gave her a golden halo and bathed the scene in an otherworldly glow.

He had never before pictured himself as a response to someone's prayer. It was a humbling experience, especially when he was uncomfortably aware of his own designs for Miss Feeney's future. Looking at her, he felt almost as if he had stumbled across some beautiful wild creature in a wood; she was as lovely, as graceful, as fascinating, and as unconscious of her charm as a wild thing would be. And he, the predator, planned to ruin this trusting creature with no more regret than he wasted on shooting a pheasant.

It was not a comfortable thought. He struggled to banish it. After all, if he failed to seize his opportunity, some other man would have her—a man who might mistreat her, or eventually cast her off penniless. She deserved better. And who better than Trevor Whitlatch? It was nonsensical for him to suffer these qualms. Conscience be damned! The chit was completely and utterly unmarriageable.

Clarissa Feeney was born to be bachelor fare, and by God, he was going to be the bachelor.

"Do as you wish. I'll light the lamp," he said abruptly. He suddenly found he could no longer meet her eyes, and turned away from the sight of her.

They spent the next forty-five minutes cobbling together a meal. Clarissa began by rather nervously confessing that her only real talent in the kitchen was brewing tea. Once it was clear she had no more notion than he how to cook a dinner, Mr. Whitlatch unearthed a bread knife and decreed that toasted cheese would be the order of the day. Clarissa, delighted, expressed confidence that toasting cheese would not overtax her culinary skills. She began slicing bread and carving cheese with a will, and sent her host to forage in the larder. He emerged victorious, triumphantly bearing a bowl of fruit, another of nuts, and half of a large apple pie.

Assembling a meal was a novel experience for both of them. Since Mr. Whitlatch was uncommonly fond of novel experiences, he tackled the project with an enthusiasm that reminded Clarissa strongly of a puppy fetching sticks. He was not offended by her stifled giggles—on the contrary, her amusement seemed to please him. The funnier she found him, the more outrageous he became, until the kitchen rang with their united laughter.

After an exhausting and increasingly hilarious search, they found plates in the butler's pantry, silver in a drawer of the adjacent dining room, and napkins in the linen closet. The dining room was discovered to be cold and dark, and it seemed silly to eat their humble fare in its arctic grandeur. They rejected the dining room, therefore, in favor of the warm, lamplit kitchen.

Perching rather precariously on wooden stools, they spread their feast on the deal table.

This cozy and cheerful meal exactly suited Mr. Whitlatch's taste for informality. It also soothed Clarissa's sensibilities. She found it impossible to feel nervous of a man while eating bread and cheese in the kitchen with him. In fact, by the time dinner had been consumed, she was chatting and laughing with Mr. Whitlatch as if she had known him all her life. She could not remember a time when she had felt more relaxed and light-hearted.

Mr. Whitlatch eventually pushed back from the table with a contented sigh, patting his elegant waistcoat. "My compliments to the chef," he said approvingly.

"I'll tell him how much you enjoyed it," Clarissa promised. She pulled the wooden fruit bowl from the center of the table and tilted it, examining its contents.

"That was your cue to rise gracefully from the table and excuse yourself," Mr. Whitlatch informed her kindly. "I am to sit here with a glass of port for twenty minutes, then join you in the drawing room."

Clarissa chose an apple and pointed it reprovingly at Mr. Whitlatch. "If you send me out of this room alone, you do so on your peril," she announced. "I have no more idea than a babe unborn where your drawing room might be."

"Probably less," he mused. "You are right. It would be cruel to send you off into the uncharted wastes of Morecroft Cottage. Daylight would find you, spent and panting, still seeking the drawing room—"

"—and very likely not ten feet from where I began," she finished, chuckling. "I always walk in a circle, however hard I try to keep a straight line."

"Well, you wouldn't be able to keep a straight line in this house, try as you might. Belowstairs it's a crazy quilt of rooms, upstairs all the passages look alike, and—"

He broke off, distracted by Clarissa's actions. She was twisting the apple with her right hand while holding the stem in her left, and apparently counting under her breath while she did so. "What are you doing?"

"What? Oh!" Clarissa stopped, looking down at her hands as if just discovering their business. She laughed, shaking her head. "Force of habit, I suppose. Pray do not regard it."

He was mystified. "What is it? For a moment I thought you were practicing witchcraft."

"Oh, dear! No, it's just a silly . . . well, game, for want of a better word." To his surprise, he saw she was blushing. She cast him a look half shamefaced, half laughing. "The girls at the academy do it. You twist the apple off its stem while reciting the alphabet. For each twist you say a letter, and the stem eventually breaks."

"What fun," said Mr. Whitlatch dubiously.

A ripple of laughter escaped her. "Well, you see, it is a fortune-telling game! The stem is supposed to break when you speak the initial of the man you are to marry."

"Ah. That sheds an entirely new light on the practice. Very scientific," he approved, seemingly much struck. "And they say female education is a waste of time! I can see your father's money was well spent."

She choked, but he went blandly on. "Am I never to marry, then? How disappointing. If my parents were still living, I would write them an unfilial letter on the subject. My future blighted! And due solely to their hideous carelessness in naming me! Really, it is quite unfair."

"How absurd you are!"

"Not at all. I defy you to twist an apple long enough to reach either of my initials without the stem coming off in your hands."

Clarissa looked thoughtful, rolling his name around on her tongue. "Trevor Whitlatch. Hm. T and W. I fear you are right, sir."

He liked the sound of his name on her lips. He smiled. "My lady will have to begin at *Z* and count backward."

Clarissa caught up another apple. "I have never tried that!" she exclaimed, laughing. "To play the game backward, I think one should hold the apple backward, don't you?"

"Oh, yes," he said promptly. "Consistency is key to any scientific experiment."

She held the fruit solemnly aloft in her left hand, took the stem in her right, and began twisting. "Z, Y, X," she counted. "W—" And the stem broke neatly off.

"It works!" she cried, her eyes dancing. She tossed him the stem and bit lustily into the apple with her perfect, white teeth. Mr. Whitlatch felt his heart turn over.

He caught the stem and tucked it solemnly in his waistcoat pocket, wondering why he had ever thought Clarissa resembled her mother in any way whatsoever. It suddenly seemed a sacrilege.

"Thank you, Miss Feeney. You have relieved my mind," he said gravely.

Chapter 8

The kitchen stools did not prove comfortable enough for protracted use. Mr. Whitlatch, spurning Miss Feeney's suggestion that they clean the kitchen for Mrs. Simmons, led her back to the library. Since he had lit a fire there earlier, the room was tolerably warm. A few seconds spent wielding the poker sent light and heat leaping cheerfully forth.

Miss Feeney was nearing the end of what surely must be the longest day of her life. Her tired eyes brightened when she spied the comfortable wing chairs before the hearth. Moving as if in a dream, she sank gratefully into the cushions of one of the chairs, curled her feet up beneath her, and rested her head against its wing, drowsily watching the flames.

Mr. Whitlatch observed these signs of relaxation with amusement. Lowering her guard, was she? Good.

The corners of the room had grown cold and dark, but the two of them were wrapped in a cocoon of warm firelight. He settled himself in the chair opposite and leaned back, idly playing with the poker. He was content for a time merely to watch the light play on Clarissa's lovely face. Soon a slight frown began to mar the serenity of her features. Ah, thought Mr. Whitlatch: an opening.

"What troubles you, Miss Feeney?" he asked softly.

Her eyes focused, and she lifted her head, blinking at him. "What troubles me?" she repeated. The ghost of a laugh shook her. "I wonder you can ask, sir."

She returned to her contemplation of the dancing flames. "It is very kind of you to treat me as a guest tonight," she said, in a low voice. "Very kind."

He shrugged. "There's nothing wonderful in that. You are my guest."

Clarissa shook her head. "No. It cannot be. If there is no employment for me here, I must seek it elsewhere. And I cannot stay here while I seek it. You know that as well as I."

"I know nothing of the kind," he said lightly. He leaned forward and busied himself for a moment in replacing the poker among the fire irons. Diplomacy had never been Trevor's strong suit, and he was keenly aware that he must tread carefully in the next few minutes. He kept his tone casual and friendly. "In fact, I was hoping to extend a more formal invitation to you, now that you have seen Morecroft Cottage. You have stepped inside the dragon's lair and discovered it is not so dangerous after all. Why should you not stay awhile, as my guest? It is a pleasant enough place."

She looked up at him again. "Oh, it is a lovely place!" she said quickly. "You know that is not the reason why . . . it has nothing to do with . . . oh, surely there is no need to explain it to you!"

"You are speaking of the proprieties." Mr. Whitlatch relaxed into his chair again, stifling an elaborate yawn with one hand. "I never think of them."

Clarissa's small hands clenched in her lap. "Why should you think of them? You are a man. However long I stay beneath your roof, *your* reputation will not suffer." She looked bleakly back into the fire. "It is very different for me. I do not need to tell you how different. You must see for yourself how impossible it is."

Mr. Whitlatch yearned to tell her what he really thought— that there was no point in protecting her fair name. She had none! It seemed ridiculous to him, to pour effort into "saving" a reputation that her birth had placed forever beyond her reach. But, with an effort, he kept his tongue between his teeth. This was no time for blunt truths. He must turn her thoughts down another path.

"You are frightened of shadows, Miss Feeney. Only think how your situation has improved already! I hope I am not a great coxcomb to say so, but I can't help feeling that being a guest of Trevor Whitlatch is pleasanter than being a prisoner of La Gianetta."

A faint smile curved the corners of her mouth. "Yes, it is. But I cannot stay a guest of Trevor Whitlatch indefinitely."

"Well, I don't know why not." He stretched his booted feet toward the fire. "I'm a very rich man, you know. One is not supposed to mention it—God knows why!—but under the circumstances I feel compelled to just point it out, in case you are fancying that your presence here imposes a hardship on me."

This time he did not succeed in coaxing a smile from her. Her expression was desolate as she stared into the flames. "It imposes a hardship on me, sir. My destiny is dependent upon the opinions others form of my character. I have no hope of securing respectable employment if I am known to be living here at your expense! Nothing could be more ruinous to my future."

"I disagree," he said softly.

She looked up at that, her brows knitting. "How can you disagree? I have only stated what must be obvious to anyone."

Trevor straightened in his chair and leaned forward, his eyes holding hers. "Your views are very clear, Miss Feeney, but it's my belief you have formed them with blinders on. You have not considered all the angles because you have not seen the entire picture. I am asking you to remove those blinders and look round a bit, before making any firm decisions about your future. You must open your mind to the possibility that you have been wrong."

Confusion flickered in the blue depths of her eyes. "Wrong about what?"

He sat back in his chair, a wry smile twisting his mouth. "Why do you wish to be a governess? Let us start there. Do you know anything about the life of a governess?"

"Why, certainly! It is the only respectable profession for a woman in my circumstances. It is the only alternative for an educated single woman who lacks family or fortune."

His expression hardened. "It is a life of drudgery, poverty and loneliness."

"But—surely not! I enjoy children. I enjoy teaching."

"You won't enjoy being a governess! It is a miserable life. A governess' station is slightly above the other servants, and slightly beneath the family, which places her outside the social sphere of either. She must endure the resentment and hostility of the rest of the staff, and the snubs and condescension of the lady of the house. For this she is paid a pittance, barely a subsistence wage in more cases than not. She is frequently required to help with housework. She must tolerate the children's tantrums, and then be blamed for their bad behavior. A governess finds herself the butt of jokes, the scapegoat for all the children's various failings, and an object of scorn or pity to the young ladies who owe her their accomplishments! She must sometimes fend off the sexual advances of her employers, or their sons, or their male guests. And she will have no ally, friend, confidante, or champion anywhere in the house to comfort her. Is this the life you want?"

Clarissa's eyes reflected bewilderment and pain. "Why do you tell me these things?" she said faintly. "I have studied all my life to become a governess."

"Just as I thought!" he exclaimed, leaning forward again. "You have aimed your life in this one direction, never looking to the right or left to see if there was any alternative. You have not considered that you might find a superior situation. An easier life. A better life."

She cocked her head to one side, as if to hear him more clearly. Her brow was still knit with puzzlement. "Is there such an alternative? I do not understand."

"Not for everyone. For you, there is."

Clarissa's gaze suddenly sharpened, and her nostrils flared like an animal scenting danger. "What are you saying?" she asked coldly. "That I should become someone's mistress after all? Yours, perhaps?"

By God, the wench was magnificent. Mr. Whitlatch, caught between admiration and annoyance, swore under his breath. He had rushed his fences! Clarissa knew exactly where he was heading with his devil's arguments. Well, hang it all—if that was the case, it was time to take the gloves off.

"In a word, yes," he said bluntly. "Why not?"

Clarissa shrank against the back of the chair. *"Why not?"*

Mr. Whitlatch realized he had frightened her, as well as angered her. "Take a damper!" he advised her testily, crossing one booted leg negligently over the other. "I'm not going to attack you."

She did not visibly relax. Her expression was eloquent of horror, incredulity, and revulsion.

"And you needn't look at me as if I'd suddenly turned into a scorpion!" he added. "I know you think I've insulted you, but I haven't. It's those blinders you're wearing that make you think so."

"Blinders!" she cried. "I don't know what you mean!"

"No, I can see you don't. I'll explain it to you, if you give me half a chance."

"No, thank you!" she said, her voice shaking. "I don't want to listen. I don't care what you say. It's wicked."

"Is it?" He forced himself to shrug. "Then let us drop the notion. I will exert myself instead to secure you a post as a governess, or a nursemaid, or whatever appeals to your wooden-headed sense of respectability. By all means, Miss Feeney, waste your life, destroy your beauty, ruin your health, and die in poverty! It's all one to me."

Taken aback, she blinked at him in bewilderment. Had she angered him? He sounded so fierce! Why was he contemptuous of her desire to be respectable? Woodenheaded, he called it. She had never encountered such a sentiment in her life.

"You have the most extraordinary ideas!" she exclaimed. "What is so odd about my wish to find honest work? How can anyone sneer at such a simple ambition? All I desire is to live respectably. You seem to think that is foolish."

"Yes, by thunder! I think *your notion* of respectability is foolish. I think you have drawn boundaries for your life that are too narrow, Miss Feeney. I believe you have, without thinking, ruled out certain occupations—one in particular—that deserve your rational consideration."

A spurt of anger shot through Clarissa. "Without thinking!" she cried. "You may be right. But only because 'certain occupations' are unthinkable."

"Oh, for God's sake!" Mr. Whitlatch flung himself out of his chair and took a hasty turn about the room.

"Yes, sir, for God's own sake!" she countered swiftly. "You cannot advance your cause by pursuing this line of conversation, believe me! I will not, I will *never* follow the path my mother took!"

He stopped pacing, an arrested look in his eyes. "Will you not, Miss Feeney? That is fine talking! You sound so superior! So very right! But have you ever stopped to think what might have become of you, had your mother followed some other path?"

A bitter laugh escaped Clarissa. "Daily!"

"Indeed?"

"Yes! I might have been born with a *name*, sir!"

"You would not have been born at all!"

He seemed to be under the impression he had flung down an unanswerable argument. She stared at him, shaking. He did not understand. He could not understand.

"Yes, I would not have been born at all. And I tell you truly, sir, that would have been for the best."

She had shocked him, she could tell. What did it matter? She suddenly felt very tired indeed. Exhausted, she leaned her head once more against the chair's silk-padded wing. She heard his swift tread crossing the floor toward her. The footsteps halted beside her chair.

"Now, *that*," he said quietly, "is wickedness."

She stared up at him. Baffled and shaken, she could not think of a reply. She was so tired. And her future was so uncertain. And he had—yes, he had hurt her, she realized with faint surprise. She felt not only insulted, she felt betrayed. It wounded her, to hear him suddenly revert to this idea of making her his mistress. Why was that?

As she looked at the harsh-featured face frowning down at her, the answer came immediately. She had begun to think of him as a friend. She liked him. He was clever and funny, and she had thought him kind. He had made her laugh out loud for the first time in many weeks. She had started to trust him. And then he had presented her with this shocking idea—why, he was actually *propositioning* her! And in one stroke, she felt, he had destroyed their budding friendship.

To her, it was a crushing blow. But of course it would not strike him the same way. If she packed up and left tonight, he would forget about her in a week. Trevor Whitlatch doubtless had many friends. But Clarissa would feel a loss. She would feel it keenly. She felt it keenly now. Friends had been few, far between, hard to make, and hard to keep, for the baseborn daughter of a trollop.

Tears came to her eyes. Annoyed, she tried to blink them away. This would never do! She returned her gaze to the fire and tried to get a grip on herself.

But her emotions were defeating her. She was too tired to fight them off. Curled in the wing chair, she hugged her knees tightly and laid her cheek against them, closing her eyes against the tide of tears. She found herself struggling not to sob. Dear God, what would Mr. Whitlatch think of her? This was disastrous. She was humiliating herself. She must stop. She must stop.

Gazing sternly down at Clarissa, Mr. Whitlatch saw the confusion and anger in her eyes melt into pain. That surprised him. Why pain? Then suddenly her face crumpled, and she was hugging her knees and weeping.

Remorse and chagrin rose up to choke Mr. Whitlatch. He shoved the heels of his hands over his eyes and groaned. Idiot! Bully! Oaf! He upbraided himself savagely. What a cowhanded way to go about seducing an innocent girl!

Without further thought, he knelt beside her chair, taking her rather clumsily into his arms. "I'm sorry," he whispered, rocking her like a child. "I'm so sorry. Shh! It's all right. I'm sorry, sweetheart. I'm sorry."

Somehow she slid, or he pulled her, off the chair and onto the hearth rug with him. Now she was crying in earnest. She clung to him and sobbed as if her heart would break. He continued to rock her and murmur soothingly, inwardly cursing himself for his clumsiness. Why the devil had he tried to reason with her? Reason with a woman! And from a distance! What was the matter with him? This misstep might set him back weeks.

On the other hand, he couldn't have alienated her entirely. She was plastered against his waistcoat and showed every inclination to stay there.

Mr. Whitlatch fumbled in his pocket and managed to extract a handkerchief. He pressed it against as much of her face as was available to him. She was evidently trying to speak, but her words were impossible to make out between the sobs.

"What?" he asked.

She repeated it, but again he could not understand her. Grasping her shoulders, he pulled her firmly away from his chest. "When you address your remarks to my armpit, Clarissa, I cannot understand them."

She uttered a loud sniff, gave a watery chuckle, and wiped her face with his handkerchief. "I'm sorry," she gulped. "I d-don't know what c-came over me."

"Come, that's better! Are you feeling more yourself now?"

She nodded. He could not resist pulling her back against him. He held her with one arm in what he hoped would feel to her like a brotherly gesture. She seemed to interpret it thus, for he felt her relax against him.

"I did not mean to make you cry," he told her. "It was thoughtless and stupid of me, and I beg your pardon."

"Oh, no! I never meant to be so troublesome. It is I who should beg your pardon, Mr. Whitlatch."

"Trevor," he said firmly.

She sat up, distracted. "I cannot call you by your Christian name! We are not related in the slightest degree."

He assumed an air of mock solemnity. "Even in the best circles, once a lady has wept all down a gentleman's waistcoat it is considered high time to dispense with formality."

He saw refusal in her eyes, and reached out to place one finger gently against her lips before she could speak. "You need not, if you don't wish to," he told her quietly. "But it would gratify me very much."

She eyed him doubtfully. "I don't think I have ever called a man by his Christian name."

Somehow that pleased him. "Really?"

"I have no male relatives, you know."

"Ah. That would explain it." He pulled her back into his arms, trying to make the gesture seem casual, and propped his back against the sturdy seat of the wing chair. He was delighted when she snuggled against him and rested her head on his shoulder. Her innocence definitely had its advantages.

"Tell me something," he murmured.

"What?" she asked sleepily.

"Why were you crying?"

A short silence fell, while the fire popped and crackled. One log fell softly into a heap of smoldering ash.

"I was sad," she said finally.

"Did I say something to make you sad?"

Her shoulders shrugged against him. "I was already sad. But you made me . . . you made me think of it."

He spoke as gently as he could. "I meant what I said, Clarissa, about wickedness. Do you really think it would be better for you to have not been born? God has given you many gifts. I know women who would sell their souls to possess your beauty."

"I suppose so," she said listlessly.

"Tell me. Why would it be so wrong, merely to use the gifts

God gave you? Did he mean for you to waste them? Each of us is given something, Clarissa. Everyone has some special gift, and we all trade upon what God sees fit to bestow upon us. If I'm not mistaken, somewhere in the Bible we are adjured to do precisely that."

He felt tension running through her now, and did not attempt to pull her back when she sat upright and frowned down at her hands clasped lightly in her lap. "I don't know if I can explain to you," she said quietly. "You want to know the reasons why I . . . why I am so adamant about . . . protecting my virtue."

"Yes. Is that a stupid question?"

A faint smile played around the edges of her mouth. "To speak truth, it wounds me that you would ask it. After we had been so friendly together, I thought you had discarded the idea. So it . . . affected me . . . when I learned that you had not."

He groaned. "I am a blackguard!"

She laughed a little. "I daresay! But now that I am able to consider it more rationally, I do not think it is a stupid question. It must seem strange to you that I have no wish to—what was it you said? 'Trade upon' my beauty?"

"That is what I said."

She looked up at him thoughtfully. "Setting aside the moral question," she said slowly, "I wonder if you can understand what my life has been, dwelling in the shadow of my mother's notoriety. Escaping that shadow has become almost an obsession with me. But I have never been able to escape it, try as I might. All my struggles have been in vain."

She looked back into the fire, as if seeking words in it that would make it clear to him how she felt, and why.

"It is more than hateful to me," she said, almost inaudibly. "It is blighting. I have no family. I can form no friendships. The shadow of La Gianetta pushes people away, colors their perceptions of me regardless of anything I say or do. My life has been completely dominated by a circumstance I did not choose and cannot change—the accident of my mother's identity."

Her voice hardened. "The thought of emulating her is more repellent to me than I can possibly express. I will starve in the street before I follow in her footsteps. I will go to the workhouse, I will throw myself upon the mercy of the parish—anything!—rather than embrace a life of harlotry as she has done."

Mr. Whitlatch almost winced. Damn. This was going to be

harder than he had thought. Clarissa had erected barriers against seduction that might keep her safe despite a determined siege. He hoped the barriers would not prove insurmountable. At the moment, however, he felt considerably dashed-down.

But she had turned back to him. It was clear, from her expression of surprised reproach, that she had seen his grimace of chagrin.

He grinned sheepishly at her. "Rather hard luck for me," he explained.

Clarissa was so startled by his honesty she burst out laughing. "Yes, it is," she gasped. "I am so sorry!"

Really, he was the most disarming creature!

Now he was leaning back on his elbows, smiling at her in a way that made her suddenly feel a little breathless.

"Well, if I cannot hope for better things, I still hope you will honor me with your friendship, Clarissa."

She smiled warmly at him. "Of course. Trevor." She stumbled a little over using his name, and blushed. It felt so strange! It did seem to please him, though. He rose, and extended a hand to help her up.

"I'll light you to your room," he announced, picking up the lamp they had brought from the kitchen.

"Thank you," she said shyly. He did not let go of her hand, which was odd, but she decided not to remark upon it. She supposed it would be churlish to pull back after she had just offered him her friendship. Besides, she rather liked the feel of her hand in his. Strange how much comfort could be found in human touch. When she had burst into tears in that stupid way, it had been so kind of him to hold her until she felt better. And clinging to him had, indeed, made her feel surprisingly better.

So hand in hand, they mounted the stairs in companionable silence. He led her to her bedchamber and waited politely at the door while she carried in the lamp and lit a candle. When she returned to hand him back the lamp, he was leaning against the doorjamb and smiling lazily down at her.

It was the same smile that had turned her breathless in the library a moment ago. Now she had the oddest sensation that her knees were turning to butter. Clarissa realized, to her dismay, that she was far more attracted to Trevor Whitlatch than was good for her.

He thanked her as he took the lamp from her. But he did not

move from his place in her doorway. He still leaned there, his eyes alight with some strange emotion.

She felt paralyzed on the threshold, mesmerized as his eyes held hers.

"Good night," she whispered.

She ought to step back. She ought to shut the door. She ought to do that right now. It was foolish to stand here staring into his eyes. But she could not move. She could scarcely breathe. What was wrong with her?

She watched as his eyes traveled to her lips. Her mouth felt heated by his gaze. His eyes flicked back to hers and she knew now that what she saw there, glittering in the dark depths, was desire.

Oh, dear God in heaven—was he going to *kiss* her? Her heart leaped at the thought and began pounding crazily. But it wasn't fear she was feeling. It was something else, some emotion she could not name. The effect was bewildering, terrifying—delicious.

She shivered.

"You are cold," he murmured, reaching up to push a stray lock of her hair back into place. "I should not keep you standing in the passage."

She could not speak. Her face tingled where he had touched her. A slow smile curved the edges of his mouth, as if he knew the effect he was having on her. She gazed wordlessly at him, trembling. Waiting.

"Good night," he said softly.

And he was gone.

Chapter 9

Clarissa drifted awake on a sea of contentment. She sighed, snuggling deeper into the most comfortable bed she had ever slept in. My, it felt good. Hazily she tried to remember where she was. She felt safe and oddly happy. What was different?

Her eyes flew open when she remembered. Heavens above!

Why did she feel safe and happy? She'd be safer in a tiger's den!

Of course, she supposed, anything was an improvement over her situation yesterday morning. Having awakened several mornings in a row to find herself locked in a strumpet's garret, it was naturally a relief to awaken somewhere else. Anywhere else! That didn't quite account for the glow of happiness she felt, but still, her fortunes had indeed altered—and with dizzying speed.

After yesterday's hair-raising events, a person might expect to lie awake for hours, nerves humming. Instead, Clarissa had fallen asleep the instant her head hit the pillow. For the first time in weeks she had enjoyed sound, undisturbed, utterly refreshing sleep. She felt wonderful.

She struggled to sit upright against the soft heaviness of the feather bed. Daylight was pouring through chinks in the closely drawn draperies. The fireplace was stone cold. What time was it? As if in answer to her unspoken question, she heard faint chimes float down the hall.

Nine o'clock! Impossible! Why, she must have slept for— what? Eleven hours? Twelve? And without even the excuse of illness!

Horrified at her own slothfulness, Clarissa fairly jumped out of bed. She made a hasty toilet, smoothed her braids, pinned them closely round her head again, donned her second-best morning dress, and hurried downstairs. In the daylight, the main staircase was easy to find.

Mr. Whitlatch, on the other hand, was not.

Clarissa hesitated at the foot of the stairs, one hand resting uncertainly on the banister. Suddenly a stout woman in a white apron materialized. The effect was so like that of a jack-in-the-box that Clarissa gave a squeak of fright. She then gasped, "Oh, I beg your pardon! You startled me."

"M'sorry, I'm sure."

The aproned female did not look sorry. She was a middle-aged soul of generous proportions, neat and tidy in every detail, with a rather intimidating air of crisp efficiency. At the moment she wore an expression so forbidding that it approached a scowl, but the frown lines marking her features were not scored into her face. She must not use that frown very frequently.

If she were smiling, Clarissa thought forlornly, the woman

might appear quite motherly. This was the face of a kind and softhearted person. Instead, alas, the plump domestic was staring very hard at Clarissa, suspicion and disapproval writ large in every line of her stiff posture and tight-lipped glare.

Clarissa swallowed painfully. She had been the recipient of such glares before, but one never became accustomed to them.

"Would you happen to be Mrs. Simmons?" she inquired as politely as she could.

An infinitesimal nod was the only reply.

"I am Miss Feeney." She tried a rather wavering smile. "I am . . . I was Mr. Whitlatch's guest last night. I wonder if you would be so good as to tell me where I might find him?"

"With pleasure. He's gone back to Lunnon." Mrs. Simmons seemed grimly gratified by the expression of dismay crossing Clarissa's face. "I dessay you'll be returning there yourself soon?"

The housekeeper's tone was waspish, but the inference that Miss Feeney must have failed to please Mr. Whitlatch was lost on Clarissa.

Clarissa pressed a hand to her brow, trying dazedly to think. "Returning to London? Oh, I hope not! That is—well, I hardly know. I cannot stay here, that is certain. What would people think?" She caught herself then, remembering that she was speaking to Mr. Whitlatch's servant. Clarissa drew herself up a little, clutching the shreds of her dignity around her. "Mrs. Simmons, would you show me to the breakfast room? I know I am shockingly late, but I would be very grateful if you could arrange for a little something to be brought there."

Mrs. Simmons's expression had altered slightly. It seemed that Clarissa's speech was puzzling the woman. As if moving automatically, she dipped a slight curtsey and said, rather grudgingly, "Follow me, please." Clarissa did so, feeling absurdly meek and guilty.

Mrs. Simmons showed her to a small but sun-filled chamber where a sideboard graced the far wall and a breakfast table had been placed in a bay window. It looked out onto a garden that would be glorious to behold five months from now.

"Oh, what a pretty room!" Clarissa exclaimed impulsively. "Even so late in the year, the prospect is pleasing."

Mrs. Simmons's air of puzzlement visibly increased. "Yes,

miss. Mr. Whitlatch is very particular about that garden. Very particular, he is."

Clarissa smiled shyly at her. "I understand he is equally particular about the house. He tells me he is a very exacting master, but that you and Mr. Simmons perform your tasks flawlessly."

What was left of Mrs. Simmons's glare vanished. "Imagine that! Well, we do try. But he never said such a thing to my face, and that's the Lord's truth."

Relief flooded Clarissa as she saw the housekeeper thawing. "It has probably not occurred to him that you might like to hear it," she suggested. "That is often the case. Especially with gentlemen, I believe."

" 'Flawlessly,' " repeated Mrs. Simmons, apparently overwhelmed.

"Of course, Mr. Whitlatch gave me the impression that he would not tolerate less," ventured Clarissa, her eyes twinkling.

Mrs. Simmons actually chuckled. "No, that he wouldn't! I've seen him dismiss a junior housemaid for coming to work in a dirty apron."

"Well, you mustn't think he doesn't appreciate you and Mr. Simmons, for indeed he does."

"Fancy that!" murmured the housekeeper, shaking her head in wonder. Her gaze sharpened as she focused it on Clarissa again, subjecting her to a close scrutiny. Doubt and puzzlement returned to her features. She seemed about to say something, then seemed to think better of it. "I'll see to your breakfast, Miss Feeney," she said primly, and exited.

Clarissa gazed round the pretty room. Everything at Morecroft Cottage was perfect. She sank into one of the two chairs at the breakfast table and ran her hands reverently over the thick and glossy tablecloth. She had never felt such a glorious texture in mere table linens. And fresh flowers adorned the center of the table. In November!

Was this what Miss Bathurst had meant when she cautioned her charges against the world's temptations? Heavens, what a thought. Clarissa had believed herself immune to the allure of worldly riches, but somehow . . . somehow she had expected the siren's song to sound a little more decadent. The melody Morecroft Cottage hummed was as sweet and peaceful as an angel's prayer.

...discover that she might have steeled her-...against the *wrong temptations*.

...g carnal affluence, she had pictured grandeur and ...nd ostentation. If Morecroft Cottage had been more ...imagined Versailles to be—covered in jewels, say, or enc...usted with gold—she would have felt no attraction. If Mr. Whitlatch had tried to lure her with diamonds and expensive trinkets, she would have spurned his offerings with loathing.

But she had not been picturing the bait aright. She was being tempted not by voluptuousness but by simplicity. The serene vista beyond these windows, this quiet, comfortable home, the chiming clock and polished wood and cozy loveliness that filled her heart with contentment—ah, these were temptations indeed. She gazed wistfully out the breakfast room windows and dreamed for a moment of what it might mean to live here.

By April, the garden would be a riot of fragrant blooms. The air would be sweet and fresh. The wood nearby would ring with birdsong. The land would become green and lush and full of promise. Summer would be . . .

This dangerous daydream was interrupted by Mrs. Simmons, pushing a teacart through a swinging door at the other end of the room. It was laden with more breakfast items than Clarissa could eat in a week. A spare and dour man wearing a rather haphazard attempt at livery followed in her wake. This individual began moving covered dishes and steaming pots onto the sideboard. He moved with surprising fluidity and speed for such a mournful-looking man.

Clarissa wished to introduce herself, since he was undoubtedly Mrs. Simmons's husband, but wondered if it was appropriate for her to converse with Mr. Whitlatch's staff. She had little notion of the manners prevailing in great houses. She also was not sure of her place in this household; it was most awkward. Was she a guest, or a potential co-worker?

Her heart sank as she realized the answer. She had allowed the staff to wait on her! That simple, unthinking act doubtless placed any situation at Morecroft Cottage outside the realm of possibility.

She now perceived it had been idiotic to describe herself as a "guest," and to ask Mrs. Simmons to show her to the breakfast room! Far better to have accompanied her to the kitchen, where she might have broached the subject of employment.

Why, Clarissa might have replaced the junior housemaid with the dirty apron!

This was a calamity. Clarissa had been here less than twenty-four hours, but already the thought of leaving to seek employment elsewhere gave her a pang. She could picture herself polishing the sideboard there and taking pleasure in its beauty, carrying pans of hot water up the stairs with a will, dusting the library with secret enjoyment of the smell of books and leather and the distant sound of that chiming clock. . . . Daft! she scolded herself. There are other houses.

But Mr. Simmons had finished arranging the sideboard. "Breakfast is served, miss," he announced, bowing with great formality.

Well. Whatever her future held, a position as Morecroft Cottage's next junior housemaid was out of the question. She was not completely ignorant; she knew that once he had addressed her as "miss," she could no longer think of him as "mister."

"Thank you, Simmons," she replied, surrendering to the inevitable.

Breakfast was delicious, but it seemed very strange to leave the table without clearing her place or carrying the serving dishes back to the kitchen. During the years she had shared Miss Bathurst's tiny cottage, the academy's cook had prepared their meals, but she and Miss Bathurst had done their own domestic tasks without assistance.

What was she to do all day? Why had Mr. Whitlatch gone back to London? And when would he return? Odd that he did not mention his plans to her last night. Perhaps he had, and she had been too tired to take note of it. The memory of her last moments with him rushed back, and her cheeks flushed with sudden heat. Why, she had *wanted* him to kiss her! Madness! She pushed the alarming recollection away.

Mrs. Simmons interrupted her thoughts by returning noiselessly to the breakfast room. One of the dailies accompanied her, a buxom country wench who eyed Clarissa covertly. The girl began piling dishes back onto the teacart, her avid curiosity imperfectly concealed.

Mrs. Simmons stepped forward, her own expression neutral. "Will there be anything else, miss?"

Clarissa hesitated. Nothing ventured, nothing gained, she reminded herself. "Mrs. Simmons, I really have no plans for the day. Is there something useful I might do?"

Mrs. Simmons, startled out of her impassivity, goggled at her. The daily dropped a teacup.

"Lawks!" uttered the daily.

Mrs. Simmons seized on this distraction with every appearance of relief. She rounded on the unfortunate girl, scolding her for her clumsiness and shooing her out of the room. After closing the door, Mrs. Simmons turned back to her unusual houseguest. She tucked her hands into her apron and gazed searchingly at Clarissa, her expression troubled.

"Beg your pardon, miss, but Mr Whitlatch gave us no notice of your coming here. Now, I hope I know my place, and it's not for me to question things, but—bless me, miss, I'm fair bewattled! Three years he's had this house, and never once has he brought anyone to it but gentlemen and . . . and . . ." Mrs. Simmons was turning slowly pink. "Well, he never brought a lady here. Not even his own sisters, which I know he has, but nary a one has crossed the threshold. So when I found you in the hall this morning, all alone as you are, and knowing you had been here since yesterday as Dawson tells me, and no maid with you, and no other guests to bear you company—well! I'm afraid I jumped to conclusions, miss, which is more than any Christian woman ought to do, and I beg your pardon. It'll be a lesson to me, I'm sure."

Clarissa blushed faintly. "Do not upbraid yourself, Mrs. Simmons. This is a bachelor household, and I ought not to be here alone. My situation is unusual, but perfectly innocent, I assure you. Mr. Whitlatch has merely offered to stand my friend. Still, under the circumstances, anyone might form a . . . an unfavorable impression."

"Very good of you, not to take offense," Mrs. Simmons said gruffly. "Bess tells me now you slept in a guest room, and Dawson's boy told Simmons you stopped Mr. Whitlatch fetching us back from the village last night. There, then! I ought to have known you was Quality."

Clarissa's blush deepened. She changed the subject hastily. "And how is your daughter today?"

She watched, a little wistfully, as Mrs. Simmons's features instantly transformed into the beaming, motherly face Clarissa had suspected was her natural demeanor. "Ah, she's that proud of herself!" said Mrs. Simmons fondly. "A beautiful, strapping grandson she's given us, and her good man ready to nap his bib for joy."

As if sharing her son-in-law's sentiments, the housekeeper's eyes suddenly sparkled with tears. "My Peggy's a strong lass, and she did well, but a girl wants her mother at such a time. If Mr. Whitlatch had sent for me yesterday I might have lost my situation, miss, for I wouldn't have left her, not for worlds. Thank you."

Clarissa was touched. "I am glad," she said simply.

Mrs. Simmons dabbed fiercely at her eyes with the corner of her apron, and recovered some of her professional crispness. "Well, then! If it's useful you want to be, miss, I am sure we can find you something genteel-like to do. D'you fancy a bit of sewing?"

Clarissa brightened. Sewing was a restful, soothing sort of employment that occupied the fingers but left one's mind free to think. Exactly what she needed. "I'd like that very much."

By the time Mrs. Simmons had her settled in the library with a cozy fire and a basket of darning, the housekeeper's attitude toward Clarissa had undergone a sea change. She bustled and clucked as if she had known Clarissa all her life and nursed her in her cradle. Clarissa rather liked the experience of being taken under that worthy's ample wing.

"If there's anything you want, miss, you just pull the bell," said Mrs. Simmons at last, indicating the bell rope at the side of the fireplace.

The housekeeper headed for the door, and Clarissa felt suddenly bereft. "Mrs. Simmons, do you know when Mr. Whitlatch will return from London?" she asked, sounding a little forlorn.

Mrs. Simmons halted in the doorway. "He'll come back by the end of the day, dearie. And when he does," she added grimly, "I'll have a word or two to say to him!"

With that cryptic remark, she exited. Clarissa picked up a needle and threaded it, frowning thoughtfully. Why had Mr. Whitlatch gone to London?

Chapter 10

M r. Whitlatch had gone to London to seek something he
normally despised: advice.

Unlike Clarissa, he had awakened early, and with a definite
plan for the day. He took care to move stealthily and make little sound as he dressed and shaved by the light of a single candle—just in case. Clarissa had struck him as the sort of person
who could be depended upon to rise with the chickens, and he
rather cravenly hoped to sneak out of the house before she
caught him.

Bates was on his conscience. He had left Bates yesterday,
vowing to avenge him, and had failed. Dismally. Mr. Whitlatch
had little experience of failure. He discovered that it annoyed
him. Bates must have been expecting his friend's return yesterday evening, probably looking forward—as much as he looked
forward to anything these days, poor fellow—to hearing Whitlatch's story. Well, he should have it. It wouldn't be the story
Bates was expecting, but Mr. Whitlatch owed his friend the
telling. He would ride in, perform his unpleasant errand, then
retrieve his curricle from Grisham's and drive it home.

He also meant to solicit some information from Bates. If his
friend recognized a description of the fair Clarissa, that would
tell Mr. Whitlatch a great deal. It would tell him, for example,
that Clarissa was an even more accomplished actress than her
mother had been. That would be information worth having. He
could then cut to the chase, so to speak, with a clear conscience.

Odd that he found the idea depressing.

Padding down the dark stairs in his stocking feet, boots in
hand, Mr. Whitlatch pondered the possibilities. If Bates identi-
fied Clarissa as one of La Gianetta's employees, he need not go
through a tiresome and time-consuming seduction. Also, of
course, he could drive a very hard bargain with her once it was
clear she had tried to force her price up through deception.

But the thought that Clarissa might have been lying to him
was an extremely unpalatable idea. He did not want it to be
true, even if it served his own purposes. Perhaps La Gianetta
was right, Mr. Whitlatch thought wryly. I might be something
of a romantic after all.

He remembered the way Clarissa had nestled so sweetly against him in the library, and a smile played across his features. He'd go bail she was a genuine innocent. And her observation that they had been "friendly together" was right. Hang it all, he liked the chit.

The smile broadened. This girl—if she were telling the truth—would not fall easily, but she would be worth the wait.

Also, of course, seducing Clarissa would give him a chance to rehearse the rituals of courtship before seeking a bride in the spring. He had never tried his hand at such delicate work. The women he had bedded thus far had all thrown themselves eagerly at his head. He couldn't expect that from the well-bred daughters of the *ton*, and he meant to lay determined siege to such women in a few months. It would be well to practice dealing with a girl who was disinclined to fall into his arms on his say-so.

Although the house had been completely dark and silent, Dawson was stirring about the stables when Mr. Whitlatch arrived, and saddled a hack with his usual swift efficiency. As Mr. Whitlatch flung himself into the saddle he told Dawson, "I'm off to London, by the way. You may tell Simmons to expect me later." This was more information than his staff was accustomed to receive about their master's whereabouts, so Mr. Whitlatch rode off with the pleasant impression that he had behaved with extraordinary courtesy.

"Inconsiderate employer" be damned!

He arrived at Bates's tiny flat just as his friend was rising from his breakfast table. Not that one could rightly call it a breakfast table. As this was the first time Mr. Whitlatch had visited Bates in his new lodgings, he stood in the doorway for a moment unseen, and eyed the dark and cluttered room with perturbation.

Fred Bates had fallen on hard times. He had taken as many of his possessions with him as possible, however, and crammed them into a space less than a third the size of his prior residence. The remains of a meager breakfast were spread across a rickety surface that obviously served as either a writing desk or a card table when not supporting a meal. It pained Mr. Whitlatch to see a stack of papers thrust aside to clear a corner for a teacup, an inkpot resting dangerously close to the sugar bowl, and a battered deck of playing cards half buried beneath a collection of bills and correspondence. He frowned.

"Had I known you were living in squalor—" he began.

But Bates started, a glad smile lightening his features. "Whitlatch! By Jove, old fellow, I had almost given you up!"

He rushed forward to wring Trevor's hand with great enthusiasm, and cleared a chair for him by shoving a pile of books onto the floor. Mr. Whitlatch sat gingerly on the edge of the chair, his frown becoming more pronounced.

"I see now why you wanted to meet me at Grisham's yesterday, rather than invite me here. Good God, man! This is no way for you to live."

Bates sank into the chair opposite, a rueful grimace twisting his features. He was several years younger than Mr. Whitlatch, but this morning he appeared older. He had always been a tall and gangly fellow, but he had grown even thinner, and his usual merriment had been displaced by a haunted look.

"It is certainly a change for me," Bates agreed, smiling with a palpable effort.

Mr. Whitlatch pushed the stack of books farther away with the toe of his boot. "This flat is too small."

"It isn't bad, once one becomes accustomed. The landlady shows me a very flattering degree of attention."

Mr. Whitlatch snorted. "So I would hope! It isn't every day she acquires a tenant of your quality. Why the devil didn't you apply to me for assistance?"

Bates stiffened. "Because I do not require assistance."

His friend's scowl became ferocious. "Stow it!" barked Mr. Whitlatch. "There's no need for you to live in such straitened circumstances. My purse is always open to you. Don't you know that, man?"

"Of course I know it," said Bates testily. "It doesn't make a ha'porth of odds. I'll pull myself out of River Tick, thank you."

"Why? You didn't fall into that river," said Whitlatch bluntly. "La Gianetta and that little tart of hers pushed you! Let me throw you a rope, old fellow. You'd do the same for me."

A brief, affectionate smile flitted across Bates's shadowed face. "I can't imagine you ever needing it, but yes, I would. And you'd refuse my help, just as I am refusing yours. Give it a rest, Whitlatch! Tell me what happened yesterday. Did you beard La Gianetta in her lair, as the saying goes?"

Trevor rose restlessly and paced across the room, but three strides brought him to the opposite wall. Thwarted, he strode back and dropped into the chair again.

"Yes," he said shortly.

Bates waited expectantly. Whitlatch's frown grew even fiercer. "It didn't go as I'd planned, Fred."

To his surprise, Bates threw back his head and uttered a crack of laughter. "It never does! Oh, she's good—she's the best there is! Piqued, repiqued, and capotted, begad! Trevor Whitlatch, of all people!"

Mr. Whitlatch grinned. "Well, it wasn't as bad as that," he amended.

"How bad was it?"

Mr. Whitlatch looked thoughtfully at Bates's honest, freckled face. "Tell me something," he said abruptly. "Did you ever meet a girl there by the name of Clarissa?"

"Clarissa? I don't think so."

"Mayhap they change their names from time to time," said Trevor grimly. "This is a black-haired wench. Blue eyes, fair skin. Loveliest creature you ever laid eyes on. You'll remember her if you've seen her."

The sadness returned to Fred Bates's eyes. "I only had eyes for Bella."

A sick dread clutched at Mr. Whitlatch's heart. "What did Bella look like?"

Fred sighed, passing his hand over his eyes as if to shield them from a painful memory. "The sweetest smile this side of heaven. A plump little thing, no taller than my shoulder. Blond curls."

Mr. Whitlatch felt he could breathe again.

In a few terse sentences, he outlined his adventures since leaving Bates yesterday, becoming loquacious only when describing Clarissa's manifold perfections. At that point in the tale, he waxed rhapsodic.

By the end of his recitation, Bates was staring at him in horrified disbelief. "You've installed her at Morecroft Cottage?"

"Yes. Why not?"

"How in God's name are you going to find her a respectable position once that becomes known?"

"I'm not going to find her a respectable position!" said Trevor, exasperated. "I mean to give her a carte blanche."

"You're mad," said Bates with conviction.

Mr. Whitlatch blinked at Fred in astonishment. "What?"

"Get her out of your house, man," said Bates earnestly. "Get her out of your sight! The woman is poison."

Bates leaned forward, clasping his hands until the knuckles turned white. His voice shook. "Oh, I know you don't believe me! You don't think it can happen to you. But it can. It will, if you don't take care. She'll tie you in knots. You won't know whether you're on your head or your heels! A month from today you'll be screaming for mercy."

Trevor had never seen Bates so moved. It was disturbing. Doubt assailed him. "Are you saying I should find a situation for her after all?"

"Yes, if you can! Yes! She says she wants a governess post or some such nonsense. Well, find her one! Call her bluff! And the sooner the better. Can't you fob her off onto some female of your acquaintance?"

Trevor punched a fist into his palm. "Hell and the devil confound it! I don't want to fob her off onto anyone!"

Bates leaned forward and gripped Trevor's knee, shaking it. "You must! If you could only hear yourself, old man! You're halfway in love with her already."

"Rubbish!" snorted Mr. Whitlatch. "What a thoroughly revolting idea! Don't sit there and mouth that pap at me. When I fall in love, if I ever do, it will be with a woman of birth and breeding. I hope I have more sense than to make a dashed cake of myself over a baseborn bit o'muslin! I've had a dozen such women in my keeping. None of 'em has made any dent in my heart."

"You think I don't know that?" said Bates impatiently. "You'd be in far less danger if they had! You'd know the warning signs. You'd be on your guard." He spread his hands beseechingly. "Learn from my experience, Trevor, I beg you. If I never do you another favor in our lives, let me do this for you. Get that girl out of your sight! And do it quickly."

Mr. Whitlatch's mouth twisted in a skeptical smile. "I make every allowance for what happened to you, dear chap, but my circumstances are altogether different. Clarissa's not using her charms to lure me into a gaming hell. Absent that, it will be extremely difficult for her to reduce me to a pauper!"

"There are other kinds of poverty, Whitlatch," said Bates quietly. "Worse kinds. She'll ruin your health. She'll cut up your peace. She'll steal your soul. You won't be able to sleep the night through without dreaming of her. There will be an ache in your heart that never goes away. You'll reach the point where you can't remember what it felt like to laugh, or sing, or enjoy the least thing—"

Fred suddenly stopped speaking and covered his eyes with his hand.

Trevor had never seen carefree, jovial Bates so unmanned. It was a terrible sight. He looked away, embarrassed.

"All right, Fred, pull yourself together," he said gruffly. "I'll think on what you said. And in the meantime, rest assured that I will make Gianetta pay for what she has done to you. I swear it."

Bates waved his hand listlessly in a gesture of dismissal. "It doesn't matter. What's done is done. I walked into the trap. I took the bait. Thank God I escaped as lightly as I did."

"Lightly!"

Bates's smile was bitter and full of self-mockery. "Oh, yes. I was going to make Bella an offer of marriage. Can you believe that? What a cawker I was!"

Trevor was shocked into silence.

"Beware," said Bates bleakly. He was pointing, and Trevor almost felt that the finger of doom was aimed at his chest. "Any man can be brought low by the right female."

Mr. Whitlatch left Bates's flat in a tumultuous mood. The last thing on earth he felt inclined to do—even supposing it was in his power to do it—was pack Clarissa off to some Queen Square seminary, or secure her a governess post where she would be completely out of his reach. On the other hand, with Bates's warning still ringing in his ears, the very strength of his disinclination now alarmed him.

His disinclination, he found, was very strong indeed. In fact, the idea of abandoning his plan of spending a pleasant winter holed up in Morecroft Cottage with the prettiest bed-warmer he had yet beheld, made him sulky as a bear.

By the time he reached Grisham's, his aspect had becoming so forbidding that the host, flustered, forgot that his best private parlor had already been reserved and ushered Mr. Whitlatch into it. A cold collation had been laid upon its table in expectation of the party who had reserved the apartment, but Mr. Whitlatch took no notice of this oddity. The preoccupied frown still marking his features, he seated himself at the table and moodily shook out his napkin. The host bit back the apology that had risen to his lips, bowed silently, and left Mr. Whitlatch to his unordered luncheon. The host would have to set a second collation out in another parlor, and finish the task in record time— but he was too well acquainted with Mr. Whitlatch to risk disturbing him in a black mood.

Trevor worked his way methodically through the beef and bread before him, thinking. By the time he had finished his repast, he had reached a decision. It was not a decision he relished, but he had made it, and by God, he would stick to it.

Bates was right. He was right for all the wrong reasons, but he was right. Trevor must get Clarissa Feeney out of his house. Not because she was a dangerous adventuress, but because she was virtuous, intelligent, and well educated. However base her birth, she had earned a chance at the life she wanted. He would try to find her a situation.

If he failed, so be it. But he would try.

The task presented certain difficulties to a bachelor. Especially to a bachelor with few respectable female acquaintances. A martial gleam appeared in Mr. Whitlatch's eyes, somewhat lightening the grimness of his expression. By God, he did love a challenge!

And one pleasing aspect of the situation had occurred to him. If he sincerely tried to secure Clarissa respectable employment, *but failed,* perhaps he could take his failure as a sign. A sign that he had been right in the first place, and that his only duty to Clarissa was to treat her well while their relationship lasted, and give her an expensive present when it ended.

A crooked smile crossed Mr. Whitlatch's features. It occurred to him that his father would have called his plan of action, "laying a fleece before the Lord." Papa would have expressed vehement disapproval, and warned his headstrong youngest son that the Lord rarely gives clear signs. Never mind; Papa would have disapproved of every facet of Trevor's plans for Clarissa!

If we are to speak of fleece, thought Mr. Whitlatch, I'd as lief be hanged for a sheep as a lamb.

He rang for his curricle.

Chapter 11

Augusta Applegate burst into her morning room like a thrush from a covert, barely taking time to set down the baby before hurling herself into the arms of her favorite brother. "Trevor!" she squealed, pounding him playfully with her fists. "You *wretch*! I know perfectly well you have been in town above a fortnight, and this is the first we've seen of you! How dare you use me so?"

Mr. Whitlatch returned her fervent hug, but then held her firmly at arm's length. "You smell of turpentine," he informed her.

"Of course I do," she replied composedly, patting her cap, which had been knocked askew by the violence of her welcome, back into place. "James has sprained his ankle, the poor poppet, and there's no use asking Nurse to rub the turpentine on it. He won't allow her to touch him whenever he is in the least pain."

"Which one is James?" inquired Mr. Whitlatch politely.

Mrs. Applegate's dimples appeared. "The eldest—which you know as well as I do! Sssh, sssh, Jeremy," she crooned, picking up the child she had deposited on the ottoman. "It's only your uncle Trevor, darling."

"So this is Jeremy!" remarked Mr. Whitlatch, in a tone of mild surprise. "He is much improved since I saw him last. A fine set of lungs," he added, as Jeremy apparently took exception to his uncle's backhanded compliment.

"All newborns are hideous," agreed the fond mother, patting and soothing Jeremy with great efficiency. "He's grown lovely though, hasn't he? Sssh, darling, yes! Such a pretty baby, yes! He's a bit shy of strangers now, you know, but"—shooting her brother a look of reproach—"I daresay he'll be well past that stage by the time you see him again." Mrs. Applegate seated herself on the ottoman with a martyred air.

Mr. Whitlatch laughed. "Give over, Gussie! Is it my fault a sailor has to go to sea?"

She wrinkled her nose at him. "You are *not* a sailor, Trevor! I have never understood why you need spend so much time at sea. I don't mean in the early days, when we all know Uncle

Zachary was teaching you your trade, or whatever it is—but nowadays, when you have simply *pots* of money, why can you not pay someone else to do that? Uncle Zachary did."

Mr. Whitlatch, amused, sat on the ottoman beside his sister. "Are you calling me baconbrained, or merely clutchfisted? I've a gift for business, Gussie. I enjoy it."

"Yes, but you don't enjoy being at sea! I've heard you complain about that part of it forever."

"No, very true," agreed Mr. Whitlatch, pinching his nephew's bootied toes. The baby gurgled happily at this treatment. "In fact, Gussie, I've a mind to stay in England now—at least for the present. As you say, I have the ability to pay someone else to captain my ships. I've been doing so, to some extent, all along. Even I cannot captain more than one ship at a time."

Augusta laughed. "Had there been a way, I feel sure you would have found it! You always believed yourself the only person capable of doing anything correctly."

Trevor grinned at her. "You're behind the times, Gussie! Inheriting Uncle Zachary's concerns and finding myself the head of a dozen ventures, all with scores of employees, soon cured me of that particular illusion."

Gussie shook her dark curls in mock sympathy. "How shattering that must have been for you!" she remarked. "But now that you have joined the ranks of lesser mortals, do you propose to live among us? Are you really staying in England now? I am glad."

Jeremy expressed his sentiments by removing his left bootie and dropping it upon the floor. Mr. Whitlatch deftly retrieved the soft object and began working it back onto the baby's fat foot.

"For the time being," he told her. He shot her a speculative glance. "Tell me, Gussie, have you ever been presented?"

His sister's dark eyes grew round with astonishment. "What, at Court?"

"Certainly," he replied, his attention seemingly fixed upon Jeremy's wayward bootie. "Your husband is a Fellow of the Royal College of Physicians, is he not? You certainly may be presented."

Augusta laughed. "I may, if I ever find the time! Four boys are a handful, you know. Never tell me you are acquiring social ambitions, Trevor! Must I make a push to introduce you to the Polite World?"

He grinned at her. "If you please," he said meekly.

"Gracious!" His sister looked a trifle harassed. "Well, it's something I always meant to do, of course—presentation, and all that—but you know, Robert and I were married in the autumn, and by the time the Season started I was increasing, and then James was born, and the following year I was increasing again—"

"Yes, you may spare me the details!" interrupted Trevor. "I see that you have never found the time to advance yourself socially."

"Well, I was never ambitious in that way," explained Augusta. "Of course, Robert meets a great many important people in the course of his work. I daresay it would not be difficult for me to insinuate myself into a few dinner parties. But as for pursuing the acquaintance of fashionable hostesses—trotting all over Town, leaving my card and paying morning calls—heavens, how exhausting! The boys take so much of my time—" She bit her lip, patting the baby as if it would be very hard indeed to let him go. Jeremy's eyes began to drift shut.

"The truth is, you enjoy motherhood far more than is good for you, and more than is good for the children," said Trevor firmly. "You must think of cultivating the *ton* as an investment in the boys' future."

Augusta sighed. "I suppose so," she agreed reluctantly. "And of course it is my duty to assist you as well."

"That's the dandy!" said Trevor approvingly. "Think of your brother, for a change! I cannot crash the gates without your help."

"Why do you wish to?" inquired Augusta. "Are you thinking of acquiring a knighthood, or some such thing?" Her eyes brightened. "I must say, that would be an excellent thing for my boys."

"Of course it would, my single-minded sibling! Keep that thought firmly in mind and the task will become much easier for you. Not only sons of Dr. Applegate, but nephews of Sir Trevor Whitlatch! Doors will fly open at their approach!"

Her eyes twinkled. "You haven't answered my question," she observed. "It must be matrimony you have in mind. Do I know her?"

"If you do, I rely upon you to introduce me."

"Oh." Augusta was disappointed. "You haven't met someone, then."

"No. But that's a situation I trust can be remedied—with your help, dear sister."

Augusta grew thoughtful. "This becomes serious! If you wish me to find you a suitable bride—"

"Not suitable," interrupted Trevor. "I have no desire to make a suitable match. I wish to make a *splendid* match. Above my station, in fact! I need you to locate an aristocrat who is willing to make a shocking *mésalliance*."

His sister waxed indignant. "If that isn't just like you!" she exclaimed. "Asking me to hit the mark, then setting the mark too high! Really, Trevor, this is the outside of enough! I don't share your ambitions, and I haven't your wealth—"

"Oh, I will bankroll the project! Never fear."

"But I haven't the *time*!" she wailed.

"I can help you there, too," suggested Trevor.

Augusta, cradling her sleeping child, gazed at Trevor in astonishment. Her usually formidable brother suddenly looked self-conscious. He rose and crossed to the window, his color a trifle heightened.

"What you need, Gussie, is someone to help in the nursery," he said, facing her with an enthused expression she instantly recognized as false. "I fancy I know just the person."

"You do!"

"Yes, I think I do. A young schoolteacher who recently lost her situation. Through no fault of her own, mind you!" he added hastily.

She regarded him fixedly, and he cleared his throat.

"I am speaking of a girl—a woman—who is well-educated, virtuous, intelligent—a charming young lady, I assure you! You will like her."

Augusta watched him carefully. "Will I?" she said cordially. She was well aware that the women most likely to enter her brother's orbit were not persons she would be inclined to take into her home. "Where did you find this paragon?"

There was a perceptible pause before he answered. "I only came across her yesterday," he said, rather lamely. "She was brought to my notice through a set of . . . of rather extraordinary circumstances."

"Indeed! What sort of circumstances?" Her eyes narrowed. "And did these 'extraordinary circumstances' have anything to do with her losing her previous situation?"

"No! Certainly not!" he said vehemently. Then he hunched one shoulder pettishly. "Or rather—yes, I suppose. In a way! I believe the school dismissed her because her birth is not respectable, and because her appearance is alluring. But neither of those circumstances is any reflection upon her character! Or her qualifications, for that matter. It's just that—"

Trevor distractedly ran a hand through his hair and, looking much harassed, crossed the room toward her. "Hang it all, Gussie, I can't explain it to you! I know what you are thinking—I thought the same when I first met her. But I was wrong!"

Augusta was slowly turning pink with indignation. "Trevor, have you lost your mind? I do not want a nursemaid whose birth is not respectable, and whose appearance is alluring!"

"She cannot help her birth! And I don't mean to imply that she is seductive; it's just that she is so damnably beautiful—"

He broke off, apparently realizing that this train of argument was failing to advance his cause, and paced the room agitatedly. "Well, I can't keep her! She's a respectable female. If you won't give her a situation, I don't know what's to be done with her."

Augusta closed her eyes for a pregnant moment. "Trevor," she said faintly, "are you telling me this hussy is currently living under your protection?"

"Yes, but she's not a hussy! It's all a mistake, I tell you! She seems to like children; tells me she wants to seek a situation as a nursemaid or a governess. Well, how the devil am I going to find her a situation? Help me, Gussie! I'll pay her salary—"

"Pay her salary!" gasped Augusta. "Oh, thank you, Trevor, you have relieved my mind considerably! I need not *pay* this creature—I have only to entrust my children to her care!"

Trevor dropped into a chair with a groan. "I will tell you the whole story," he promised. "You will see for yourself that this girl is perfectly innocent. You may entrust your children to her with a clear conscience."

Augusta waited expectantly, if a trifle skeptically. Trevor placed his fingertips together, in the manner of a solicitor explaining a difficult legal matter, and poured into her incredulous ears a tale so fantastic that she thought it worthy only of the

Minerva Press. By the end of it, she was tapping her foot with impatience.

"I see that you believe her, but I cannot say the same! Has she any references?"

"References?" He looked blankly at her.

Augusta's eyes snapped dangerously. "Yes, *references*! If she hasn't any, her last employer turned her off without a character! Really, Trevor! I always thought you a clever man, but it appears to me that this minx has completely pulled the wool over your eyes. How can you be so green?"

Her brother's aspect became thunderous. "You haven't met her, Gussie. I have. You may take my word on it that the girl is honest."

Augusta sniffed. "If she is, I sincerely pity her."

He leaned forward hopefully. "Then you'll take her on?"

"No, I will not," she said firmly. "Nor will anyone else! And *that* is why I sincerely pity her!"

Neither coaxing nor bullying succeeded in changing Mrs. Applegate's mind; Augusta shared her brother's indifference to the opinions of others. She was also a tigress when it came to protecting her loved ones. She refused to offer a post of any kind, let alone a position of influence over her darling children, to a baseborn beauty whose only recommendation came from her rake of a brother!

Trevor eventually slammed out of his sister's house in high dudgeon, flung himself savagely into his curricle, and drove north at a rattling pace. Gussie's inflexible prejudice, coming on top of Bates's dire warnings, was infuriating. Their attitudes, he realized, were exactly what Clarissa had been talking about last night. She had faced such bigotry all her life. Seeing it for himself—and in Bates and Gussie, of all people!—was eye-opening. He felt a keen desire to show them how wrongheaded they were, but could not immediately think of a way to do so. Perhaps someday he would force Clarissa's company on them, by God! An hour spent in her sweet, modest presence would do more to dissolve their preconceived ideas than any argument he could make.

On the other hand, he was more certain than ever that persuading Clarissa to join the *demimondaine* was the best way to secure her comfort and security. It was the only profession where her birth would be no hindrance. Quite the contrary! La

Gianetta's daughter would have a distinct advantage over other aspirants to the top ranks of the Fashionable Impures.

A cold mist was creeping up from the river, and soon Mr. Whitlatch's driving coat was covered with tiny droplets. He turned up his collar and wiped the moisture from his face, swearing under his breath. What a damnable climate! He thought longingly of a pretty Spanish property he had recently declined to purchase. An opportunity wasted, b'gad. He could have spent the winter there and returned to England only for the Season.

But then he pictured himself trying to oversee his many business ventures from Spain, and grinned at his own folly. Spain would have driven him mad within a week.

And, of course, he would never have met Clarissa. The eternal optimist residing within Mr. Whitlatch's buoyant soul still believed that meeting Clarissa had been a stroke of astonishing good luck. Once he persuaded her to abandon her silly notions of respectability, she would easily reconcile him to spending the winter in England. And he was now convinced that the sooner she banished virtue, the better it would be for her.

This prospect was, naturally, cheering. He beguiled the tedium of the journey to Morecroft Cottage with pleasant visions: Clarissa hanging breathlessly on his every word, held spellbound by the genius of his arguments; Clarissa falling into his arms, begging forgiveness for the stubbornness that had kept her from his bed; Clarissa discarding the wardrobe she currently owned, which—from what he had seen of it—had been chosen to quell her beauty, and arraying herself in raiment befitting her loveliness.

Better yet: Clarissa wearing garments specifically designed to inflame a man's desire.

Best of all: Clarissa wearing nothing whatsoever.

But however enjoyable one's musings, a lengthy drive in an open carriage is a miserable way to spend a drizzly November afternoon. By the time he reached Morecroft Cottage, Mr. Whitlatch was stiff with cold. The lamplit windows had never looked more welcoming.

Chapter 12

Mr. Whitlatch, always dismissive of details, had forgotten his early-morning mention to Dawson that he would return by nightfall. He was therefore agreeably surprised to discover that the household was on the lookout for his arrival.

The contrast to yesterday's reception was striking. Dawson nipped out and took the curricle without his setting up a shout; the front door opened magically as he approached; the dour visage of Simmons greeted him and relieved him of his gloves, whip, and driving coat; Mrs. Simmons popped out of nowhere with a steaming mug of tea laced with brandy; and Mr. Whitlatch was whisked into the library, where a roaring fire awaited him. He was so overwhelmed by his staff's efficiency and solicitude, it was not until the library door closed behind him that he remembered he had a bone to pick with the Simmonses.

He halted on his way to the fireside, on the brink of ordering them to return and hear exactly what he thought of housekeepers and butlers who deserted their posts, when a soft voice spoke from one of the wing chairs.

"Mr. Whitlatch!" Clarissa said, her voice warm with delight. "I am glad you have arrived safely home. I missed you sorely today."

He turned and saw her rising gracefully from her seat by the hearth, the loveliest of smiles lighting her face, her eyes sparkling. He caught his breath. All irritation was forgotten. It was worth coming home tired and chilled to be greeted by such a sight. Her genuine pleasure at seeing him again warmed him more thoroughly than the snapping fire. The day's annoyances fell from him like a stone, and he smiled.

"It's Trevor," he reminded her, taking her hand in his for a moment and dropping a light kiss on her cheek. "I don't deserve to be welcomed. But thank you."

Clarissa's hand traveled briefly to her cheek, as if unconsciously, and she appeared confused. "Trevor," she murmured obediently, then gave an uncertain laugh. "I am still unsure whether it is right for me to—"

He moved away before she could retreat farther.

"What a wretched host I have been!" he said lightly. "I mean to make it up to you in future." He dropped into the chair across from her and yawned, watching her covertly.

She sank slowly into her chair, doubt in her eyes. He hid a smile. Why had he always thought women baffling? Clarissa was as transparent as glass. He felt he could almost hear her thoughts as she tried to convince herself that his casual kiss had been perfectly innocent and friendly. In a moment, Trevor thought, she'll be ashamed of herself for having thought it could be anything else.

Sure enough, a faint blush mounted her porcelain cheeks, and she bent hastily over the sewing basket beside her. Trevor allowed himself a momentary grin of triumph, but hid it carefully behind his steaming mug.

"What are you doing?" he asked, gesturing toward the cloth in her lap.

"Only some sewing for Mrs. Simmons."

He sat upright, startled and a little displeased. "For Mrs. Simmons!"

Clarissa laughed at him, her nose wrinkling delightfully. "It is not her sewing, precisely! It is household sewing. At the moment, I am hemming table linens."

"You are not an employee here," he growled.

"No, unfortunately. I am only a guest," she replied, her composure unruffled. "But as I am an uninvited guest, this seems the least I can do to repay my host's generosity. I had as lief be useful, you know. I cannot sit idly all day."

He relaxed again, amused. He could not help contrasting her serenity and industry to the last occupant of Morecroft Cottage, who would probably have been screeching and throwing things by now to demonstrate her opinion of being left alone all day with no explanation and no entertainment.

"No wonder you missed me," he commented. "I hope you did not spend the entire day sewing."

"Certainly not," she replied, a gleam of mischief disturbing her gravity. "I also wound your clock, sorted your spoons, and polished your epergne."

Trevor groaned and clutched his heart dramatically. "If your object is to make me sorry I abandoned you, you have succeeded admirably! Sackcloth and ashes would hardly suffice to express my dismay! Good God, Clarissa, how can I ever make it up to you?"

She laughed. "No need!" she assured him, neatly snipping a thread. "I enjoyed myself thoroughly. And I was not alone. Mrs. Simmons is a sensible woman, and her conversation was most interesting. Do you know, sir, her sister's husband's second cousin married a Feeney? Only fancy! She and I might be related."

Trevor, who had just taken a mouthful of hot toddy, choked. When he had somewhat recovered, he fixed his watering eyes upon Clarissa and said grimly, "I wouldn't run away with that idea, my girl! Nor would I encourage Mrs. Simmons to make inquiries as to your connections among the various Feeney clans. She is perfectly capable of discovering *which* Feeney you are descended from."

Clarissa's cheeks had turned a becoming shade of pink. "I know nothing of my Feeney connections," she said with great dignity, "but as it is a common name, Mrs. Simmons and I have agreed that it is unlikely I could be related to these particular Feeneys."

"Most improbable!" he snapped.

Her eyes were on her sewing, but she shot him a mischievous glance from beneath her lashes. "Well, I don't know why the notion should upset you," she said demurely.

Trevor carefully unclenched his jaw. "It does not *upset* me."

"After all, it would be very convenient. If I were Mrs. Simmons's guest, rather than yours, my staying here would be quite unexceptionable."

Trevor smiled through his teeth. "Yes, provided you have no objection to vacating your chamber, since it is an apartment reserved for my guests, and removing to the servants' quarters."

The chit had the impudence to chuckle! "I would have no objection at all," she replied.

The conversation was fast slipping out of Trevor's control. He found himself hanging on to his temper by the slenderest of threads, but he would be hard put to explain why. Somehow the picture of Clarissa being related to his housekeeper, however distant the connection and however farfetched the notion, irritated him past bearing.

He glowered at her for a moment. Clarissa serenely threaded a needle and began work on another piece. Trevor was seized with an idea. "I see what it is!" he exclaimed. "You are punishing me. Very unhandsome of you, Clarissa! I have already apologized for leaving you here alone."

She stared at him, distress and astonishment in her gaze. "I am only teasing you a little. Punishing you! How can you think so? What an odd notion!"

Her sincere bewilderment told its own tale. It struck him like a thunderclap that Clarissa, unlike every other female he had known, dealt straight up. There was nothing oblique about her. Had she been angry, she would have raked him over the coals the instant she saw him.

Trevor hastily begged pardon.

She was frowning. "Yes, but I think I understand now what you were accusing me of, and I must say, Mr. Whitlatch, I think it most unhandsome of *you*! What cause have I given you to suppose that I would behave so—so *ungentlemanly*? And pray, what I have said to throw you into whoops?"

"Forgive me! I have never before had the privilege of acquaintance with a *gentlemanly* female."

"Hmpf!" she sniffed, but her lips twitched. "It is entirely unfair, in my opinion, that a word embodying so much virtue should have a solely masculine application."

He grinned at her. "I shall keep my inevitable reflections to myself."

God, she had a delightful laugh. He suddenly realized he was beaming as fatuously at her as a schoolboy in the throes of his first calf-love, and Bates's warning clanged jarringly in the back of his mind. He dismissed the thought immediately, but it had already wiped the grin from his face. Sobered, he watched as she neatly set swift, tiny stitches in the hem of the tablecloth. Her fingers moved with a rapidity and sureness that spoke of great skill.

"You seem to have done this sort of work before," he observed.

She flashed him another quick smile. "Many times."

"Do you enjoy it?"

"Yes, in a way. There is something about sewing that soothes the spirit. Of course, hemming tablecloths is not as interesting as dressmaking."

"Good Lord! You make your own dresses?" He ran his eyes over her with renewed interest. She was wearing another one of her modest, high-necked frocks, this one a gray wool of some kind. Like the two others he had seen, it fit her beautifully. It was the color and style of her clothes, not the workmanship, that was unflattering.

He tried to picture how Clarissa would look right now if that unappealing fabric were, say, claret-colored. The image fairly made his mouth water. "Would you like some unsolicited advice?"

"No, I would not!"

"What a pity." Trevor leaned back in his chair, stretching his long legs toward the fire, and lazily crossed his ankles. "By the by, aren't you going to ask me where I went today?" he inquired. "I am still waiting for you to treat me to the tantrum I deserve."

"Mrs. Simmons told me you had gone to London," she answered, contentedly stitching.

His brows climbed. "Was that sufficient information for you? I admire your lack of curiosity. You have just the sort of well-bred indifference my mother tried in vain to instill in her daughters."

She must have heard the laughter lurking in his voice, for she looked up, her eyes twinkling. "So! You did *not* tell me anything about it! I thought perhaps you had mentioned your plans to me last night, and I had been too sleepy to retain it."

He laughed out loud at this. "You don't flatter a man, at any rate! Did you slumber through all my remarks, or merely the later ones?"

"Only the later ones, I believe," she replied mischievously.

"Come, that's encouraging! I held your interest for a while."

"Just at first," she reminded him. "Are you going to tell me where you went today, or must I first minister to your vanity and beg you to disclose the whole?"

He grinned at her. "I dare not wait for you to minister to my vanity! A man grows old eventually."

He paused expectantly, waiting for her to prompt him with a demand to continue. She did not rise to his bait, however, but remained tranquilly sewing.

He chuckled. "Very well, Miss Feeney! Although you pointedly refrain from asking, I will tell you. I did indeed go to London today, where—among other errands—I spoke to my sister about offering you a post as nursemaid to her children."

He was unprepared for the intensity of her reaction. Clarissa

cried out, dropped her sewing, and clapped her hands to her
suddenly burning cheeks. Tears started in her eyes.

"Oh, how *good* you are!" she gasped. "Thank you, thank
you!"

She must have seen the guilty dismay in his face; something
warned her that her joy was premature. The blaze of gratitude
in her eyes dimmed, and her hands returned to her lap. Her fingers clenched tightly. Then a valiant attempt at a smile wavered
across Clarissa's face.

"I suppose . . . I suppose she told you she has no need for a
nursemaid . . . at present."

Trevor shifted uncomfortably in his chair. This was one of
the conversations he had mentally rehearsed while driving
home in that deuced cold curricle. Unfortunately, the real conversation was failing to follow the script he had written. Telling
Clarissa of his sister's views ought to have been the wedge that
would open her mind to the idea of accepting his carte blanche.
But he had, as usual, not taken the listener's probable emotions
into his calculations. And it had not occurred to him that
Clarissa would know his sister's views without being told.

In the face of her naked vulnerability, it did not seem possible to immediately bring forward his arguments and offers. In
fact, even a Philistine like himself could see that it would be
nothing short of cruel. He decided to skate past the issue. For
the moment, he promised himself. Only for the moment.

"The devil of it is, my sister does need a nursemaid. But she
won't admit it," he said gruffly. "Augusta has four wild little
boys, and the most incompetent nurse it has ever been my mis-
fortune to meet. But if the truth be known, Gussie enjoys dancing attendance on her children! She gladly pays the boys' nurse
to do nothing, so that she may have the privilege of cosseting
and scolding them herself all day."

Clarissa's smile was wistful. "I would feel the same."

He snorted. "My sister has a thousand amiable qualities, but
where her children are concerned she is completely bird-witted.
She pays a nurse to do nothing, so I supposed she might pay a
nursemaid to do nothing as well! Besides, I offered to pay your
salary."

He saw the shock on Clarissa's face and added testily, "You
need not take offense! I am at least partially responsible for the

coil you find yourself in. It was a reasonable offer for me to make. But she would have none of it."

"Of course she would have none of it!" exclaimed Clarissa. "Good God, sir, you must have given her the impression that . . . that . . ." She buried her face in her hands.

"No such thing, I assure you! I told her outright you were a virtuous girl."

Behind her hands, Clarissa uttered a sound somewhere between a moan and a laugh. "And this failed to convince her? How extraordinary."

A reluctant grin briefly flashed across Trevor's face. "Yes! The silly creature wanted references."

The silence that greeted this remark was deafening. It spun out for a moment while Trevor's jaw set grimly. "Well? Have you any?"

"No." Clarissa raised her face tiredly from her hands and regarded her companion bleakly. "I thought I told you. Miss Bathurst passed away quite suddenly."

Trevor swore under his breath. "I cannot secure you employment without references! What of her successors? The cousins, or whatever they were. Did they not provide you with any sort of letter?"

"They told me they could not."

"Could not!" Trevor, goaded, rose and took a hasty turn about the room. "Why could they not?" he tossed over his shoulder at her.

Clarissa answered in a small, shamed voice. "They said they felt unqualified to recommend me, because they were unacquainted with my work."

Trevor flung himself back into his chair. He regarded Clarissa from under fiercely beetling brows. "In other words, they turned you off without a character."

"They believed I had none, sir." She hung her head, obviously wretched.

Trevor's hands clenched wrathfully on his knees, but his wrath was not directed at Clarissa. "So these ugly customers not only dismissed you, they refused to provide you with the means to secure a post elsewhere. And I suppose you meekly packed your bags! I would have camped on their bleeding doorstep until they coughed up a letter of recommendation!"

That brought her head up. "Why did I not think of that?" she marveled. "A pity you were not there to advise me, sir! Such rough-and-ready tactics would doubtless have caused them to *instantly* capitulate, and we might have been spared this conversation!"

His lips twitched, but he firmly repressed the urge to grin at her sally. "It seems to me," he told her sternly, "that you would be hard-pressed to prove you were ever within five miles of Bathurst Ladies' Academy, let alone that you resided there for years, completed your studies, and were kept on as a teacher."

She flushed, straightening in her chair. "As you say," she said stiffly. "Unless my word be taken, I cannot."

"Well, don't poker up!" he advised her. "I don't doubt your story, after all. But what did you plan to do before I stumbled into your life? You can't peddle an education door to door as if you were selling pins!"

"No, but I heard there were registry offices in London, where one can apply for governess positions and the like. I had hoped to interview at such an office."

His brows arched sardonically. "Without references? Your name would be placed at the bottom of the list—if they agreed to list you at all! Women are cautious, you know, about the sort of persons they put in charge of their children. You should have heard Gussie! I never knew she could be so pigheaded. She's generally an easygoing sort."

Clarissa raised puzzled eyes to her companion's face. "Is it really so difficult to obtain a post without references? A governess cannot be *born* with references. She must earn them somewhere. I understand that I cannot expect to receive a prestigious situation, or a high-paying one, but surely even a beginner like myself—"

Trevor interrupted her impatiently. "You are mistaken! Governesses are, in fact, born with references! It is the only occupation open to genteel women in impoverished circumstances. Believe me, Clarissa, the market is glutted with such women! And they are generally hired because they are somebody's cousin, or somebody's sister, or because Aunt So-and-So's dear friend Miss Such-and-Such has known the applicant's family all her life, et cetera."

A short silence fell. Clarissa picked up her sewing again, her hands not quite steady.

"My father secured me the best education money could buy,"

she said in a low voice. "He believed he was providing for my future. I, too, thought he had given me the means to avoid both poverty and disgrace. Now it appears he did not succeed, and I must choose between them."

He frowned. "Choose between what?"

"Poverty and disgrace." Her fingers trembled as she set another stitch.

Trevor felt a stab of exasperation. "There is no need for these heart-burnings! I won't pretend to misunderstand you. You speak of choosing between life as a menial, and the kind of life I offered you yesterday. A menial's life is certainly one of poverty, with all its attendant miseries. But I still cannot fathom why you think becoming a gentleman's *chère amie* would be such a disgrace."

A mirthless laugh escaped her. "If you do not understand why prostitution is disgraceful, I cannot explain it to you!"

His eyes gleamed; this was the opening for which he had hoped. He might be able to make her an offer tonight after all. "Try."

He waited, feeling like a cat crouching before a mouse hole.

Clarissa's fingers stilled. She seemed taken aback. He watched, not unhopeful, as she struggled for a moment to find words and then shrugged helplessly. "Some truths simply *are*. One cannot give a reason. I could refer you to the Bible, of course—"

"Yes, I've no doubt you could. But those are not your words. A parrot can quote scripture! I want to know why *you*, Clarissa Feeney, believe it is wrong to trade pleasure for income."

She had put the sewing away in the basket, folded her hands in her lap, and leveled her gaze at him accusingly.

He held up one hand as if fending off her reproach. "Forget the ulterior motive you are ascribing to my question! I only ask you to explain your views to me as you would explain them to any friend."

"Very well," she replied icily. "Prostitution is wrong because it divides married persons, whom God has joined together as one flesh. It is wrong because it causes men to break faith with their wives. It causes them to spend money wastefully, money that would be better spent on their families. It wreaks havoc on the lives of innocent women who are betrayed, abandoned, or even impoverished through their unfaithful husbands."

"I am not speaking of married persons," Trevor countered. "I have told you already that I have no patience with men—or women!—who hold their marriage vows lightly. But what of arrangements between unmarried persons? Whom do they harm? For myself, I confess it seems a completely different matter. I see nothing wrong with a convenient and pleasant liaison, if there is no third party to consider."

Clarissa's eyes flashed. "There is always a third party to consider! My entire life has been an object lesson in why prostitution is wrong! Even in such an arrangement as you describe, do you not, at the very least, run the risk of creating new life?"

Mr. Whitlatch was silenced. A hit, he acknowledged wryly to himself. A palpable hit.

He tossed off the last of his drink and set down the mug. It was time to try a fresh approach. He leaned forward, elbows on knees, and spoke gently.

"I know your views on the matter, but for good or ill, my dear, you have been born. Now that you are among the living, you must want something from life. What is it?"

She looked up at him warily. He was reminded once again of a wild creature, scenting danger. "What do you mean?"

"I know what you planned your life to be. And I know what you expect your life to be. But what do you *want* your life to be? Surely no one dreams of becoming a governess. Is that really the height of your ambition?"

Her apprehension seemed to fade. To his surprise, a shy smile flitted across her features. The effect was charming. "Of course not."

He returned her smile. "Well, then?"

She played with the edge of her sewing a little nervously. "One cannot always have what one desires. It is better to seek . . . achievable goals."

"Ah," he said softly. "You must secretly cherish some goal you believe is *not* achievable."

She laughed a little, self-consciously shaking her head. "Well, it is certainly not in my hands!" Her eyes met his fleetingly, then dropped. "I suppose I want what every woman wants."

"And that is . . . ?"

She blushed again. "It does no good to speak of such things.

But of course I would rather marry than be a governess. Anyone would."

Trevor folded his hands across his waistcoat and crossed his legs, watching her from under hooded lids. Best to get her secret hopes out in the open—where he could pull them to bits. He hoped she wouldn't take it too hard. An unfamiliar, uncomfortable feeling of guilt stirred within him, but he quashed it. This was no time to grow a conscience! Not now, when he could sense his quarry weakening.

"Tell me," he invited. "Do you think you might marry someday?"

Clarissa looked doubtfully at him for a moment, but seemed to decide his question was innocent enough. Her sewing dropped as if forgotten, and she gazed into the fire.

"It is not impossible. We spoke of God's gifts the other day. I know that the gift of love and marriage is not given to everyone," she said slowly. "But it is often given to . . . unlikely recipients."

"Such as yourself?"

She nodded. Her expression became wistful again. "I enjoy other people's children, but I would dearly love to have children of my own."

He kept his tone encouraging. "And when you picture marriage, what sort of husband does your imagination conjure? What kind of life would you fancy? In your heart of hearts."

Her eyes were wide and misty. She gazed into the flames as if she could read her future in them. Her pensive reverie was lovely to behold, but Trevor found himself chafing with impatience as he watched her. He knew she had been harboring some idiotic, schoolgirlish fantasy! This was it.

"He need not be handsome, or rich," she said dreamily. "A kind man. Perhaps a scholarly man; a reader of books. I believe I could be happy with very little. A small garden would be nice, and a few chickens or geese."

Trevor could not repress a sneer. "Love in a cottage, in fact!"

Clarissa took no notice of his sarcasm, but continued to gaze tenderly into the fire. "Yes," she agreed, sighing, "that would be lovely."

"You are aware, I trust, that such cottages are far more pleasant to look at than to live in. And that they generally house farm laborers."

The jeering note that had crept into his voice seemed to penetrate her consciousness at last. Clarissa's eyes refocused and returned, somewhat apprehensively, to her companion. "Yes, I suppose. Not always."

"Clarissa, you are far too well-educated to be happy with an illiterate clodhopper!"

Her temper flashed again. "Yes—more's the pity! And you need not tell me that I am no fit wife for a *gentleman*. I know that, too."

"Then whom do you picture sharing this rustic life with you? Where will you find your gentle, scholarly—yet oddly impoverished!—companion?"

She lifted her chin defiantly at him. "You asked me to describe my ideal, and I have done so! I did not say I expect to find it."

"You won't!" he told her bluntly. "In fact, Clarissa, here is your dilemma in a nutshell: Every man whom you could possibly consider marrying will deem you unmarriageable."

He leaned back in his chair, certain that he had just flung down the card that would take the trick. But he had not. Clarissa's hands clenched on the arms of her chair, and her voice shook with emotion.

"That is not true! You speak as if everyone was reared to consider only the surface—to seek only worldly gain! For that is what *you* seek, in marriage and in everything else! You have made that clear! But not everyone is brought up so. Not everyone is taught to study *only* their own advantage! It may be difficult for you to believe, Mr. Whitlatch, but there are people who place a high value on inner qualities! On . . . on . . . character! And temperament! And virtue! And . . ."

Her voice became wholly suspended in tears. She dug fiercely in the mending basket at her feet, extracted a handkerchief, and defiantly blew her nose.

Trevor was thrown off balance. He found himself struggling once again to suppress the pangs of conscience. Blast the wench! He had injured her rubbishing *feelings* again! But it was for her own good. The sooner Clarissa faced reality, the better off she would be. It would do her a great disservice to encourage such a dangerous fantasy. The mores of the world were universal. Unalterable.

He scowled. "Marriages may be made in heaven, but so long

as they are contracted here on earth, they will remain what they have always been—commercial pacts."

He had meant to adopt a patient, firm tone with her, suitable for pointing out the magnitude of her error, but somehow he missed the mark. Even to his own ears, he merely sounded sulky.

Clarissa's wet eyes widened accusingly. "You told me yourself you hoped to marry for love!"

He stifled an impatient exclamation. "I *hope* to marry for love! But I *plan* to marry well. I intend to have both if the two are not incompatible. But only a fool lets his heart rule his head! That is the way of the world, Clarissa."

"No one is more aware of that than I!" She sniffed, refolding the damp handkerchief with shaking hands. "I do not expect to marry, but I do not concede that it is impossible. I am sure there are educated, virtuous, gently bred men who might overlook my . . . my lack of connections."

He stared incredulously at her. "This is delusion! Only the lower classes marry solely for love. One of the things an educated man learns while being educated is to seek a bride as high as he may! Where will you find an intelligent man who is indifferent to his wife's background? What sort of a man is reared to care for virtue alone in his bride?"

Clarissa's spine straightened. Her eyes blazed in her lovely face. She looked magnificent. "A vicar's son!" she cried, in the manner of one throwing down a gauntlet.

Trevor's jaw dropped. So this was the secret wish of Clarissa Feeney's heart—to marry a vicar's son. She dreamed of someday meeting a mild-mannered, unworldly nincompoop who would place his trust in Heaven and wed her for love.

He threw back his head and roared with laughter. He laughed until tears gathered in the corners of his eyes. He laughed until he choked. Then he wiped his streaming eyes, shaking his head and gasping. "Oh, Clarissa! Oh, Clarissa, that's rich!"

"I fail to see the joke," said Clarissa. Her voice was small, and shook a little.

Trevor looked at her, and the sight of her hurt feelings sobered him a bit. His laughter subsided into a lopsided grin.

"The joke," he explained, "is that I am a vicar's son."

This time it was Clarissa's jaw that dropped. The door swung noiselessly open, and Simmons stepped into the room. "Dinner is served, sir," he announced in sepulchral tones.

Chapter 13

Clarissa set down her fork with a sigh. "Two persons cannot possibly do justice to this dinner," she said, with real regret. She gazed at the barely touched platters of food arrayed before her, and shook her head in disturbed wonder. The unnecessary magnificence of this meal struck her as decadent. It was costing her a severe struggle to hold her tongue on the subject.

Mr. Whitlatch had offered her a hasty apology when dinner was announced, and she had swallowed her distress and accepted it. No good alternative had presented itself to her; she was, however unwillingly, a guest in the man's home. And once she had consented to dine alone with a single gentleman, an action she knew perfectly well would ruin her if it ever became known, she was in a poor position to object to the uncalled-for lavishness of the dinner. Or, for that matter, to cavil at the seating arrangement. Mr. Whitlatch was seated at the head of the table, with Clarissa at his left hand rather than at the foot—improper for dining tête-à-tête, but, as Trevor had pointed out, far more convenient. Her host had yet again chosen convenience over propriety. He was certainly consistent.

Now he was grinning at her over the rim of his wineglass. "You sound as if you don't approve."

"I do not," she said earnestly, relieved to speak her mind at last. "It is a shocking waste, sir. There are many hungry people in the world."

Her companion appeared utterly unrepentant. Even at dinner he lounged at his ease, leaning on one elbow in a way that would have earned him instant dismissal from the table at Miss Bathurst's Ladies' Academy. His dark eyes gleamed with amusement.

"I am happy to say that you need not add this meal to the list of my iniquities. Whatever was not grown in my own gardens was purchased at fair market value."

She blushed for her rudeness. "I beg your pardon! I did not mean to criticize you."

His swarthy features lit with that peculiarly engaging grin of his. "You didn't offend me."

No; she was fast reaching the conclusion that it was impossible to offend Mr. Whitlatch! He seemed to have no notion of the rules governing polite conduct. Why did she find his utter lack of propriety *attractive*? Really, the effect he had on her was inexplicable.

She eyed him doubtfully. "Are you truly a vicar's son?" she asked.

He chuckled. "Shocking, isn't it? To have fallen so far!"

She flushed scarlet. "Oh, dear! I ought not to blurt out such a question. I beg your pardon."

He set his wineglass down and took up his fork again. "You know, I wish you will rid your mind of the notion that I am a fragile fellow, forever needing to have my pardon begged."

Clarissa watched, fascinated, as he carved off a bite of roast chicken with as much relish as if he had not already eaten enough for two people. "Oddly enough, I was just thinking that," she said politely. "You are amazingly thick-skinned, sir."

"Um," he agreed, chewing. "Never take offense where none was meant. 'S'one of my rules."

Her eyes twinkled. "What an excellent rule. I imagine you frequently wish that others followed it."

Good heavens, the man did not even take offense at *that*! He chuckled, and lifted his wineglass to her! Despite her best intentions, she burst out laughing.

"That's better," he said approvingly. "The way you were eyeing that ham and yawping about the poor, I thought you were planning to read me a lecture. I'd much rather you laughed at me."

"I ought not to laugh, sir," she said ruefully. "It is no laughing matter, after all! I am sure my time would be better spent in reading you a lecture, as you call it."

"On the contrary! Your time would be completely wasted."

She smiled. "I cannot believe you to be completely lost to virtue, Trevor, after all your kindness to me."

A swift frown momentarily darkened his features, and she felt him withdraw from her in some indefinable manner. The moment passed so quickly, however, she was not sure she had seen it. Almost immediately he was teasing her again.

"I am immune to rudeness of every sort, Clarissa. I go further: I welcome it! I draw the line, however, at sermons delivered over dinner. My kindness, as you have erroneously called it, does not extend that far."

She laughed. "You have patiently borne with my preaching already, I think! I do not blame you for desiring a change. What rudeness shall I inflict upon you next?"

He chewed thoughtfully, pretending to consider the possibilities. "You had begun very nicely, I think," he suggested.

She bit her lip, dismayed. "Oh, dear! Had I?"

He swallowed another mouthful of wine. "Yes," he said simply. "You were expressing doubts about my parentage."

She choked. "You know perfectly well I never meant it so! I expressed only my amazement that someone so—so unconventional—began life as a vicar's son."

"Ah. Perhaps it will clarify matters if I explain that I was my father's *third* son. By the time I arrived, it was abundantly clear that both Phillip and James were going to follow in Papa's saintly footsteps. It would have been redundant for me to do the same."

"Whose footsteps did you follow, then?"

"My uncle's. They led me, originally, to the East India Company."

Clarissa coaxed the tale from him, so engrossed that she barely noticed the servants' silent removal of the dinner plates. Her host's casualness had its natural effect, and she soon abandoned decorum, placing her elbows on the table and leaning her head on one hand, raptly watching the candlelight flicker across the strong planes of Mr. Whitlatch's face as he talked.

He spoke with affection of his dashing, eccentric uncle, Zachary Whitlatch, and the knack for business he had apparently inherited from him. Pious Philip and scholarly James had felt themselves marked for the Church at an early age, but young Trevor had taken to his uncle's seafaring vocation like a duck to water. With his parents' fond blessing, Trevor accompanied his uncle on several trial voyages, and then left home for good at the age of sixteen to become his childless uncle's protégé and heir.

By the time he had described his early career, the candle set between them was burning low in its socket. He picked up a pair of snuffers and leisurely removed part of the wick. As the light intensified slightly, Clarissa sighed and blinked a little.

"It must be wonderful to be a boy, and go to sea," she said dreamily. "I have always longed to see the world."

He shot her an amused glance. "It's wonderful only so long as one remains, in fact, a boy," he told her, finishing his attentions to the candle. "These days, I only enjoy being at sea for the first week or so. Then it becomes a dead bore."

"A bore!" she exclaimed. "How is that possible?"

He tossed the snuffers back onto the tablecloth and leaned back, grinning at her indignant expression. "Bad food, low company, cramped quarters, nothing to do—and by the second week, I promise you, one is well advised to stay upwind of the crew."

She had not thought of that. "Oh, dear. But then, at the end of the voyage—India!" The sparkle returned to her eyes.

He laughed. "Sometimes. Sometimes other places."

"Tell me about India. Tell me *anything* about India."

"India? Faugh! I dislike India. It is a sad, moth-eaten sort of place."

She placed her hands over her ears. "No! Oh, you horrible man. You are teasing me!"

He laughed out loud at her reaction. "Shall I bore you with tales of my business ventures? I'll grant you, those who never leave England miss a great deal. If it weren't so tedious to cross the sea, I believe I would recommend travel to everyone. Travel for pleasure, that is."

"I have never been anywhere," Clarissa said wistfully.

He reached over and caught her hand in his. "Where would you like to go, Clarissa?" he whispered, in the voice of a conspirator. His eyes gleamed with mischief and he waggled his eyebrows, forcing a giggle out of her.

"Gracious, I don't know!"

"Bombay? Marseilles? Venice? Boston?"

"Oh!" she cried, her eyes like saucers. "Have you been to all those places?"

"Not Boston," he admitted. "Now *there's* a continent for you! It might be worth the trip, to see America."

Clarissa wondered if she ought to pull her hand back out of his, but he was playing absently with her fingers. It was clear his mind was elsewhere, so obviously he meant no harm. And she rather liked having her fingers played with, she discovered. She decided to let him hold her hand a moment longer.

"I would like to see Italy one day," she confided shyly. "I am sure I never shall, but—oh! The pictures one sees! It seems the sun is always shining there."

"I like Italy myself. Are you fond of art? Paintings, and sculpture, and architecture, and all that?"

"I've never had an opportunity to find out," confessed Clarissa. "I rather fancy I would be. I'm very fond of history."

His grin flashed at her again. "Then you must definitely see Italy."

"Oh, I dare not set my sights so high! I would count myself fortunate merely to see Bath one day." As she spoke, she carefully drew her hand out of his clasp. She half feared he would say or do something that would embarrass her, but he seemed to take no notice. He certainly made no attempt to retain her hand. An odd pang of disappointment mixed with her relief.

"Bath! Your goals are far too modest." Trevor reached for the half-empty wine bottle and refilled the glass at her elbow. "Italy was the first foreign country I visited. My uncle chose well in taking me there. Venice whetted my appetite for travel in a way that Bombay, had I seen it first, would not have done."

He set the wine down and regaled her with the tales of Venice, Florence, and Rome that fired her imagination and filled her with wanderlust. He had traveled through Italy many times, sometimes on business but often for pleasure. He had been fourteen when he saw it first, and for the first few days had been miserably homesick. She exclaimed at that, and questioned him eagerly about the home he had left.

So Trevor, amused by her air of avid interest, told her of his early life in a peaceful Devonshire vicarage. This tale was as wondrous to Clarissa as any of his adventures abroad. He had arrived late in his parents' life, with his older brothers already fifteen and seventeen years of age, and his oldest sister, Theresa, twelve years his senior. But he and Augusta, born only eighteen months apart, had formed a close bond in childhood that persisted to this day. The stories of the mischief the two youngest members of the Whitlatch family had gotten into, their wild escapades and the pranks they had played, made Clarissa laugh heartily and wish she could meet Madcap

Gussie, as the family called her. It all sounded idyllic to Clarissa. She envied him his childhood, and told him so.

"Life held its charms," Trevor admitted. He smiled at her a bit quizzically. "It still does, you know. I'm not the sort of sap-skull who moons about, mourning his lost boyhood."

"Oh, no!" she said quickly. "How silly, to be sure! And I don't mean to complain of my own situation. I only meant . . . well, I don't know what I meant." Clarissa blushed faintly and looked at her hands. "I suppose I was comparing my own childhood to yours. Absurd! I was—I *am*—very grateful for the opportunities I was given."

"A roof over your head, three meals a day, clothes on your back, and an education."

"Yes. I had everything I needed." She smiled at him, but knew her smile did not reach her eyes. The stories of Trevor's adventurous life, and the warm family affection he had taken so much for granted, revealed the barrenness of her own existence in a painful light.

She would have looked away to hide her shameful envy, but his eyes held hers.

"Oh, Clarissa," Trevor murmured softly. "You break my heart."

Her eyes widened in surprise. His features had harshened into a strange mixture of anger and sadness that she recognized, startlingly, as pity. He reached out a hand and brushed his fingers against her cheek, a gesture so unexpectedly tender that she felt sudden tears welling.

Clarissa was embarrassed by her odd surge of emotion. "You are kind," she whispered. A ragged smile curved her mouth. "I don't know why kindness should make me cry."

Trevor's eyes darkened, and a softer expression than she had yet seen in him made him seem, for the first time, compassionate. "You haven't known much kindness, have you, Clarissa?" he murmured. "A girl of such loveliness. Such intelligence. Who wishes she had never been born. God, what a waste."

His hand moved slightly, cupping her cheek. His fingers felt warm and strong, for all his gentleness. She wanted to protest, especially in light of the language he had used, but her protests died in the warmth of his touch.

She was so unused to human contact that the simple act of touching, skin against skin, caused another confusing rush of emotions. Longing spilled from somewhere deep inside, as if his touch had opened a floodgate in her heart. Her breath caught. She wished she could lean into his warm palm, lose herself in it, wrap it round her like a quilt.

Trevor's fingers moved lightly, caressing her cheek, then slid into her hair. She closed her eyes like a cat being petted, and shyly, tentatively, raised her own hand to touch his. He whispered something inaudible; she caught only the word "sweet." His hand moved again beneath her fingers, turned, and captured hers.

"I think you need a little kindness, Clarissa," he said softly. "I think you need a holiday."

She opened her eyes slowly. "A holiday?" she asked, confused.

"Have you ever had one?"

"Well, no. That is, I . . . I'm not sure what you mean. I don't always behave like a watering pot, I assure you! Pray do not regard it."

"But I do regard it." He pulled their linked hands away from her face and leaned in to her, resting his elbows on the table. His thumb stroked the back of her hand comfortingly. "I think you have suffered a great many upheavals in your life in a short amount of time. You need a respite."

Clarissa smiled. "Are you proposing to take me to Italy?"

Trevor's eyes darkened swiftly. "Would you go with me if I did?"

For a moment her heart pounded crazily. "No," she managed to say, but her voice sounded, to her own ears, suspiciously faint. Fortunately he did not press her, but transferred his gaze to their linked hands.

"I think you can afford to wait a while before seeking employment. Let me take care of that. I'll make a few more inquiries on your behalf. In the meantime, Clarissa, I think you should relax a bit and enjoy yourself."

Enjoy herself! What a strange idea. She considered it warily, examining the concept as gingerly as if it might bite her. "I am no hedonist, Mr. Whitlatch."

He looked pained. "I am no hedonist, *Trevor*," he corrected her, making her laugh in spite of herself.

"Very well!" she said, trying to draw her hand out of his. "I am no hedonist, Trevor!" But this time he not only thwarted her attempt to pull away, he captured her other hand as well. Clarissa decided resistance would only make her appear foolish, and sat passively, reproof in her gaze.

But he did not see it, since he continued to regard their hands. "It's an attractive picture," he mused, toying with her fingers. "I would give a great deal to see you frisking about the house like a kitten."

Clarissa gasped, and began to laugh helplessly. "How ridiculous!"

"You could use a little absurdity, my dear." He suddenly flashed her a crooked grin that made her heart skip a beat. The gleam of mischief in his eyes was so inviting she had to fight to keep herself from responding to it. "In fact, I have never met anyone who needed absurdity as much as you do. A healthy dose of frivolity would speedily cure what ails you."

"Nothing ails me!" she said shakily.

His hands tightened on hers. "Are you so accustomed to suffering, Clarissa, that you no longer recognize it?"

Her amusement faded. A sharp little frown creased her forehead. "Trouble comes to every life. It would be vain to deny that I am worried about my future, or that I mourn the loss of my home and my friend. But you mustn't teach me to feel sorry for myself, Mr. Whi—*Trevor*."

"No danger of that. After all, they say trouble comes in threes, and you have had your three. You lost Miss Bathurst, you lost your situation, and you fell into the clutches of a wicked abductor. For the time being, your troubles must surely be over."

A brief smile flickered across Clarissa's face. "Unless I immediately start another set of three," she suggested.

"Not under my roof!" commanded Mr. Whitlatch in mock horror. "You are going to have a holiday, Clarissa. No arguments, now! Remember that I am your wicked abductor. I might force you if you resist."

"Wicked abductor, indeed! Generous benefactor is more like it." But the smile was tugging irresistibly at the corners of her mouth. "Oh, dear! A real holiday! I wouldn't know how to begin."

For a moment she pictured what it might be like, to toss her burdens aside for a time and play like a child. It sounded delicious. Trevor must have seen the temptation in her eyes, for that wickedly attractive grin flashed across his features again. "It's quite simple," he assured her. "You'll pick it up in no time."

"But what must I do?"

"Whatever you please. You can read novels, and dawdle, and sketch. You can ride through the countryside when the weather is fair, and laze about the house when it is not. You can eat far more than is good for you, and sleep late in the mornings, and anything else that takes your fancy."

A bubble of laughter escaped her. "It sounds wonderful," she admitted. "But it can't possibly be right. What would become of the world, if people followed their own inclinations all the day?"

Mr. Whitlatch dropped her hands and made a derisive noise. "You should have been born two hundred years ago."

"I am not a Puritan!" she cried, stung.

He pursed his lips and regarded her, one eyebrow raised. Clarissa was suddenly aware that her gray merino, high-necked and long-sleeved, was not only dowdy but, perhaps, excessively modest. And she supposed there was no real need to dress her hair so unbecomingly.

"Very well! Your point is taken," she said stiffly. "But I would ask you to remember my circumstances, sir! My wardrobe is perfectly appropriate for a rural schoolteacher."

"A rural schoolteacher of advanced years and no beauty," he scoffed.

"A rural schoolteacher of limited means," she countered with dignity.

"Aha! Is that the problem? In that case, I have something to show you." Trevor seized her hand again and rose, pulling Clarissa to her feet and tucking her hand in his elbow.

"Where are we going?" she asked, surprised by this sudden burst of activity.

He took a candle from the sideboard and grinned down at her. "Upstairs, my innocent!"

It said much for her trust in him that these fell words failed to alarm her. "You are never serious!" she complained.

"I am frequently serious, as you will soon learn," he promised, releasing her hand to open the door. "Come along!"

"Now, *really*—!" she exclaimed, hands on hips.

Trevor burst out laughing. "There is an excellent carving

knife in the cupboard there, if you would like to arm yourself first."

Her lips twitched. "No, thank you. If you are really taking me upstairs, I know exactly where my hat pin is."

She allowed Trevor to take her hand and lead her from the dining room. She supposed he would explain what he was about in his own good time.

But his footsteps slowed on the stairs, and Clarissa glanced up to see him frowning thoughtfully down at her.

"Having second thoughts, Mr. Whitlatch?" she teased.

He smiled, but absently. "No. But it has occurred to me that what I am about to propose may offend you. I hope it does not."

"Propose? I thought you were going to show me something."

"Yes, but after I show it to you, I intend to give it to you." His frown vanished, and devils suddenly danced in his eyes. "Do you have any idea how suggestive this conversation is becoming?"

Clarissa gasped, and bit her lip. "Pray do not explain!" she begged.

His shoulders shook. "No, that would ruin it," he agreed. "Besides, I have every hope that when you actually see what I am going to show you, you will find it so irresistible that you will *want* me to give it to you. I am hoping, in fact, that your desire will overcome your scruples."

Clarissa stopped dead on the stairs. "I am not going another step farther until you tell me what we are discussing!" she declared in a strangled voice.

His grin became, if possible, even more devilish. "We are discussing my latest proposition, Clarissa."

She stood her ground. "Well? What is it?"

Trevor's left hand held the candle, but his right arm suddenly slid round her waist, pulling her close against him. She froze, so astonished she could not move.

"I am taking you upstairs, Clarissa. To the Tudor Room," he murmured, his mouth nearly touching her ear. She shivered involuntarily as his warm breath stirred against her neck. "We are going to remove some clothing there, you and I."

Laughter quivered in his voice, but Clarissa saw nothing humorous. She struggled on the narrow stair to turn and glare at him, outraged. "How dare you?" she gasped. "Let me go!"

"Careful!" he warned, releasing her enough so she could catch hold of the banister. "I am less dangerous to you than the polish on these stairs."

Clarissa clung to the banister, breathless. She felt she had been knocked off balance in more ways than one. But Trevor kept one hand at the small of her back to brace her. His hand felt as strong and steadying as the wood beneath her fingers, and his face showed genuine concern.

"Are you all right?" he asked.

She glared at him in speechless indignation. The man was impossible! But had she slipped, she was completely sure he would have caught her.

"You chose a dangerous place to frighten me half out of my wits," she told him, her voice unsteady.

He appeared much struck. "So I did. Let's go up to the landing."

Clarissa choked. "Where you can begin again, no doubt?"

"You read my mind," he told her. Really, it ought to be against the law for a man to have such an attractive grin!

She kept one hand on the banister, and gathered her skirts in the other. "I am going up to the landing," she told him with great aplomb, "because it is nonsensical to stand on the stairs. But you are *not* going to take further liberties with me, Mr. Whitlatch."

"Am I back to being Mr. Whitlatch?" he mourned, trailing after her. "Must I apologize?"

"It would certainly do no harm if you did. Taking me to the Tudor Room to remove our clothing, indeed!" She halted at the top of the stairs, bristling.

"To remove 'some' clothing," he corrected her, assuming a ridiculously innocent expression. "I only meant we are going to remove some clothing *from the wardrobe*. What did you think I meant?"

She could not think of an adequate reply. Her host crossed to the door of the lavish bedchamber she had glimpsed yesterday, flung the door open, and bowed as if ushering her in. Clarissa, flummoxed, remained at the top of the stairs.

"Why did you say such outrageous things to me?" she demanded, feeling extremely foolish.

Trevor strolled back to her and flicked her cheek with one careless finger. Expecting only mockery, it unsettled her to see the warmth in his smile. His expression invited her to share his mischief, and she felt her defenses crumbling. He cupped Clarissa's chin in his hand and forced her to meet his eyes. "You didn't really think I would force my attentions on you."

His directness pulled an answering honesty out of her. "No."

Trevor's expression was suddenly completely serious. "Thank you," he said gravely. "I will never do so."

She smiled softly at him. "I know that. You are a man of honor."

A soundless laugh shook his shoulders. "Oh, Clarissa, do not trust me too far! Your definition of honor differs somewhat from my own."

She pulled his hand away from her face and tried to look severe. "I do not think it right, for example, for you to tease me as you did a moment ago."

Humor lit his features again. "You'll be glad to know there was a method to my madness."

She could not help smiling. "There was? What was it?"

He winked. "I planted shocking thoughts in your brain so my true intent will seem tame by comparison."

Trevor then walked away from her and into the bedchamber. He did not pull her hand, seize her elbow, or use any physical means to compel her. He simply took the candle with him. She had, perforce, to follow.

Chapter 14

Trevor was careful to leave the door open behind him. He knew perfectly well that leading Clarissa into this particular chamber was highly improper, and wasn't sure how far her natural curiosity would bring her. She did step rather nervously over the threshold, but then halted immediately, as if fearing the room held some contagion she might catch.

The last thing he wanted was for Clarissa to bolt like a frightened filly. He strolled casually away from her as if her presence was a matter of complete indifference to him. It was rather like taming a fawn, he thought.

His footsteps noiseless on the lush carpeting, he crossed the floor and flung wide the gilded doors of the enormous wardrobe. His mouth twisted wryly at the sight of the empty shelves and pegs. The last time he had seen the inside of this wardrobe, it had been crammed with expensive garments. Expensive pink garments, he recalled with an inward shudder. Now there were exactly two frocks, lonely and discarded, hung on pegs at the back of the wardrobe. Neither of them were pink. Apart from those, the wardrobe contained nothing but a large box. He lifted this out and carried it to the bed.

As he set the box carefully down, he glanced over his shoulder and saw Clarissa still in the doorway. She was apparently rooted to the spot. Chuckling, he strolled over to her and handed her the candle. "The room won't bite you," he assured her.

She rewarded this sally with a slight, apprehensive smile. "I suppose not," she admitted. "I don't know why it should affect me so."

"Come along, then! Let me show you what is in the box. I promise you it is nothing alarming." He placed a hand in the small of her back and propelled her toward the bed.

She stopped when she reached the bedside and glanced fearfully overhead. "The mirror will not fall on us, will it?"

Trevor, recalling the activities that had been vigorously pursued beneath the mirror without dislodging it, coughed. "I feel reasonably certain it will not."

He removed the top of the box and pulled out a riding habit. Drifts of tissue paper floated to the floor around them as Clarissa's eyes widened in wonder. The light jumped and wavered in her hand, and Trevor, with great presence of mind, removed the candle from her suddenly nerveless grasp.

"Oh, the gorgeous thing!" she breathed, reaching for the garment as if in a dream. He placed it in her arms and then strolled leisurely around the room, lighting the wall sconces. By the time he returned and set the candle on the bedside table, she appeared to have forgotten her surroundings. She was perched on the pink satin coverlet, examining the cut of the jacket with a combination of eagerness and reverence that made him smile.

"Such beautiful work!" she exclaimed.

"It ought to be. I would hate to tell you what I paid for it."

Clarissa's voice dropped to an awestruck whisper. "And it is made of velvet. I have never touched real velvet before."

She was petting the sides of the jacket and the heavy folds of the skirt as tenderly as if they were alive. Watching her caress the material gave Trevor an odd, disembodied sensation. He stared, mesmerized, at her soft hands running lightly over the velvet, at her gently stroking fingers.

"Do you think it will fit?" he managed.

Her fingers faltered. "Fit whom? *Me?*" she gasped.

"No, the Grand Turk!" he retorted, jamming his hands in his pockets before they could reach for her of their own accord. "Of course you! Don't you ride?"

Clarissa dropped the garment as if it might burn her. "I cannot accept a gift of *clothing* from a gentleman!"

Trevor snorted. "I've no patience with such stuff. Do you need a riding habit, or don't you?"

"What has that to do with anything?" stammered Clarissa, horrified. "No lady could accept such a gift. It would be *most* improper, sir!"

He knew it, but feigned astonishment and hurt. "It has never been worn," he offered.

Trevor saw temptation flash in her eyes, but she swiftly quelled it and pressed her lips firmly together. "That is neither here nor there," she informed him loftily. "I am sure you meant no offense sir, but I must refuse it."

"Very well," he said, trying to appear wounded. "But you made such a point of your being an impoverished schoolteacher, I thought you might not own a riding habit. If you do, of course, there is no harm done."

"It is not *that*," said Clarissa, appearing much harassed. "As it happens, I do not own a riding habit. Well, of course I do not! But that does not mean you can *give* me one! It is far too expensive, and far too personal an item—oh, heavens! Even *you* ought to know better!"

That surprised a laugh out of him. "Even I!" he agreed, abandoning his injured posture and hopping up beside her on the bed. "Oh, the devil fly away with propriety!" He seized her hand and petted it, coaxing her. "Can't you take it, Clarissa? Won't you? As a favor to me? It does no one any good, sitting in the bottom of a wardrobe. And I would like to go riding with you tomorrow, if the weather is fine."

His honest cajolery seemed to melt her resolve more effectively than his pretended hurt had done. She visibly softened,
and bit her lip. "Oh, dear!" she said ruefully. Her fingers
reached again for the edge of the velvet jacket and played with
it lightly, longingly. "It's lovely," she said, and sighed. Then she
pulled her hand away, as if with an effort, and shook her head.
"But I cannot."

Trevor had an idea. "What if you borrow it?" he suggested.
"You needn't accept it as a gift, if that compromises your prin-
ciples. For all I care, you may give the silly thing back to me
when you are done with it."

He thought he discerned a flicker of hope in Clarissa's troubled eyes. He continued quickly, before she could speak and
talk herself out of it. "You will probably need to alter it, of
course." Trevor ran his eyes over her figure. It occurred to him
that he had created an excellent excuse to do that, so he allowed
his gaze to linger. He was careful to hide the pleasure it gave
him.

Clarissa now appeared more thoughtful than alarmed. He
rose and lifted the garment away from her, holding it up so its
folds fell naturally into the lines it would assume when worn.
He grinned when awestruck desire leaped in her eyes. She
itched to wear the thing, that was certain.

"What do you think?" he asked her innocently. "It may not
be possible to alter it sufficiently, but you will be a better judge
of that than I."

"It looks as if it might be a fair fit," she admitted. "But even
if it were proper to borrow it, I . . . I cannot imagine myself
wearing it!"

"Why not?"

Clarissa rose and took the jacket from him, gazing at it with
longing. "This is much, much finer than anything I have ever
worn. I couldn't possibly don such an expensive garment,
merely to ride a *horse*!"

She sounded scandalized. Trevor threw back his head and
laughed. "You'll look nohow if you wear it for anything else!"
he advised her.

"Yes, but—"

"But nothing! It's a riding habit." He took the jacket from her
and tossed it, together with the skirt, carelessly into the box. "If
you won't wear it while riding a horse, it goes back in the

wardrobe," he told her firmly. "I won't have you making a figure of yourself by wearing it to play whist with the bishop."

That coaxed a reluctant laugh out of her. "Well, I can't do
that! I haven't been invited to play whist with the bishop."

"No. You've been invited to go riding with me."

Her eyes had not left the riding habit. "So I have." Smiling
softly, she walked back to the bed and began to straighten and
carefully fold the garment he had tossed there in a heap.

While she worked there, lost in thought, the unconscious
sweetness of her expression made her appear as incorruptible as
one of Raphael's Madonnas. And her chaste gray gown was as
incongruous against this background of noisy pink as a Quaker
in a brothel.

Trevor felt a sudden stab of disgust at himself. He ought
never to have brought Clarissa in here. He could easily have
taken the box to her in the library. Even with the door open, this
was no place for a virtuous female. He rose and scowled down
at her.

"Let me carry the riding habit downstairs for you. There is no
need to give me your decision immediately."

A discreet cough sounded. Trevor looked up to see his housekeeper standing in the doorway, lifting a lamp and frowning accusingly at him. She looked exactly like Diogenes, searching in
vain for an honest man. Mrs. Simmons had obviously taken in
the situation at a glance, and was stiff with disapproval. All she
said, however, was, "Will you be needing anything more this
evening, sir?" She delivered this query in minatory tones, gazing balefully at her employer.

It was certainly not the first time Trevor had seen Mrs. Simmons outraged by his introduction of a female guest into his
home, but the quality of her disapproval was somehow different this time. With a shock, he realized her condemnation was
directed for the first time at *him*, rather than his guest!

He hunted in vain for an appropriate response to his house-
keeper's reproachful gaze. But while he stood dumbstruck,
Clarissa turned round, glowing with relief. "Mrs. Simmons!
The very person we need!"

Mrs. Simmons perceptibly thawed as she turned to Clarissa.
"Yes, miss?"

Clarissa carried the velvet riding habit to her, and the two
women immediately bent their heads over it, clucking and wor-

riting and discussing together, in incomprehensible female terms, the nuances of propriety, dressmaking, and God alone knew what. Trevor watched, fuming, as Clarissa and his house-keeper—*his* housekeeper!—closed ranks against him in that inimitable feminine way.

"I daresay if I retired to the library, neither of you would miss me!" he announced sarcastically.

Clarissa spiked his guns by beaming radiantly at him. "Oh, *would* you?" she cried, her pleasure and gratitude instantly de-flating his annoyance. "Mrs. Simmons agrees with me that I ought not to accept the riding habit as a gift, but she thinks it might not be wrong to *borrow* it—and I would so love to go rid-ing!"

The sight of her sparkling happiness floored him. Not only did it enhance her loveliness tenfold, it was strangely touching. Such a little thing, to thrill her so completely! He thought, be-musedly, that he had frequently bestowed far costlier baubles on other women as outright gifts, and none was received with half the joy that this "loan" of a riding habit gave Clarissa.

"If you would not mind waiting downstairs, sir, I will join you after I try it on. But I cannot do so here!" Clarissa added, looking around the room with a barely repressed shiver.

"Certainly not!" sniffed Mrs. Simmons, placing a protective arm around Clarissa. "This is no place for the likes of you, child. If there's anything else you need from the wardrobe, why, you've only to ring for someone to fetch it. No need for you to come in here again." She directed a quelling stare at her em-ployer. "There was no call for you to bring Miss into this room in the first place, sir, if you don't mind my saying so."

"Thank you!" said Trevor with awful sarcasm. "Shall I beg her pardon, or yours?"

"Oh, pray—!" blurted Clarissa, blushing.

Mrs. Simmons patted Clarissa's arm comfortingly, but the severity of her glare did not abate. "Tsk! I daresay you meant nothing by it, sir, and if Miss Feeney has taken no offense, far be it from me to suggest she should. As for begging my pardon, I trust we haven't come to such a pass as that! I hope I know my place! But this much I *will* say: you hadn't ought to have brought Miss Feeney to this house alone, and her with no maid to wait on her, and no decent women to bear her company! Such goings-on! Why, you should be ashamed, sir, exposing her to wicked gossip! Anyone might look askance at her. I did, myself, though it shames me now to say it. I *had* thought you might bring some company back with you from Lunnon, and it fair bowled me over to see you drive up in that curricle tonight as solitary as when you left this morning."

Trevor felt his cheeks redden. "And what business is it of yours, I should like to know?" He instantly felt the surliness of this response and hastened to add, "You may leave Miss Feeney's fate in my hands, Mrs. Simmons! I assure you, I will do my utmost to find her a—a *suitable* situation."

Clarissa interjected in her gentle way, "Indeed Mrs. Simmons, it is very good of you to champion me, but I feel sure there is no need."

Mrs. Simmons looked as if she would like to say more, but contented herself with a sniff. "Well! Do you hand me that riding habit, then, and I'll light you to your room. High time you was in bed! There will be time enough to try this on in the morning."

"But I wish to take her riding in the morning!" Trevor protested, sounding lamentably peevish.

Mrs. Simmons ruffled like a disgruntled hen. "The idea! Miss Feeney has been sewing all day. I'll not have her wearing her fingers to the bone!"

Clarissa laughed. "I am not such a poor creature," she told her newfound ally, but meekly allowed herself to be shooed out the door.

Trevor watched in grim amazement. Mrs. Simmons, who had served him for years and his family before him, and whose fierce loyalty to the Whitlatches had withstood even the strain of being asked to serve in a house where he sometimes kept his bits-o-muslin, had just flown in his face defending a chit she had met only this morning. Clarissa's swift conquest of his redoubtable housekeeper was unprecedented, and oddly disconcerting. It was daunting to picture what life might be like if, through bedding Clarissa, he incurred Mrs. Simmons's displeasure. Good Lord—what if the Simmonses gave notice? Unthinkable!

Mr. Whitlatch, unaccustomed to worry, found it infuriating to have second thoughts about a course of action he had not only already decided upon, but had been looking forward to with no common degree of pleasure. He retired in a very foul mood indeed.

Chapter 15

The next few days were heaven on earth for Clarissa. She had never considered what it might mean simply to be transported to a place where *no one knew her*. When she realized that she had been liberated, at a stroke, from the stigma of her illegitimate birth and her mother's notoriety, she experienced a relief so profound it bordered on exhilaration. Joy quickened her step and sparkled in her eyes.

Mr. Whitlatch had promised that he would begin taking steps to find employment for her the very next week. This made her feel as if a burden was lifted from her and shifted onto shoulders much stronger than her own. Freed from her most pressing concerns, freed from the burden of her identity, freed, for a time, from all responsibilities and encouraged by her host to do nothing but please herself, Clarissa found herself, literally and figuratively, *carefree*. Happiness flooded her heart.

Morecroft Cottage spoke to something in Clarissa's starved and homeless soul. Everything about the place seemed utterly perfect to her. Sometimes, when alone, she would close her eyes and gently press her fingers against a windowsill, a banister, a piece of wainscoting—wishing she could leave her fingerprints on this lovely, peaceful house the way, she felt, it was leaving its mark on her. She knew these sweet November days would be short, and an endless winter might follow. It was important to cherish whatever moments were granted to her here. And to never, never, forget this place and time.

With the constraints usually imposed upon her banished, Clarissa's natural friendliness asserted itself. She was interested in everyone, from the stables to the kitchen, and soon made herself so popular with the staff that Trevor began to grumble. Mrs. Simmons fussed over her, Dawson's boy eagerly ran her errands, Hogan labored mightily to find late blooms among the flowerbeds for her, and one morning Trevor waited in vain for someone to bring him his shaving water. After ringing unavailingly for ten minutes, Trevor raged onto the landing in his dressing gown and set up a shout. Webster, the stalwart individual who normally performed this necessary task, was discovered on the stairs, lugging two enormous buckets of steaming water, which he informed Mr. Whitlatch, respectfully but firmly, he was not allowed to have. Webster was engaged in supplying Clarissa's bath. The shaving water would have to wait, in fact, while Webster made two trips more.

That Clarissa's wishes should take precedence over Mr. Whitlatch's seemed natural to everyone but Mr. Whitlatch.

This annoyed Trevor, but did not seriously anger him—partly because it appealed to his sense of the ridiculous, and partly because he found himself in sympathy with his besotted staff. There was something endearing about Clarissa. It was a quality that had nothing to do with her beauty. He was amazed to see how rapidly her sad primness dissolved; within forty-eight hours of her arrival at Morecroft Cottage the somber, strained expression that had seemed her habitual demeanor when he met her, completely melted away. She lost none of her dignity, but gained a vulnerable sweetness that seemed to touch the hearts of everyone around her.

Trevor swiftly developed a secret obsession: making Clarissa laugh. Her laughter was delightful, unaffected and hearty, but what tickled him was how surprised she always seemed by it. Her laugh was invariably accompanied by a sudden, startled, widening of the eyes that spoke volumes about the rarity of laughter in her short life.

It was deeply gratifying to discover this new kind of power. He had been able, with very little effort or expense, to effect a complete change in Clarissa's drab existence. None of the charities he had sporadically underwritten had inspired him with philanthropic zeal, but now he thought he understood how a man might dedicate himself to that sort of work. It was a heady feeling, this power to transform another's life.

In a matter of a few days, he had turned a sad-eyed woman into a merry, glowing girl. He did not preen himself on this overmuch; he knew the transformation was not entirely his own doing. A man can scrub the grime off a windowpane, but he can't take credit for the light shining through it. The enchanting creature who romped in the garden with Dawson's spaniel and laughed out loud at Trevor's jokes was doubtless the "real" Clarissa Feeney. Under Mrs. Simmons's fond mothering and his own teasing, she was blossoming like a cherry in spring.

Trevor was unable to abandon his business concerns entirely merely to dance attendance on Clarissa, much as the notion appealed to him. Still, his stature in the City empowered him to handle his affairs however he chose. He ordered two or three of his underlings to drive out daily and meet him at Morecroft Cottage, rather than go, himself, into town. He was closeted with them for a portion of every afternoon. During these sessions, he found his attention sometimes drawn from the droning voices and rattling papers by the sound of Clarissa's feet running exuberantly on the stairs, or her distant voice raised in a brief snatch of song. Her singing always stopped abruptly in mid-phrase. Trevor would grin, picturing Clarissa guiltily catching herself and placing a hand over her mouth. But it pleased him mightily to think that her happiness was so complete, her heart would overflow in song.

It was fortunate that Trevor enjoyed Clarissa's society for its own sake. It certainly gave him none of the pleasures he had originally anticipated. Every night he would retire, baffled and out of temper, and berate himself for the opportunities he had missed that day. Alone in his bedchamber, it always seemed that he had behaved like a perfect gudgeon. Had he done *this* differently, or *that*, surely Clarissa would have responded thus-and-so, and he would not now be lying between cold sheets alone! Every night he vowed that tomorrow would be different. Tomorrow he would corner her, kiss her, and find the magic words to make her his own.

It wasn't that the opportunity to make such a move had not yet presented itself. His innate honesty forced him to admit that. Pacing before his bedroom fire in his stocking feet, he would recall the myriad opportunities he had had, and call himself every name he could think of. What was the matter with him? Lack of nerve? Impossible! Well then, what?

Trevor had no answer for this home question.

One night he glumly pondered the possibility that he was losing his mind. Unlikely, he supposed. There had never been anything like that in his family. But apart from madness, he really had no explanation for his actions—or lack of action—that afternoon.

He had left an unusually dull session with his hirelings to stretch his legs. Rounding a bend in the path, he spied Clarissa. The sight of her brought an instant grin to his face, and an intense feeling of satisfaction. *Ah, there you are!* he thought—and realized, with an inward sense of his own foolishness, that his real purpose in leaving the meeting had been not to stretch his legs, but to seek Clarissa.

She was picking apples. Trevor halted on the path and watched her for a moment. She was wearing a brown print dress, very plain and somewhat faded, and was engulfed in one of Mrs. Simmons's aprons. The sash, since it contained far more material than was needed to encircle Clarissa's slender waist, was tied behind her in an enormous, lopsided bow. One of the bib straps was sliding down her arm. The dress was hideous, and the apron worse. She looked adorable.

This was obviously no desultory search for a ripe apple. Mrs. Simmons had been teaching her the art of pie-making, so Clarissa clearly meant business and expected results. She was armed with a two-handled straw basket and a rickety stepladder.

The lower branches of the tree had been denuded weeks before. The only apples worth picking were well out of reach. Undeterred, Clarissa had set up her stepladder and dragged the basket up it. When he first spied her, she was balanced atop the stepladder, grasping one of the gnarled branches over her head with one hand. The basket swung precariously from the other.

Her back was to him, so he was able to watch, undetected, while Clarissa cautiously raised herself up on her toes. She then reached both arms over her head, shoving the basket among the branches while still clinging with one hand. This maneuver disclosed spotless white stockings and worn black slippers to Trevor's interested gaze. He wondered if she would actually climb the tree. If she did, he wondered how she planned to get down again. He also wondered how she planned to get the basket down, once it contained apples. His grin widened.

She lodged her basket in the branches and shook it a little. Once satisfied that the basket was secure, she let go of it, grabbed the overhead branch with both hands, tested her weight, then swung her feet up off the stepladder onto a neighboring branch.

Catastrophe struck. Clarissa had failed to take into account the trajectory her swinging skirts would trace. Several pounds of flying calico and muslin slapped the stepladder broadside. It promptly toppled over.

Clarissa, hanging in the tree by her hands and feet, squeaked. It was not an elegant sound, but it was so far from the profanity he would have used under like circumstances that Trevor had to bite his lip to keep from laughing aloud. Delighted, he waited to see how she would extricate herself from this predicament. He was rewarded by the sight of Clarissa cautiously lifting her hips, bending her knees, and sliding slowly forward onto the branch where her feet were. This stretched her lovely body lengthways and, since it was still necessary for her to cling to the tree with both hands, he was treated to an example of exactly *why* mothers forbade their daughters to climb trees. Clarissa's body slid forward, but her skirts stayed where they were. First her ankles, then her shapely calves, then her knees, then a pair of ribbon garters all presented themselves in turn as she slid onto the branch. Unfortunately, once her thighs touched the branch, the show was soon over. She gripped with her knees, sat on the branch, dangled her feet, let go of the overhead branches, and hurriedly struggled with her skirts. They were voluminous enough to give her a fight, but eventually succumbed.

"What a pity that hoops have gone out of fashion," Trevor remarked.

Clarissa gasped, and nearly fell out of the tree. "M-Mr. Whitlatch! Heavens, what a start you gave me!"

"Trevor," he corrected her, for the umpteenth time. He strolled up to her, grinning. "The ladder has fallen over," he pointed out.

"I see that," she said crossly. She tried to tuck her skirts more closely round her ankles, but almost lost her balance in the effort. Another squeak escaped her, and she gave up, clinging to a nearby branch with as much dignity as she could muster. "Pray do not stand directly beneath me!"

"Very well," said Trevor obligingly. "The view is almost as fine from here."

Clarissa's cheeks reddened prettily. She feigned indifference, however. "Actually, it is a very good thing you have arrived, sir," she said airily, waving a careless hand. "Would you kindly set my stepladder back up?"

"Oh, is that your stepladder? I thought it was mine."

She choked. "Of course it is yours!"

"Then we need not discuss absurdities. I like it where it is."

She tried to glare at him, but burst out laughing instead. "You will not be so rude as to leave me up here!"

"Won't I?" he teased, placing one hand on the trunk of the apple tree and leaning toward her so suggestively that she squeaked again, scrambled higher on the branch, and clutched her skirts. "What is the chivalrous thing to do, do you think? Shall I come up after you?"

"Never mind chivalry, sir; try for the *sensible* thing!" she begged. "Do put the stepladder up—and then go away!"

"Go away? I am not so poor-spirited. I will stay and help you out of the tree."

"If you set the ladder up, I will not need your help."

"On the contrary! How will you get the apples down? Aha! I see you had not thought of that."

Clarissa bit her lip. "No," she admitted. "But I haven't any apples yet."

"After taking so much trouble, it would be a pity to leave without them." He straightened himself leisurely and strolled beneath her branch. "Hand me the basket."

She eyed him uncertainly. "Are you proposing to help me pick the apples?"

Trevor grinned crookedly at her. "It wasn't my first choice, you know, but you have refused all my other proposals."

He saw her expression soften and knew he had somehow scored a hit. "Hand me the basket," he repeated, and reached up for it. To his surprise, Clarissa leaned down and touched his hand lightly with her own.

"I think you are the kindest, most honorable man I have ever met," she told him, her voice sounding a little tremulous. Before he could recover from his surprise and react suitably to her advance, she had pulled away, as if embarrassed, and begun tugging briskly at the basket. She had lodged it in the branches a little too securely, however, and it refused to budge.

Trevor opened his mouth to say, "Allow me—" but suddenly Clarissa uttered a strangled cry and slipped. Quick as thought, Trevor braced himself beneath her and caught her legs. In her terror, however, Clarissa was clinging to the tree trunk and futilely struggling to recover her balance.

"Let go," he commanded.

"I am falling!" she gasped.

"Yes, very well, fall!" he said calmly. "I have you."

Clarissa closed her eyes and obediently let go. She tumbled immediately into Trevor's arms. "Oh!" she cried, convulsively clutching him round the neck.

"Are you hurt?" he asked.

"Oh!" she clung to him, shuddering.

"Clarissa, are you hurt?" he repeated, more sharply.

She opened her eyes. "N-no," she managed. "I don't think so."

But she made no move to get down. And he made no move to set her down. His arms tightened round her as he gazed at the exquisite face so close to his. Her skin was extraordinary— lush, creamy, and flawless. Her color fluctuated deliciously as she stared into his eyes; she seemed embarrassed by her predicament, but somehow—hallelujah!—he had mesmerized her. He could feel it. She wasn't going anywhere.

For a moment he forgot to breathe. God, she was lovely. He could scarcely believe his good fortune. It seemed he had been waiting for this moment forever. Now it was here. Clarissa, this girl of all girls, in his arms. Her heat and softness and beauty all his. It was intoxicating.

He watched, spellbound, as her porcelain cheeks flushed a delicate shade of pink. Her lashes swept down against the soft curve of her cheekbones like fluttering moths.

"You must think me a perfect fool," she whispered.

No, Clarissa, I just think you are perfect. The answering words rang so forcefully in his mind that he thought for an instant he had said them aloud. But his tongue seemed stupidly thick; he felt unable to speak or move. All he could do was stare drunkenly at the girl in his arms—her skin, her hair, her scent, her mouth.

Ah, God, her mouth.

This was it. This was the moment. He was going to kiss her. Every instinct shouted *now*!

But the seconds ticked inexorably by while Trevor Whitlatch, that master of timing, froze. What in the hell was the matter with him? He had never wanted anything so much as he wanted to taste this girl's lips. He wanted it so much it made him dizzy. But her very nearness robbed him of rational thought, robbed him of all ability to act.

Damn. *He* was the one who was mesmerized.

He gazed, paralyzed, at Clarissa while her pink cheeks turned pinker. Eventually she began a modest struggle to get down. The opportunity had clearly passed him by. Bemused and baffled, Mr. Whitlatch set her on her feet, still unable to believe what had just happened. Clarissa had tumbled into his arms, had almost *encouraged* his advances, and he had stood there like a stick.

That was the night when Trevor Whitlatch paced before his bedroom fire in stocking feet and grimly entertained the possibility that he was going mad. Brain fever. He had heard terrible things about brain fever. What were the symptoms, anyway? What would his brother-in-law, Dr. Applegate, say about a normally fearless man suddenly shaking in his shoes at the prospect of stealing a kiss from a pretty girl? Brain fever would be the least serious diagnosis!

He flung himself into a chair and poured himself a dollop of brandy from a decanter on the side table. He tossed it down his throat, poured another, and moodily swirled it in the glass, watching the light play through the amber liquid. On Tuesday, he had rashly promised to find the wretched girl employment next week. Now it was Friday night. He was running out of time.

It occurred to him that the notion of seeking a bride in the spring might be preying on his fancy overmuch. The seduction of Clarissa had become, in his mind, an essential test. Despite her birth, in many ways Clarissa was a woman of refinement. Educated, intelligent, modest, virtuous—just the sort of female he hoped to win next year. If he could conquer Clarissa's heart, he could, he thought, face the women of the *beau monde* with equanimity.

Yes, that must be what was unnerving him. It had nothing to do with Clarissa herself. Kissing her had taken on this strange, unnatural importance only because he was mentally preparing himself for kissing other, truly important females.

His brow cleared. This problem would be easy to solve. A pleasure, in fact, to solve. Clarissa was no totem. She was a girl, a girl just like any other. And tomorrow he was going to kiss her. No more waiting for the right moment. No more hesitation.

Just grab her and kiss her. This mysterious power she had over him would instantly be broken. What could be simpler?

Tomorrow, he promised himself. And this time, he meant it. A slow smile of satisfaction unfurled across his features. He silently toasted the resolution, tossed the brandy down his throat, and set his glass down with a decisive click. Tomorrow.

Chapter 16

A cloudless morning had dawned, and the riding habit was finished. Clarissa had spent a great deal of time over the past several days carefully altering the garment, which had been made for a slightly larger and taller lady, to fit her own form. The trick had been difficult to pull off, since Clarissa was anxious not to harm the expensive garment or ruin the exquisite tailoring it evinced. After all, since she was *borrowing* the habit, as she continually reminded herself, she was determined to make no irreversible changes. But at last the alterations were completed to her satisfaction, and this, finally, was the day Clarissa would go riding with Mr. Whitlatch.

She donned the riding habit in a fever of nervous excitement. Mrs. Simmons had sent the youngest of the dailies, Bess, to help her dress. Bess shyly confessed a secret ambition to one day be a lady's maid, and instantly entered into the spirit of the momentous occasion. Her enthusiasm was contagious as she tucked and patted and laced Clarissa into the costume. She even manifested a genius for hairdressing, and insisted on brushing Clarissa's hair until it shone, curling it with hot irons, and draping the fat sausage curls dashingly over Clarissa's left shoulder. Bess grew bolder as her confidence increased, and refused to allow Clarissa to peek while she worked. Eyes shining, expression intent, Bess finally placed the little velvet hat with the jauntily curling feather high atop Clarissa's massed curls, pinned it precisely into position, and stepped back to view her handiwork.

Bess drew a deep breath, swelling with pride, then let her

breath go in a sigh. "Oh, miss, you do look a picture!" she breathed reverently.

Clarissa laughed at the girl's awestruck expression. "May I look now?"

Bess nodded. Clarissa stepped before the cheval glass and halted, eyes widening. Was this fashionable creature really Clarissa Feeney? It seemed impossible!

"Merciful heavens," murmured Clarissa, staring at her own reflection.

It was a shock to see herself dressed all in pink velvet. Why, she had never worn such a color in her life! She had been half afraid the effect would be vulgar. It was a relief to see that the severe cut of the habit, and the fact that the color became her extremely well, softened the impact. And, after all, the shade was more a dusty rose than an outright *pink*. Her hair looked almost blue-black against the roseate hue, and the warm, soft color definitely flattered her complexion. My goodness. She had never known she could look so well.

The hat was simply darling. The new way Bess had done her hair was as stylish as it was pretty. And the habit fit perfectly now. In fact, Clarissa wondered nervously if it fit a little too well.

Bess caught the sudden worry in Clarissa's eyes and drew closer. "Is something wrong, miss? Don't you like it?" she asked anxiously.

"Oh, you've done beautifully!" Clarissa assured her quickly. "It's just that—" She patted the bodice, turned sideways, glanced again at her reflection, and blushed. "Do you think the jacket might be a bit too snug?"

Bess's wide brown eyes appeared over Clarissa's shoulder in the mirror. "No, miss, it looks ever so nice. Does it pinch you?"

Clarissa's expression turned thoughtful. "No." The high-waisted silhouette that emphasized her breasts did look very much like illustrations she had seen in *The Lady's Magazine*. She also remembered seeing similar form-fitting garments on well-dressed persons in London. This must be the order of the day, she supposed.

Then she remembered Mr. Whitlatch teasing her about being a Puritan. That made up her mind.

"We won't change a thing," Clarissa announced. "This is the

most elegant outfit I have ever worn. I shall stop fancying myself conspicuous, and simply enjoy it."

Bess clapped her hands, giggling. "Aye, miss, right you are!"

Clarissa then reduced Bess to speechless bliss by thanking her, praising her, and recklessly withdrawing a sixpence from her slender store of funds to press into the girl's palm. Clarissa had no idea if sixpence was considered adequate largesse in the first circles, but then, she was fairly certain Bess didn't know, either. Her stammering gratitude made Clarissa feel that the precious money had been well spent.

There was something magical about wearing new clothes, especially clothes in which one felt oneself looking one's best. Clarissa's eyes sparkled with anticipation as she caught the velvet train up over her arm, exited the bedchamber, and fairly danced to the top of the staircase. She paused at the top and leaned over the rail. Mr. Whitlatch was waiting in the hall below. Clarissa was seized with a sudden, mischievous impulse to make a dramatic entrance.

"Mr. Whitlatch!" she called.

"Trevor," he responded automatically, turning and looking up at her.

She smiled saucily. "Trevor," she repeated obediently, and then moved lightly down the stairway, one hand gracefully trailing on the banister.

She had the satisfaction of seeing his jaw drop. Her heart gave a happy little leap at the sight, and she beamed at him. This seemed to complete his stupefaction. Clarissa reached the foot of the stairs, dropped the train behind her, and twirled once, laughing with delight.

"Isn't it fine?" she exclaimed. "Thank you so much for allowing me the use of it."

Trevor's jaw worked soundlessly for a moment. "Fine," he repeated hoarsely. He cleared his throat. "You have a genius for understatement."

"Do you like it?"

"Very much."

"I am glad." She spread her hands and pointed one toe, showing him the costume. "The only garments you see that are mine are the gloves! I had to stuff tissue in the toes of the boots, but everything else I was able to alter tolerably well."

His eyes narrowed for a moment, and then he grinned. "Do I recognize that lace at your throat?"

Clarissa blushed. "Oh, dear! Mrs. Simmons assured me that you had thrown the shirt out, sir. Gentlemen haven't worn lace for years."

"Quite right. I am pleased to see it put to good use. It looks far better on you than it ever did on me. What a thrifty soul you are."

"Lace is very dear," she said with dignity. "I am not generally a nipfarthing."

"Oh, no! Not a cheeseparer," he agreed. "It's just that you don't live beyond the door. Very commendable!"

She suspected that he was roasting her, but before she could demand to know his meaning, he bowed and offered his arm. She was glad to let the subject go, so she tucked her hand companionably in the crook of his elbow.

He led her outside. Dawson waited there with two beautiful horses. Clarissa eyed them a trifle nervously. One was an enormous chestnut with his coat polished to a high gloss; the other, smaller, horse was a soft dapple gray. She was relieved to see that it was the smaller animal that bore a sidesaddle. She could not imagine herself atop the chestnut, whose size alone was intimidating. When the huge horse reinforced the terrifying portrait he presented by rolling his eye at her and snorting, Clarissa instinctively stepped a little closer to Mr. Whitlatch. She peeped anxiously up at him.

"Did I explain to you, sir, that I am not an accomplished horsewoman?"

His grin flashed down at her. "I didn't suppose you could be. Come! I'll help you up."

He transferred his hands to her waist, but Clarissa hung back. "Ought I . . . ought I, perhaps, to pet the gray horse a bit? Give him a chance to become acquainted with me?"

"Her," corrected Trevor. "She's a mare. Certainly you may pet her if it makes you feel more comfortable."

Clarissa, with Trevor's hands still lightly holding her waist—to reassure her, she supposed—reached out a gloved hand and timidly patted the mare's glossy neck. "What is her name, Dawson?"

Dawson touched his forelock to her. "Daisy, miss. She's a ladies' mount, so she ought to give you a comfortable ride."

Trevor made a rude noise. "In other words, she's a slug! Beautiful manners, though. You won't win any races, but you needn't fear she'll throw you into the nearest hedge."

Clarissa stepped out of Trevor's encircling hands to stroke the mare's nose. She ventured a smile. "I cannot imagine you buying a *slug,* sir, let alone keeping her once you had done so."

"I didn't buy her for me," he said shortly.

Clarissa flushed scarlet. What a ninnyhammer she was! The mare was bought for the female whose riding habit she was wearing. Some of the magic that had surrounded her this morning suddenly faded.

But the glow returned once Trevor flung her up into the saddle and Dawson handed her a riding crop. The saddle was surprisingly comfortable, and after Dawson had adjusted the stirrup for her, and she had arranged the skirt of the riding habit to drape properly, she felt much more secure than she thought she would. The mare was perfectly docile, and it was rather glorious to be perched high on Daisy's back, feeling the animal's muscles bunch and move beneath her, carrying her effortlessly forward. Trevor, perched even higher atop the chestnut, led the way out of the yard and toward the lane. Clarissa, following on gentle Daisy, laughed aloud from pure pleasure.

Trevor swiveled round in the saddle to grin at her. "Enjoying my slug, Miss Feeney?"

"Slug, indeed!" cried Clarissa indignantly. She leaned forward to pat Daisy's neck. "Don't listen to him," she advised the mare. "You're a love, aren't you? Yes, good girl, then! We'll show him."

"A *love,* is she?" said Trevor musingly. He pulled his horse alongside Clarissa and pretended to regard Daisy with new appreciation. "I don't believe I've ever chosen a mount using that particular yardstick."

"Very well, then; she is a *sweet-goer.* Is that better?"

He laughed. "Spoken like a right one!" he agreed. "Although how you arrived at that conclusion so quickly, I cannot conjecture. You must be a wonderful judge of horseflesh."

Clarissa rolled her eyes mournfully. "You are forever roasting me! I haven't ridden a horse above half a dozen times in my life, if as much! And I am sure you are well aware of that."

"No. How should I be?"

She cast him a skeptical look. He appeared serious; merely interested. "Well, I had to borrow a riding habit."

"True."

"And I was a little afraid of Daisy, just at first."

"No! Were you? You astonish me."

She burst out laughing. "There must be any number of clues that give me away!"

Trevor ran his eyes over her appreciatively. "Not at all. You carry yourself very gracefully, Miss Feeney. You don't appear awkward in the least."

Clarissa beamed. "Really?"

His eyes ran over her again, raking her. He leaned toward her. "Shall I gratify your vanity by telling you exactly how beautiful you look in that saddle?"

She blushed, and bit her lip. "Let us talk of something else!" she begged.

They had turned down the lane. Overarching branches of trees formed a canopy of yellow and gold above their heads. Daisy paced daintily across the carpet of leaves underfoot, but Trevor's horse danced and tossed his head. Clarissa stole a glance at Trevor, admiring how easily he controlled the restless animal. She was glad he liked the way she looked on horseback, but believed she couldn't possibly look as good as he did. He appeared perfectly at home, very much in command, and devastatingly handsome.

They spent the next hour riding companionably through the crisp, clear morning, laughing and chatting together like old friends. Clarissa could not remember enjoying any morning of her life more than this one; everything conspired to make it perfect—the weather, the novelty of being on horseback, the pretty clothes she was wearing, the beauty of the countryside, and, best of all, the friendship growing between herself and her host. It seemed the more she was around Mr. Whitlatch, the higher he rose in her esteem. His manners might be unconventional, but beneath his odd abruptness she was sure he had a kind heart. And he was such good company when he chose to be!

Trevor took her on one of his favorite rides through the surrounding countryside. It delighted her to feel she was sharing a part of his life that few others saw. He hadn't lived there long, having only purchased Morecroft Cottage a few years ago, and he had no close friends in the neighborhood. She suspected that the reason for this was the use to which he had put the house, but she did not like to say so. Still, his affection for the area and pride in his home was apparent; he spoke enthusiastically of the improvements he had made to the property, and gave her the history of many of the interesting items she had seen in the house. As he talked, it became clear to her that Morecroft Cottage's manifold perfections were largely due to Trevor Whitlatch's own taste and eye for beauty. He had evidently chosen everything, from the design of the stables to the furnishing of the rooms, and by imposing his own clear vision on the house and its contents he had created a home of surpassing loveliness. She felt her heart warming to this unexpected side of him, but it also seemed so strange to her, somehow, that she hardly knew how to comment. She could not reconcile her concept of the reckless, ruthless Mr. Whitlatch with this sudden glimpse of him as a gifted domestic artist.

But Trevor chanced to look at her while describing the difficulties he had encountered in choosing just the right carpet for the dining room, and caught her expression of doubt and wonder. That swift, disarming grin flashed across his face.

"I know what you are thinking. No, don't blush and disclaim! You're quite right. It's odd that I would care about that, isn't it?"

"Well, I don't know if 'odd' is the right word," Clarissa temporized.

"Effeminate."

Clarissa threw back her head and laughed heartily. Trevor's grin widened. "Thank you!" he said.

"I don't know why I found it so surprising," she remarked after she had recovered somewhat from her laughter. "When one comes to consider it, this quality is completely consistent with what one knows of you. You simply imposed your will on the house—exactly the way you impose your will on everyone and everything around you."

"What an unflattering way of expressing it! But it's true, of course, that I have definite ideas. I always have definite ideas, whether running a business or decorating a mantelpiece."

"How fortunate that you have the means to indulge your ideas!" she said in a tone of congratulation.

He grinned at her again. "I have the means, Clarissa, largely because my ideas are good ones."

She laughed, throwing up one hand in the gesture of a fencer acknowledging a hit. "I am silenced, sir! I find I cannot disagree. If your businesses are run as beautifully as Morecroft Cottage is, you have indeed deserved your success."

He led the way uphill and stopped at the top of a rise where they could turn and admire the view. Clarissa exclaimed at its beauty. From here, Morecroft Cottage and its peaceful setting looked like a glimpse of heaven itself, and she told him so. Trevor nodded with satisfaction, gazing past her at the pretty house nestled in the dell. His expression was such a mixture of pride and tenderness, she scarcely recognized him.

"It has turned out well," was all he said. Then a rueful laugh shook him. "A pity I didn't save it for my bride! I'm really fonder of it than any of my other properties. In hindsight, it was a catastrophic mistake to install Rosie here. I daresay no decent woman will deign to live in it now."

Clarissa was puzzled. "Who is Rosie?" But the instant the words left her mouth, she wished she had bitten her tongue out rather than utter them. She immediately realized who Rosie must be! But the words were out, now, and she could not call them back. She glanced at Mr. Whitlatch, shamefaced, and saw that he was watching her discomfiture with unholy amusement.

"Miss Feeney, I am surprised at you."

She felt her cheeks grow hot. "I am sorry—" she started to say, but Trevor continued as if he had not heard her.

"I would have thought that a woman of your intelligence would instantly recognize the name of the person who perpetrated that horror on my second-best bedchamber. I thought you might guess it when you first saw the room."

She understood him at once. Rose! That pink, rose-strewn bedchamber had been designed for a woman named Rose. It was so obvious, so painfully, absurdly obvious, that her blush deepened at her own stupidity.

But Trevor was shaking his head at her in mock sorrow. "Did you think *I* had decorated that room? You wound me, Miss Feeney!"

"I . . . well, really, I . . . Mr. Whitlatch, it is none of my business!"

"On the contrary," he said unexpectedly. "It is very much your business."

"H-how? What do you mean?"

He looked at her a moment, as if considering. "Walk with me," he said abruptly, and swung down from the saddle with the ease of an athlete. He led both horses to a nearby tree and tethered them, then reached up for her peremptorily. She slid cautiously off the saddle and into his waiting arms. He set her on her feet, but kept one arm around her, steadying her as he led her back to the top of the rise. Then he stepped behind her, turning her to face out over the peaceful valley, and slid both arms around her waist, holding her fast.

"Look at it," he murmured. His breath stirred the plume on her hat and set it fluttering against her cheek like a butterfly's caress. "Did you ever see a lovelier home?"

"Never," she whispered. His arms felt strong and comforting. She could not resist leaning back against her friend, and felt him cuddle her gently when she did. It was so pleasant to stand here, Trevor's comfortable strength at her back, and gaze down on Morecroft Cottage. It looked like a doll's house from this height, small and perfect and golden, slumbering in the sunlight. A magical place, infinitely desirable.

"I want you to live there," he told her. "I want it to be your home." His voice was low, husky with some strong emotion. She felt answering emotion begin to rise in her. *Home.* What a lovely word. This house. This man. She could feel it pulling her like the tide, strong, inexorable. Resistless, she let the longing sweep through her. *Home.*

She was pressed so snugly against his body, she could feel his voice vibrate against the back of her shoulders. "Would it be so terrible, Clarissa, to live for a while in that house with me?"

Clarissa tore her gaze from the lovely valley and turned her head to look into Trevor's dark eyes. They were so close to hers, the power of his personality instantly seemed to overwhelm her. It was as if her own will melted and seeped away, bewitched. The magic spell the day had woven still held her in its net; she felt drugged, suspended in time, dreaming here in Trevor's arms.

A faint smile curved the edges of his mouth. "I'll tear out all the pink. Next week, if you like. We'll replace it with blue, or yellow, or whatever you choose—although I must say," he said, cupping her cheek and looking into her face, "that pink becomes you to admiration."

Clarissa caught the faint, clean scent of his shaving soap and

felt the heat radiating from him, warming her. She knew she
ought to break away. She ought, at least, to answer him. Why
was his touch so confusing, so overpowering? She could only
stare wordlessly into Trevor's eyes while her thoughts whirled
and scattered like leaves in a wind.

"Clarissa," he whispered. "Stay with me."

The sound of his voice breathing her name seemed to shoot
through her like heat lightning. She saw his eyes darken with
desire and purpose, saw his expression change, and knew he
was going to kiss her. She parted her lips to protest, but whatever words she meant to say vanished, forgotten, as his mouth
came down on hers.

Nothing in Clarissa's life had prepared her for this experience. It was shockingly intimate, thrilling and terrifying at
once. His heat enveloped her; she felt dizzy. Her knees went
suddenly weak, and her eyes drifted shut. The world seemed to
tilt crazily, and she was grateful for the strong arm supporting
her. *Stay with me.* No words had ever sounded sweeter. She
clung to him for a long moment, yielding. Then his mouth
slanted, and she felt him pulling her tighter against him. His
kiss became insistent, demanding. Alarm clanged faintly in the
back of her mind, and she suddenly recalled the other words he
had said: *For a while.*

Sanity returned in a cold rush. Her eyes flew open.

Clarissa clutched at the lapels of Trevor's coat. "Stop! Stop!"
she managed to say in a tiny, shaking voice. She struggled
briefly and then staggered as he suddenly let her go. His hands
came up, gripping her shoulders, and she hung there in his
grasp, panting and shaken.

His expression was so queer—eager, hungry, hurt. His fingers squeezed her too tightly. He was too close; she needed air.
She could not breathe with him so close. She could not think.

Clarissa pulled away from him, frantically, and ran, half
stumbling, back toward the horses. She yanked fiercely at
Daisy's tether, freeing the animal. Tossing the reins up onto the
pommel, Clarissa scrambled somehow, anyhow, into the saddle.

She heard Trevor give a hoarse shout behind her, but she nei-
ther looked back nor waited. Sobbing now, her teeth gritted,
Clarissa hung to Daisy and urged her forward. She had to go.
She had to go.

Chapter 17

Headlong flight is all very well in its way, but eventually one's horse tires. By the time Daisy signaled her disapproval of Clarissa's inexperienced attempt to ride *ventre à terre* to nowhere in particular, Clarissa's turbulent emotions had subsided somewhat.

She slowed Daisy to a sedate walk, an instruction Daisy patently approved, and composed herself. A few seconds spent arranging her skirts, tugging on her jacket, patting at her curls, and straightening her hat did much to restore Clarissa's equilibrium. She now felt ashamed of her tears, and of the panicked impulse that had driven her to run from Mr. Whitlatch like one demented. What on earth was the matter with her? All her emotions seemed so close to the surface these days. She could neither understand them nor control them. She had never behaved so irrationally in her life; it was completely unlike her.

Of course, she had never let a man kiss her before, either. She realized now that the disgusting intimacy the music master had forced on her when she was sixteen was *not* a kiss. She had believed, based on that one horrible experience, that kissing was repulsive. Today she had learned that it was, in truth, the music master who had been repulsive. Being kissed by Trevor Whitlatch was entirely different. Not disgusting at all, actually. But as her memory stirred, those inexplicable tears began to well within her again. What *was* the matter with her? She hastily turned her thoughts in a different direction.

Daisy was taking her down a rather dusty lane that Clarissa, naturally, did not recognize. It wound through fields that were bare now, after the harvest, and consequently devoid of farm laborers. Not a soul was visible. There was no one to ask the way.

Not that Clarissa had made any final decision as to where she was going. She dreaded returning to Morecroft Cottage, but she had nowhere else to go. And there was the small matter of her trunks, not to mention the fact that she was riding a horse that did not belong to her, and wearing clothes that did not belong to her. Still, if she could only hit upon an alternate destination, she felt she would be very glad to go there, returning the horse and retrieving her things at some later date—preferably by messenger.

She reached a fork in the road and reined Daisy in, looking anxiously about her. The main road seemed to be bending to the right; the left branch dwindled almost immediately into a lane that was more a cart track than a proper road. But there was no signpost, and the landscape conveyed no information to a stranger's eye. Fields stretched to her right, and a scrubby wood to her left. Daisy tossed her head and blew softly, and Clarissa patted the animal's neck, more to reassure herself than the mare.

"Good girl, then," said Clarissa absently. She sighed. "You would *think* that some helpful person would erect a sign, would you not? Really, I have half a mind to turn down this lane. It has every appearance of leading to a farmhouse. What do you think?"

Daisy expressed no clear opinion. Clarissa hesitated, nibbling the tip of one gloved finger. Just then she heard footsteps stamping and rustling in the brush to her left, and held Daisy steady, her eyes brightening with relief. In a few seconds the brush parted and a man in leather gaiters emerged, his dog bounding beside him and a rifle slung on a strap over his shoulder. He stopped in his tracks and stared, slackjawed, when he saw Clarissa.

Clarissa smiled blindingly at him. "Oh, sir, I was never more glad to see anyone! Pray, can you tell me where I am?"

The man was very young, seemingly just past boyhood. He had a round, pleasant face dominated by a pair of large brown eyes framed in thick lashes. These goggled at her for a moment, and then he seemed to awaken from his sudden stupor. He flushed like a girl, and pulled off his hat. A lock of brown hair immediately fell across his brow. He raked it back with his fingers, stammering.

"I b-beg your pardon! We seldom see strangers in—*heel,* Sam! Sit, sir!" This to the dog, who had approached Daisy, tail wagging, and caused the mare to dance sideways. The dog obliged the lad by trotting back to him, and he grasped its collar and pressed its hindquarters until it squatted down beside him, gently panting. The young man's face was now beet red. "I'm frightfully sorry. He's still a puppy, you know, and I'm afraid he's not very well trained."

"He's quite large for a puppy."

"Oh, yes! I daresay he'll be as big as a mastiff." He thumped his pet vigorously and told it it was a good dog. Then he glanced shyly up at Clarissa again. "Did you say you were lost?"

She laughed, her nose wrinkling comically. "No, I did not—but I am! I've no sense of direction, and I have never been in this part of the country before. I haven't the least idea where I may be. I don't know what I would have done if you hadn't come along. Followed that track, I fancy, until I found someone to ask." She pointed with her riding crop.

The young man chuckled. "You'd have caught cold at that! That's the road to Mr. Manvers's farm. He's a testy old gentleman, and dislikes females. He'd be more likely to chase you off with a broom than give you directions."

"Heavens! I've had a lucky escape, then."

"Yes, rather." His shy smile returned. "I would be very glad to be of service to you, if I may."

"Thank you, you are very good. Only tell me where this road leads and I shall be very much in your debt."

He pointed ahead. "This lane joins the Pentonville Road. And behind you is Islington."

Well. It was clearly time for her to decide where she was going. She knew nothing of either Pentonville or Islington, but now that she had been told where the lane led, she would look like an imbecile if she loitered, irresolute, at the crossroads. And still she hesitated. The young man watched her expectantly. She blushed.

"And—and which way, pray, is Morecroft Cottage?" she asked, as nonchalantly as she could.

His eyes grew round with wonder and doubt. "Morecroft Cottage? Mr. Whitlatch's place?" His gaze traveled over her, and a troubled look crossed his features. Clarissa felt her blush intensify when he asked incredulously, "Are you stopping there?"

She tried to look haughty. "Yes, I am. For the present."

She watched his expression change as he palpably withdrew. She could feel his disapproval, and it stung. This well brought-up, likeable young man was altering his opinion of her based solely on the information that she was a guest of Mr. Whitlatch. She had to curb a sudden impulse to explain, to tell him exactly why she was there and her innocence of any wrongdoing, to pour out excuses and beg him to believe her. It was impossible to do any such thing, of course. So she sat in miserable silence while the admiration in the young man's expressive eyes turned to reproof and condemnation.

Neither of them had attended to the sound of approaching hoofbeats, and both jumped, startled, at the sound of Mr. Whitlatch's voice as he reined in his horse beside Clarissa's.

"Good afternoon," he said. His eyes raked Clarissa mockingly. "Let me guess: you have lost your way. It's a habit of yours, I think."

She thought she saw anger in the set of Trevor's jaw, but he seemed to be masking it in the presence of a third person. She could only be thankful. She tried her best to remain composed and speak pleasantly. "Yes, I am afraid it is. This kind gentleman seems to know the neighborhood well, however, so you find me in good hands, sir."

Trevor glanced at her companion, a sardonic gleam lighting his eyes. "So you rushed to Miss Feeney's assistance! What a noble nature you have, Mr. Henry."

Mr. Henry's young face flushed. "A-anyone would!" he stammered.

"Well, I am in your debt," said Trevor smoothly. He glanced from Mr. Henry's obvious discomfiture to Clarissa's, and the sight of their embarrassment apparently tickled his wicked sense of humor. "Shall I introduce you, or have you performed that office for yourselves? Ah, I see that you have not. Very well. Clarissa, allow me to present to you Mr. Eustace Henry." His grin widened. "The vicar's son."

Clarissa almost gasped aloud, but managed to keep her countenance while she bowed to Mr. Henry.

Mr. Whitlatch continued. "Mr. Henry, the lady you have been assisting is Miss Feeney." There was a barely perceptible pause before he proceeded. "My ward."

His *ward*! Clarissa gaped at her host in dumbstruck amazement. The effrontery of the man! But Mr. Henry was bowing very low to her, a smile of eager relief transforming his features.

"Your servant, Miss Feeney!" he exclaimed reverently. His enthusiasm invested the common courtesy with something more than its usual meaning. He straightened, beaming. "You are her guardian, then, Mr. Whitlatch? I had heard you were in the neighborhood, but—" He stopped, suddenly covered with confusion. Clarissa could easily imagine what he had heard. Doubtless that Mr. Whitlatch had brought another female out from London, with all that that implied.

Mr. Whitlatch seemed unconcerned. "Yes, I mean to stay here for a period. And Miss Feeney too, I imagine." He smiled urbanely at Clarissa. She glared at him in speechless dudgeon.

The lock of hair fell across Mr. Henry's forehead again, making him appear even more boyish as he turned his radiant smile upon Clarissa. "Then I daresay we may see each other at morning services tomorrow!" he exclaimed. His smile turned shy again. "I . . . I hope so, at any rate."

Clarissa had no idea whether Trevor attended church, but she unhesitatingly replied, "I shall certainly be present." She threw a challenging glance at her host, but he appeared perfectly unruffled. He touched his hat to Mr. Henry.

"Until tomorrow, then, Mr. Henry. Come along, Clarissa."

He turned his horse and, without a backward glance, started back the way he had come. Clarissa was thus reduced to the status of a child who must go where she is bid and suffer herself to be addressed by her Christian name. Inwardly fuming, Clarissa bowed to Mr. Henry and turned Daisy to follow Mr. Whitlatch. He had, very neatly, left her with no dignified alternative.

Mr. Henry still stood at the side of the road, watching them go. He appeared lost in some beatific daydream. She waited until he was out of earshot before addressing Mr. Whitlatch.

"I suppose you find this situation amusing!" she hissed, furious. "Whatever possessed you to introduce me as your ward?"

Soundless laughter shook him. "You are my ward. After your father's death, your mother . . . er . . . commended you to my care."

Clarissa gasped, and bit her lip. He smiled grimly at her. "It's true, as far as it goes. And you would do well to accept the story with the appearance, at least, of complaisance."

Trevor glanced at her mortified expression and his jaw tightened. "Very well. What would you have me do? How should I introduce you, Clarissa? I would be interested to know how you would characterize our relationship."

"We have no relationship!" she told him, her voice shaking a little. "And I am no one's *ward*! The idea is absurd! I'll have you know, sir, that I am one-and-twenty!"

He shrugged. "No matter. I shall tell people that you are under my protection until your twenty-fifth birthday. That ought to buy us some time."

"Buy us some time for what?" Clarissa asked, confused. Then her expression became despairing. "Oh, sir, how am I to find employment if people believe I am your ward? They will think it so odd of me!"

"Yes," he said shortly. "I think it odd myself."

"You cannot mean to keep me here until my twenty-fifth birthday!"

"Why not?" he said flippantly. Then his brows drew together. "You are not my prisoner, Clarissa. I told you I would try to find a position for you, and I will keep my word. If you still wish it."

"If I still—*if* I still wish it!" she choked. "Of course I wish it! But—will Mr. Henry tell people in the village that I am your ward?"

"I suppose he will. What does that matter?"

Clarissa pounded her fist against the pommel in frustration, and then had to rein Daisy in as the animal jumped forward. "Do you not see, sir, that if people here believe me to be your ward—to be anyone's ward!—I will not be able to seek employment in this neighborhood?"

She saw by his puzzled frown that he did not understand why this upset her. She wasn't sure, herself, why it upset her. She gazed at him in helpless frustration. "I do not wish to go back to London," she said at last.

"Very well. I had not thought about that, one way or the other. We will find you a situation in St. Albans, or Camden Town, or Uxbridge, or anywhere you like. What difference does it make?"

She took a deep and shaky breath, and expelled it on a sigh. "None, I suppose," she said listlessly. He was right, of course. What difference did it make? After this week, or next, she would never see Morecroft Cottage again. Never see Trevor Whitlatch again. Or Mrs. Simmons, or Dawson, or Hogan, or even Mr. Henry. And that was all doubtless for the best.

They rode on in silence for a few moments. Clarissa glanced uncertainly at her companion. He was sitting very straight in the saddle, gazing ahead with a most forbidding expression on his face. Still, she determined to speak.

"It is time you told me, sir, how I came to be in your power."

Trevor's eyebrows flew upwards. "What! Do you mean you do not know?"

"I know nothing. My mother's servant came to me and told me to pack my things, that I was being sent away with you. Why?"

"Good God!" He considered her for a moment, his expression unfathomable. "From what I now know of you, I am astonished you obeyed her."

Her eyes flashed. "Believe me, my case was desperate or I never would have done so!"

"I do believe you," said Trevor wryly. "I said I was astonished."

He fell silent. Clarissa waited impatiently for a few seconds, then turned to him again. "Well?"

"Well what?"

"You have not answered my question! Why was I sent away with you? I have gathered, of course, that my mother promised you I would become your mistress." It was suddenly difficult to speak past the constriction in her throat. She had to force the terrible words out. "Did she . . . did she *sell* me to you?"

Trevor uttered a startled exclamation. "Devil a bit! What do you take me for? I'm not a man who traffics in the sale of—" But he suddenly broke off, his indignant expression turning almost ludicrously to chagrin. After a short struggle with himself, he spoke again, gruffly. "Very well. I suppose I did exactly that. And not five minutes after telling La Gianetta I was no slaver! What a joke."

"Not a very funny one," she said quietly.

"No." He shot her a quick glance, and his mouth twisted in self-mockery. "You may have noticed that I am a creature of impulse."

Despite her churning emotions, that almost surprised a laugh out of her. "Yes, oddly enough, that aspect of your character has not escaped me."

"My instincts are generally sound, however. The majority of my impulsive decisions turn out well."

"Yes, you have the Midas touch, as all the world knows! What a disappointment for you, to have made such a—such an *unprofitable* investment in me!" Clarissa's cheeks flushed with mortification.

"I can't deny that I am disappointed with the results thus far." A sudden grin lightened his features. "Still, some of my richest ventures showed heavy losses in the beginning. It would be foolish to despair at this early juncture. I'll turn you to gold yet."

She shook her head resolutely. "No, sir, I fear the touch has deserted you this time. The sooner you secure employment for me, the sooner you will stop throwing good money after bad."

"What money? You haven't cost me a farthing, apart from the . . . er . . . initial outlay. I have given you nothing. In fact, I haven't dared to offer you so much as a handkerchief, for fear of offending you! You nearly bit my head off for trying to give you that rubbishing riding habit."

"You know very well I did no such thing! Pray do not expect to draw me into a foolish argument and thus lead me from the point!"

"What is the point?"

"I am living almost entirely at your expense. Nothing could be more improper! You may wipe that wounded look off your face, sir; I do not mean to imply that I am ungrateful. You have been everything that is kind, everything that is generous. I am very sensible of it, I assure you."

"You are fretting yourself to flinders over nothing."

"It is not 'nothing' to me!"

"Very well. When you leave me for your new position, I will present you with a bill for your lodging and meals."

An unwilling smile tugged at the corners of her mouth. "You have an answer for everything."

Trevor smiled, but the smile did not reach his eyes. "I have much to answer for," he said quietly.

Clarissa was tempted to reassure him, but quelled the impulse. He did, in fact, have much to answer for. Her hands tightened on the reins. "So. You purchased me." She gave an unhappy little laugh. "I don't know why the truth should upset me. After all, it is what I suspected all along."

"In point of fact, no money exchanged hands—if that makes you feel any better."

She gazed numbly at him. "Should it?"

"No. I suppose not. But I wish it would." Trevor suddenly

reached over and seized her reins, pulling both horses to a stop. His hand covered hers and his voice grew husky. "Clarissa, I am sorry. I wish I could find smooth words to make it up to you, to somehow make everything all right. But I'm a plainspoken fellow, and I've no knack for making pretty speeches."

Tears rose up to choke her. "I don't want pretty speeches," she whispered. "And nothing you could say would put this situation right."

His hand tightened over hers. "Let me try. We have always spoken truth to each other, have we not? Truly, then, the transaction between myself and La Gianetta was meaningless. She cheated me, but that does not touch you. It cannot touch you. No one can put a value on your person or your soul, Clarissa. You owe me nothing."

Abruptly, he returned control of her horse to her and headed his chestnut to the left. In a haze of conflicting emotions, she suddenly became aware that they were turning through the gates of Morecroft Cottage. She struggled to compose herself before anyone could see her. They rode up to the house in silence.

The instant Dawson helped her to alight, Clarissa discovered she was woefully stiff after spending the morning on horseback. She also felt strangely low and dispirited. She knew it was good news to learn that Mr. Whitlatch would not hold her accountable for her mother's debt. That ought to have relieved her mind, not depressed her! Mr. Whitlatch had no hold on her whatsoever. He had acknowledged it. She was free to leave with a clear conscience, at whatever time a situation offered. Trying to feel glad of this, and inexplicably failing, Clarissa drooped tiredly as she made her way upstairs.

Bess helped her change out of the pretty riding habit and into one of her plain round gowns. Clarissa ran her hand regretfully over the soft folds of rose-colored velvet as they lay, discarded, on her bed. What a pity that she would never wear it again. Then she remembered the meaning of the rose color, and that the habit had been purchased for someone else. Her spine stiffened. Just as well, she told herself. It was time she came down from the clouds and returned to the realities of her life. Soon she would obtain a post as someone's housemaid, or nursemaid, or something equally dreary. In Uxbridge. And this wonderful,

magical week of holiday at Morecroft Cottage would all seem
like a far-off dream.

Chapter 18

Mr. Whitlatch, despite his upbringing, was not a regular
churchgoer. And if he were, church services would be the
last place in the village he would choose to be seen with
Clarissa. It seemed ill-advised, to put it mildly, to flaunt
Clarissa in the face of the parish when he still hoped—however
dim the prospect seemed at the moment—to eventually make
her his mistress.

On the other hand, since she appeared determined to go, it
would be unseemly to allow her to go alone. Unseemly and a
trifle cruel, to send her alone into that lion's den! It spoke volumes about her innocence that she would even *suggest* attending church while residing unchaperoned at a bachelor's
residence. But she came downstairs on Sunday morning gloved
and bonneted, her right hand buttoning her redingote over the
white muslin she had worn her first evening at Morecroft Cottage, and a battered prayer book in her left. She apparently took
it for granted that respectable persons attended church of a Sunday.

Trevor did not care to explain to his guest the exact reasons
why the thought of attending church with her on his arm made
his hair stand on end. So he gritted his teeth and called for his
carriage. If Clarissa wanted to go to church, to church they
would go. He would find some way to deal with the consequences. After all, he reminded himself grimly, he always
enjoyed a challenge.

Trevor had braced himself to be met with stares and whispers, so he bore the villagers' scrutiny with equanimity.
Clarissa's serene indifference surprised him, however, until he
recollected that she had been used to stares and whispers all her
life. She sat through the entire service apparently untroubled by
the mild sensation her presence caused. Nothing disturbed her
poise or caused her earnest attention to waver; her sweet, seri-

ous expression was unfeigned. One had to admire both her courage and her piety.

He was amused to discover that attending church went a long way toward establishing not only Clarissa's respectability in the village's eyes, but his own as well. Mr. Henry had obviously been busy. The word had spread like wildfire that the lovely girl with the modest demeanor was Mr. Whitlatch's ward. When they stepped out of the vestibule after the morning service, they were quickly surrounded by eager well-wishers.

Trevor had not foreseen this development. Now that Clarissa seemed ready to accept the role he had recklessly assigned her, he realized that she had been right in the first place—telling the village that Miss Feeney was his ward could easily prove disastrous. To him! The wench was so damnably charming, ten to one she would have the whole village in her pocket inside of an hour. It would be a black day for Trevor Whitlatch, when and if the parish ever learned that he had compromised the popular Miss Feeney! With an effort, he banished the gothic vision this conjured up—a crowd of angry villagers marching on Morecroft Cottage with torches and pitchforks—and exerted himself to be cordial to the various persons who approached them.

Most people were friendly, many were curious, and some were frankly agog to know who, and what, Clarissa was. But a few of the parishioners swept past them coldly, disapproval writ large on their forbidding faces. Trevor discovered within himself an irrational desire to box the ears of these worthy folk, merely because they had jumped to an entirely correct conclusion.

Clarissa's lovely manners seemed to be winning the day; a small crowd had gathered; and then, to Mr. Whitlatch's annoyance, young Mr. Henry pushed his way through to Clarissa's side. He seized her hand and wrung it, his round face beaming.

"Miss Feeney! How splendid to see you again!" he exclaimed, removing his hat. His unruly brown locks had been pomaded into strict order. In fact, his entire person shone with cleanliness, and his clothing looked suspiciously new. Mr. Whitlatch felt his hackles begin to rise.

"How do you do, Mr. Henry?" said Clarissa, smiling at him in a friendly way. The degree of tolerance she was showing this silly halfling struck Trevor as excessive.

"Oh, capital! Never better! But you must allow me to present my parents to you. They are excessively anxious to make your acquaintance!"

Trevor watched in cynical amusement as young Mr. Henry, placing Clarissa's hand upon his arm with a kind of ecstatic reverence, ushered her tenderly over to where the vicar and Mrs. Henry stood. He could imagine just how anxious the vicar and his wife were to make the acquaintance of a girl whose antecedents were entirely unknown, and who had been described to them as the "ward" of the rakish Mr. Whitlatch! He saw Eustace, fairly tripping over himself in his eagerness, go through the motions of presenting Clarissa. He saw Clarissa's modest curtsey. He saw the stiffness of the vicar's bow, and the limpness of Mrs. Henry's handshake. The vicar's wife was making a palpable effort to appear civil, but it was plain as a pikestaff that beneath her rather sickly smile she was quivering with hostility and alarm.

Trevor had to cough to hide his wicked grin. Really, if Mrs. Henry's animosity had been directed at anyone other than Clarissa, he could find it in his heart to sympathize with her. No mother enjoys meeting a penniless unknown who has thrown her only son, at a tender and impressionable age, into a fever of admiration.

Eustace did not seem to notice his parents' lack of enthusiasm. His worshipful eyes never left Clarissa. He looked completely thrilled. He looked, in fact, like a prime idiot. A coterie of young men began to form, hovering hopefully on the fringes of the Henry group, and Mrs. Henry began a spirited effort to include these gentlemen in the round of introductions to Clarissa. Eustace's aspect promptly took on the semblance of a dog guarding a bone. Trevor nearly laughed aloud. He had never thought to derive so much entertainment from attending church.

His amusement faded, however, when he learned that Clarissa had given Mr. Henry permission to call upon her at Morecroft Cottage. She innocently landed this leveler on him during the drive home, and, heedless of Dawson's presence on the box, he rounded on her.

"You did *what*?" he thundered.

Clarissa opened her eyes in astonishment. "Why, what objection can you possibly have?"

"What objection! I've *every* objection! Why the devil do you think I brought you here, rather than set you up in London? I want to keep you out of the reach of—" he stopped, recognizing the shock in Clarissa's expression, and hastily amended what he was about to say. "I've no wish to trip over Eustace Henry every time I open my door!"

But Clarissa had noticed his about-face, confound it. Anger glittered in the glorious blue eyes turned up to his. "If your intent was to keep me from the society of *Eustace Henry*," she uttered disdainfully, "I should think Morecroft Cottage was a very silly place to bring me!"

Of course that was not what he meant, and she knew it. But this would be a much safer battle than a discussion of what he *had* meant.

He glared at her. "As my ward, Miss Feeney, I relied upon your sense of propriety to prevent such a misstep! Why did you not apply to me for permission, before granting that imbecile leave to run tame in my house?"

"Well, how unfair!" she gasped, diverted as he had hoped she would be. "You introduced me to him, for heaven's sake! How was I to guess you held him in aversion? He seems a perfectly blameless young man!"

"Blameless? I daresay he may be! But—"

"And as for letting him run tame in your house, I never heard anything more unjust! I gave him permission to *call,* not to move in with you! If you feel so strongly about it—although I still cannot imagine why you do—you need not meet him. I will see him alone."

"Then next, I suppose, I will have to hire some female dragon to guard your reputation!"

Clarissa gave a little crow of laughter. "Sir, you are the most exasperating person of my acquaintance! You cannot suspect poor Mr. Henry of any evil design!"

"That's not the point!"

"Well, what *is* your point? Anyone would think you expected him to descend upon us for hours at a time, or on a daily basis! If he calls at all, which is far from certain, I am sure it will be a very correct morning call of a quarter of an hour. He will very likely bring his mother with him! He is only trying to be neighborly."

Trevor gave a snort of derision. "You don't believe that any more than I do."

She flushed. "Why should I not believe it?"

"Neither the vicar, nor any member of his family, has called on me since the first week I took up residence in the neighborhood!"

"Well, I could not be expected to know that!"

"No, but—"

"And now that you have added to your household—or at least that is what you deliberately led them to believe—why should they not call again? It is only proper, after all, for the vicar, or the vicar's wife—"

"Or the vicar's *son!*" he interjected jeeringly.

"—to call upon your ward!" she finished, a martial light in her eye.

"Miss Feeney, I am a man who likes his privacy. If you intend to turn Morecroft Cottage upside down with social engagements—"

"No such thing! It is your house, sir; I am perfectly mindful of it."

He eyed her grimly. "Once you have opened the floodgates, we will be deluged."

"Oh, pooh! You are making a mountain out of a molehill. Are you really such a hermit? I must say, I think this sudden desire to barricade yourself in your home is most unaccountable! You are neither scholarly nor pious, and if you expect me to believe you are *shy,* why, I never heard such a—such a *rapper!*"

Trevor could not suppress a grin. "No, I confess I have never suffered from shyness."

"I thought not! And at any rate, it can hardly signify if we are 'deluged' for a time. All you need do is rebuff everyone, in your inimitable way! They will speedily learn to leave you alone again. I will not be here much longer to keep the floodgates open."

He was startled. "Where are you going?"

Clarissa turned to him, eyes wide with amazement. "It is Sunday," she told him carefully, in a tone suitable for teaching backward children. "Tomorrow is Monday. You promised that you would begin seeking a situation for me. You cannot have forgotten!"

He had not, of course. But he had hoped she might have forgotten, or perhaps changed her mind. It was rather wounding to hear once more how determined she was to leave him. He

hunched one shoulder pettishly. "I have found you a s.
Clarissa. You are my ward."

Her hands clenched on the prayer book in her lap. "No,
uttered, her voice sounding suddenly choked and breathle .
"No, you are not serious. I can't believe—I *won't* believe that
you have deliberately deceived me."

Trevor's eyes snapped dangerously. "Very affecting! But I
have had enough of these die-away scenes, thank you! Stop behaving as if I'd insulted you! What the devil is wrong with
being my ward?"

Clarissa's voice was barely audible. "I thought it was merely
a tale you were using to shield me from gossip." She covered
her eyes with a shaking hand. "I ought never to have acquiesced
in such a crazy story; I ought to have done something to scotch
it. Now I am in a worse fix than ever! And it is my own fault,
for I have lent credence to the tale through my own behavior.
What was I thinking?"

He pulled her hand away and held it in a strong grip. "Look
at me!" he commanded. She did so, albeit unwillingly. Her eyes
were full of pain. Trevor swore impatiently. "Clarissa, you have
made a habit of despair! I've no patience with it. Obstacles and
setbacks are not calamities—they are opportunities! With each
obstacle you overcome, you will become stronger. If you fall
into a fit of the dismals and wallow in self-reproach every time
you put your foot wrong, you will never succeed at anything.
And what is more, you will annoy me! Exceedingly."

Some of the pain left her eyes. "A habit of despair," she repeated slowly. "Is it really possible to make a habit of despair?"

"Certainly. And it is just as possible to make a habit of opti-
mism. I recommend the latter."

The ghost of a smile flitted across Clarissa's troubled features. "The Whitlatch method. You ought to write a book."

"I haven't time. I'm too busy enjoying life, and turning
everything I touch to gold."

She laughed a little. "Very well, King Midas! Now teach me
how I may turn this situation to gold, if you please! I confess, I
do not see a way out of these difficulties."

Trevor shrugged. "What difficulties? I will not renege on my
promise, Clarissa. I will put feelers out tomorrow, seeking a situation for you as governess to a tribe of spoiled children, or as
companion to some rich old harridan, or some other delightful

bit of drudgery. In the meantime, you will remain here, ostensibly as my ward. And, Clarissa—" He took her shoulders and turned her toward him. She looked up at him warily. "Let me know, if you should change your mind," he told her quietly. "You know I would be pleased to have you stay."

He felt her soften. The wariness left her, and she hung, defenseless, in his grip. Dear God, she was so beautiful. A tide of desire surged through him. It was torture to hold her like this, at arm's length, and watch her eyes go wide and misty.

"Thank you," she whispered. "I wish it were possible."

Well, this was progress! She wished it were possible. He was careful to keep the hope from his expression. Instead, he merely nodded, and let her go. They were approaching the house.

Chapter 19

"Look what I have found!"

Trevor glanced up from the charts he was studying and saw Clarissa, seeming very pleased with herself, standing in the doorway of his office and holding out a dusty box for his inspection. He eyed it with foreboding. "What is it?"

"It is a backgammon set! Someone had placed it in the back of the linen closet. I can't imagine why."

"Can't you?" said Trevor politely. "I have already thought of one likely explanation."

"It seems a strange place to store a game. Who would think to look for it in a linen closet? It might have been lost forever!"

"Precisely."

Her eyes widened in that startled look he loved, followed by her charming ripple of laughter. "Sir, you are too bad! Do you not like backgammon?"

A man could not help smiling at her. "Do you?" he countered.

"I believe I do. I have not played it often."

"Well, that explains it. I have played it too often! My uncle was fond of it, and I was frequently bored enough to indulge him in a game or two during our travels together. Backgammon is a colossal waste of time."

Clarissa's face fell. "It is not exciting, of course. I suppose you prefer games of chance. Most gentlemen do."

"Oddly enough, this gentleman does not." Trevor yawned lazily and stretched his cramped arms. Studying charts was fatiguing work. "Betting on a game strikes me as even sillier than playing the game for its own sake."

She nodded approvingly. "Now, there, I must agree with you. I have never understood the impulse to gamble."

"Good," muttered Trevor, recalling the incredible sums Rosie had managed to squander at silver-loo in London. Her addiction to gaming had been the main reason he had packed her off to Morecroft Cottage. Not that that had answered; she had immediately taken to drink. It amazed him now to think that he had ever found that redheaded harpy attractive.

But Clarissa was studying him with her head cocked, birdlike. "I am surprised, you know, to discover that you dislike gaming."

"Why?" he asked, amused.

"It appears to me that your life consists of one gamble after another! I never met anyone who relished adversity the way you do. I had thought that taking foolish risks was your favorite sport."

His eyes gleamed. "The risks I take are never foolish."

Clarissa laughed a little. "Risks are always foolish," she told him primly.

"Good God! What a tame and depressing life you must have led!"

Some of the laughter left her eyes. "Why, so I think. But I never knew it until—" She stopped, seemingly vexed with herself.

Trevor reached her in two strides and placed a finger beneath her chin, tilting her face up. Her eyes met his unwillingly. He finished her sentence for her. "Until you met me."

She tossed her head, crossly swatting his hand away. "Oh, very well—yes! But I daresay I shall quickly reaccustom myself to a . . . a more ordered existence."

He quirked an eyebrow at her. "A duller existence."

"A *normal* existence." Her face was turning pink. "You scarcely acknowledge the rules most people live by," she told him severely. "And you tackle every project, every problem, with so much . . . enthusiasm! It isn't seemly. Most people would consider the life you lead to be nothing short of harrowing!"

"But that is not your opinion, and never has been. You enjoy it here. You find my company exhilarating."

Clarissa backed toward the edges of the room, clutching the backgammon box protectively. "How dare you!" she spluttered.

He followed her, deftly pinning her by placing his palms flat on the wall on either side of her. "How dare I what, Clarissa? Speak the truth to you? I will always speak the truth to you. Life is too short for polite equivocation."

She lifted her chin at him, and her eyes flashed. "Life is too short for mannerless bullying!"

He laughed softly, delighted. "Yes, by God! Give me the word with no bark on it!"

"Don't sneer at me!"

"I'm not sneering at you. I'm admiring your spirit. You are every bit as outspoken as I am, and that's a rare quality in a woman."

She looked confused, but some of the anger left her. "You're talking nonsense. You should not praise me for intemperate speech, of all things! It has always been my worst fault."

"I like it."

She wrinkled her nose at him. "Yes, a charming quality! My hotheadedness has won friends for me everywhere I go!"

"It has won you this friend, at any rate."

"You are serious!"

"Of course I am. I like to know exactly where I stand. Don't you?"

She bit her lip, but a smile tugged at the corners of her mouth. "I have always had difficulty distinguishing between plain speech and rudeness, especially when I speak in haste. You mustn't pretend that fault is a virtue, simply because you share it!"

He grinned. "Virtue is in the eye of the beholder. We are kindred spirits, you and I. Confess! You feel perfectly comfortable with my lack of manners and my unconventional ways. My rough edges don't frighten you a bit."

Amusement lit her eyes. "You haven't succeeded in hoodwinking me, if that is what you mean."

He was startled. "Hoodwinking you?"

"Yes! The way, I fancy, you have duped your unfortunate employees. I have seen the gentlemen who visit you in the afternoons. They shake in their shoes whenever your eye turns in their direction! What a humbug you are."

He was so nonplussed, he failed to block her move as she ducked neatly beneath his arm and freed herself.

She unconcernedly walked away, approached the massive table where his charts were spread out, and began to glance over them inquisitively. Aggrieved, he followed her.

"I'll have you know, Miss Feeney, that I am an extremely powerful and terrifying individual. My word is law, and my wrath is dreadful to behold."

"Oh, yes! I daresay it is," she agreed calmly. Her eyes were on the charts, and her expression was suspiciously demure.

His lips twitched. "Beware! One day you will incur my displeasure. On that day, you will quickly learn to fear me."

"Pooh! You are all bark and no bite."

He took her shoulders and pulled her firmly round to face him. "If a dog barks loudly enough, he often does not need to bite. But the teeth are still there, Clarissa."

"Ah. I see. Your point is well taken, sir; you are a tyrant after all."

Her face was turned up to his, rosy and laughing. His senses were teased with a whiff of lemon verbena sachet. "And you, Clarissa, are a darling," he exclaimed, leaning in and kissing her swiftly.

The touch was purposely brief and light; the sort of kiss that expressed affection or greeting, not desire. But Clarissa pulled away, startled, and instinctively pressed one palm to his chest as if to hold him at bay. He pretended not to notice. With studied nonchalance, as if exchanging a kiss was a common, natural, friendly occurrence, he turned back to his work.

Clarissa was standing utterly still, blushing rosily. He kept his face impassive. He had been carefully trying, the past few days, to retake the ground he had lost when he kissed her at the ridge. He had believed himself to be beginning to re-create the friendship that he hoped would form a starting point for his siege. She had visibly relaxed more around him, permitted his touch when it was offered in an ostensibly friendly spirit, and obviously enjoyed his company more with each day that passed. She still mentioned leaving far more than he liked, but he thought she seemed noticeably less enthused about the prospect. If only he could convince her that his kiss was harmless! The less frightening she found his advances, the further he could go.

With that in mind, he gestured casually toward the papers in front of them. "What did you find here to interest you?"

"Oh . . . nothing," she stammered. His air of unconcern seemed to help her recover her tone of mind somewhat, just as he had hoped. She leaned over the desk beside him in a much more natural manner. "It all appears quite meaningless, to me. What are these curious dotted lines you are poring over?"

"Shipping routes."

The blue eyes suddenly twinkled up at him. "Well! And you think *backgammon* dull!"

He grinned at her, and suddenly he was very aware of how small the space was between their bodies. Her skirt brushed his leg. The air between them seemed charged with electricity. Their eyes locked, and Trevor's smile faded in a surge of desire. The memory of kissing her, really kissing her, rushed vividly into his mind. It took a strong effort of will to resist his impulses; the urge to take her in his arms was almost overmastering.

But what if she felt it, too? Ah, God. She did. He saw her eyes dilate and her lips part, and sensed the exact instant when she stopped breathing. His scruples vanished, and he reached for her.

But Clarissa stepped away, tension visible in every line of her squared shoulders. "Should I put the game back in the linen closet?" she asked. Her voice sounded high and tremulous.

"Blast the game," growled Trevor. He moved purposely toward her, but then was frustrated by the entrance of Mrs. Simmons. He checked in mid-stride. The housekeeper stood placidly in the doorway, ducking a slight curtsey.

"Eustace Henry has called. Shall I show him up?"

The moment was gone, as surely as if a bucket of ice had been poured over him. "Hang Eustace Henry!" snapped Trevor, exasperated. "Tell him to go to the devil!"

Mrs. Simmons folded her hands against her apron and fixed Trevor with a disapproving eye. "He has not called to see *you*, sir!" she admonished him.

"Oh, dear," said Clarissa faintly. "Pray show him into the morning room, Mrs. Simmons. I will be there directly."

As soon as Mrs. Simmons had gone, Trevor rounded on Clarissa. "What did I tell you when you invited that gudgeon to call?" he demanded. "I knew he would haunt the place!"

Clarissa peered distractedly at her reflection, showing dimly in a brass wall sconce, and smoothed her already smooth hair. "I own, I did not expect him to call here every day!" she admitted. "It is really rather awkward, with everyone believing me to be your ward. The sooner you find me a situation, sir, the better."

She whisked out of the room in a rustle of skirts, and Trevor was left to stare at the space she had just vacated. He swore under his breath, long and fluently. He was fast becoming obsessed with the chit. And he was no nearer to his goal than when she first arrived.

Well, that wasn't entirely true. He had kissed her, at least. But the only discernible effect it had had was to make him want her even more. It had done nothing to soften Clarissa's position; she was as adamant as ever.

Trevor began furiously pacing the room, pondering the problem. As a man of his word, he had, albeit reluctantly, given one of his clerks orders last Monday to find respectable employment for Miss Feeney. The ambitious underling had proved lamentably industrious, and had, in fact, apprised Mr. Whitlatch of several opportunities already. Trevor had spurned them all. And he had, moreover, told Clarissa of none of them. He was guiltily aware that she might not find them as objectionable as he did. Three he rejected as ill-paying, four because he thought the work demeaning, and one because the position offered was in Yorkshire. He knew it was irrational; once she was removed from Morecroft Cottage, she would be as far out of his reach in Finsbury as in York. But nevertheless, he threw the advertisement in the fire. No Yorkshire situation for Clarissa!

He tried to return to his charts and ledgers, but soon gave it up as hopeless. Drat the wench. She was ruining his concentration. He leaned tiredly against the table, rubbed his eyes, and wondered what the devil Clarissa was doing, holed up in the morning room with Mr. Henry. He ought to step up and see for himself, by George.

Three long strides brought him to the passage, where he

nearly collided with Dawson's boy, carrying a large parcel wrapped in brown paper.

"Beg pardon, sir," piped the boy, struggling to retain his hold on the package. Trevor reached out and steadied it for him, for which he received a gulped "thank 'ee!"

"What have you got there, lad?"

"Packet from the linen draper's, sir."

Trevor's eyebrows climbed. "Really? I don't recall ordering anything."

"No, sir. It's for Miss Feeney, sir."

The eyebrows climbed higher. "The devil you say!"

Was she finally pledging his credit? Spending his money? It was surprising, but actually a rather welcome development. Let her be beholden to him! He felt, at this stage of the game, he would take whatever meager advantage he could obtain.

"Let's have a look." Trevor removed the package from the stable boy's resistless grip and tore the paper off in one smooth movement. Several lengths of muslin and one of silk, neatly folded and stacked, met his interested gaze. On top was a ready-made round gown of dark blue kerseymere.

New clothing. And, from the look of it, finer clothing than he had yet seen her wear. The colors were not bright, but neither were they the drab hues she currently favored. One of the muslins was white, delicately sprigged in cherry. One of the muslins was a pale violet. And the silk was a pastel yellow of some kind. There was no pink to be seen, he noted with a flash of amusement.

Now, what did this portend? He rubbed his chin thoughtfully, staring particularly hard at that jonquil silk. Had he ever seen her wear silk? He thought not. Pretty high flying, for a would-be nursemaid.

Trevor became aware that the stable boy was staring at him with shocked, sorrowful eyes. "Them was Miss Feeney's things, sir," the boy said. His respectful tone was edged with condemnation.

Irritated, Trevor fixed him with the gimlet gaze that had caused many a hapless cabin boy to quail. This lad was apparently made of sterner stuff. His eyes did not drop. "Well?" demanded Mr. Whitlatch.

"We hadn't ought to open her packages, sir."

"It is not *her* package if I have paid for it!"

The boy gulped, abashed. "I thought she paid for it herself!" His cheeks reddened, and he ducked his head nervously. "I hope you won't take offense, sir; I'm that sorry."

Sudden doubt struck Trevor. "Was this delivered, or did you pick it up?"

"She sent me to the village for it, sir."

Trevor held out a peremptory hand. "Give me the bill."

"There wasn't a bill, sir. She gave me a haddock full o' beans afore I left." In proof of this assertion, he dug in his jacket for a moment and unearthed a small bag fashioned from a knotted handkerchief. A few coins still weighted the bottom of it. "I paid for it, all right and tight, sir."

He proffered the makeshift purse to his employer, who took it, frowning. It certainly was not his.

Trevor's jaw worked soundlessly for a moment, then a crashing oath escaped him. Dawson's boy fell back a pace, startled, but Mr. Whitlatch's wrath was directed only at himself. Another blunder! What in blue blazes was wrong with him? He had deliberately torn open her package and inspected her personal belongings. Now he owed Clarissa an apology. He was sick to death of owing Clarissa apologies!

He curtly dismissed the confused stable boy, stuffed the purse in his pocket, and, arms full of fabric, strode grimly to the morning room. His arrival, he discovered, was ill-timed. A cozy scene met his affronted gaze. Clarissa and Mr. Henry were seated at a small table before the fire, heads almost touching, playing backgammon.

It was a relief to direct his anger away from himself and onto a more comfortable target. What the devil was she doing, entertaining Mr. Henry with parlor games? *His* parlor games, in fact, and in *his* parlor!

Clarissa looked up when he appeared in the doorway, and he thought he saw her blush. His eyes narrowed in suspicion, but before he could utter the scathing words that rose to his lips, he recalled that they were not alone. He nearly choked, biting back his remarks. The probable reason for Clarissa's blush was present. It had risen from the table, in fact, and was bowing to him.

"Mr. Whitlatch! How do you do, sir? I wondered if I might have the pleasure of seeing you today," said Mr. Henry as he bowed.

Trevor barely heard Mr. Henry's polite blatherings. Ugly

memories were flashing through his mind, memories of light-skirted women who had done their best to fleece him, smiling and fawning and cooing in his presence, and cheating on him in his absence. Fury shook him.

"How d'you do?" snarled Mr. Whitlatch.

Mr. Henry's doglike countenance became anxious. He was clearly cudgeling his brain to discover what he might have done or said to offend Mr. Whitlatch. But Clarissa had risen, her eyes on the material in Trevor's arms.

"Is that parcel mine?"

"Yes!" snapped Trevor. He supposed he must look ridiculous, standing there like a mannequin holding several ells of yardage half wrapped in torn paper. It didn't matter. By God, Clarissa had set out to make him look ridiculous. She was playing him for a fool, just as all the others had done.

Her eyes lifted to his, puzzled. "The paper is torn."

"What of it? The contents are unhurt." He tossed the package contemptuously onto the sofa.

Clarissa studied his white-lipped countenance for a moment, then swiftly crossed to him and laid a gentle hand on his sleeve. "You are angry. Why?"

Her directness rattled him. For the first time, he almost understood what people found so objectionable about his own manners. Candor was all very well, but it knocked a man off balance to be addressed with outright bluntness. He scowled down at the lovely eyes upturned to his and tried to remember why he was angry. Bloody hell! It was a curse to be so easily bewitched by a pretty face.

He became aware of Mr. Henry's voice, like the buzzing of some annoying insect, forcing his attention.

"I beg your pardon . . . I fear I have overstayed. I don't mean to intrude. That is . . . I mean . . ." he gulped. "Really, Miss Feeney, I enjoyed our game so much that the time just slipped away! Mr. Whitlatch, I hope you will not think me hopelessly rude if I take myself off?"

The silly young chuff was as red as a beet. Trevor waved his hand impatiently. "For God's sake, man, don't stay on my account!"

Clarissa walked back to shake Mr. Henry's hand, and as he watched Mr. Henry's worshipful eyes devouring Clarissa's face, Trevor remembered why he was angry. Mr. Henry clung to Clarissa's hand just a heartbeat longer than he needed to. He even had the temerity to take her little hand in *both* of his, and press it in a way that struck Trevor as extremely loverlike. A surge of possessiveness ripped through him, turning his mood as black as thunder.

Clarissa appeared perfectly composed. She did not seem to encourage Mr. Henry's ardor, and she did not return his clasp, but, Trevor reminded himself savagely, she probably *dared* not, in his presence! She neither blushed nor pulled her hand away, blast her! Mr. Henry declared that he required no escort, since he knew his way out—evidence of familiarity that further enraged his host—and Clarissa walked with him as far as the door of the room and shut it behind him as he departed. She then turned and leaned against the door, her hands still gripping the handle behind her back.

"Well, Mr. Whitlatch," she said coolly. "What have you to say for yourself?"

Chapter 20

"Don't play the outraged innocent!" Trevor spat. "It is not you who has been injured, and well you know it!"

"No, indeed! It is Mr. Henry who has been injured. I have merely been embarrassed," said Clarissa scornfully. "I know that you pride yourself on your rudeness—Heaven knows why!—but I never saw anything to equal that performance! Whatever possessed you to storm in here and interrupt our game with your theatrics?"

"My *theatrics*! That's rich, by God!" Trevor pointed accusingly at the stack of folded yardage lying in a welter of torn paper. "Would you care to explain this interesting purchase?"

Clarissa lifted her chin defiantly. "Would you care to explain its condition?"

His jaw clenched. "Don't expect me to beg your pardon! Not now! Aye, I tore it open."

Clarissa walked crisply to the sofa and began straightening the package, her fingers trembling a little. "I knew you had done so, the moment I saw it," she said, in a low, strained voice. "But why? I do not understand you. You pretend I am a guest here, then treat me like chattel! You have no right, no right whatsoever, to inspect my personal property."

He followed her, and his long fingers closed tightly round her arm. "What rights do I have, Clarissa?" he hissed. "Or have I none?"

He jerked her around to face him, and she gasped in mingled pain and outrage. "Unhand me this instant! What has come over you? You are behaving like a lunatic!"

His features were contorted with frustration. "Have I no right to touch you?"

"None that I do not give you!" she flashed. "Let go of me!"

Instead, he took both her shoulders in a viselike grip and stared hard into her face, a queer, savage light in his eyes. "And what rights have you given Eustace Henry?"

Her eyes went wide with shock.

"I've spent the better part of a fortnight walking on eggshells around you, playing the fool, treating you like a *lady,* by God! Thinking I could win your cold little heart! And all the time, you meant to give yourself to some mewling, puling little milksop—"

"Stop it!"

"—who's not man enough to stand by you when I come into the room!"

"Stop this at once!"

"So help me, Clarissa, if I loved a woman, I wouldn't bow myself out and run away when I saw her threatened by a rogue like me!"

"No!" she agreed hotly, struggling in his grip. "I daresay you would wrestle him to the ground, or begin a bout of fisticuffs for her entertainment! Edifying!" She pulled herself out of his clutches and rubbed her arm where he had seized it. Her eyes blazed with anger. "Mr. Henry, thank God, possesses both manners and sense! He would never mortify a lady by indulging in a tantrum!"

"Oh, Mr. Henry is everything that is admirable!" snorted Trevor.

Clarissa compressed her lips in a thin line, as if struggling to control her temper. She walked back to the table before the fire and began, moving rather mechanically, to put the backgammon game away. "He certainly has many admirable qualities. You need not jeer at him, or call him names! Mr. Henry has a well-informed mind and a kind heart. Such a combination must always inspire respect."

Trevor's eyes narrowed. "And affection?"

She did not reply immediately, but bent over the table, gathering the counters with shaking hands.

"It's plain as a pikestaff. You mean to marry him, if you can." Trevor's voice was hard with disgust. He flicked the kerseymere dress with a contemptuous finger. "Where did you find sufficient funds to acquire these fribbles? Silk, and sprigged muslin! I thought you were a pauper."

"I had a little put by—not that it is any concern of yours! Why should I not spend my money as I choose?"

"Why not, indeed?" agreed Trevor bitterly. "So you have squandered your nest egg! What a risky experiment, for a woman who dislikes gambling! That decision must have cost you a good night's sleep. Still, I daresay it may prove a profitable investment, if you succeed in laying a trap for that unfortunate boy."

Clarissa flushed scarlet. "You are vulgar, and hateful, and I won't listen to you!"

"Oh, but you will! You will listen to me!" Trevor strode swiftly across the room and caught her in his arms. His violence knocked over the little table and the backgammon game went flying, scattering counters across the hearth rug. Clarissa cried out, struggling, but he held her fast.

"I will let you go, but you will hear me first. For you have never heard me out, not once, in all the little *discussions* we have had! You have told me all your reasons, all your myriad and very good reasons, all your *reasonable* reasons, for rejecting my offer unheard! But for once, Clarissa, you will hear it. You will listen to my offer in plain English, and then reject it if you can!"

She tossed back her head and glared at him. "Very well! Since you insist on tormenting me with your unwelcome proposals, I will hear them—once and for all! Then kindly refrain from insulting me with them again!"

He eased his grip on her, but did not let her go. She could have broken free, but apparently scorned to do so. Instead, she leaned passively back against his interlocked hands.

Clarissa's palms pressed against his chest as if warning him: this far, and no farther. Her expression was defiant, furious, utterly closed against anything he could say. He knew this, but there was no turning back.

God help him. She was the loveliest, most desirable girl he had ever seen or dreamed of. It seemed that every muscle in that lithe, willowy back of hers was tensed against him. He spread his fingers, willing her to relax. She did not.

He took a deep breath. "First let us consider Mr. Henry's proposal."

"Mr. Henry has made no proposal," she said coldly.

"He will. If his mother permits him! No, do not interrupt—Mr. Henry may be of age; I neither know nor care. The point is, he is smitten with you. And I believe your calculations are correct. Since Mr. Henry is too young to have recovered from boyish idealism, at some point he will probably offer you marriage."

"It is the height of impropriety to *calculate* what Mr. Henry's intentions may be! Really, I—"

"Stop interrupting, Clarissa! You waste your breath when you preach propriety to the likes of me! For the sake of argument, let us say that you someday receive an offer from the guileless Mr. Henry. It will be marriage that he offers. Are we agreed on that?"

She hesitated, then nodded, tight-lipped.

"Very well. Have you thought what marriage to Mr. Henry would mean? A life of genteel poverty with a man whom you will soon learn to despise!"

She gave a furious gasp. "How dare you! Just because *you* despise poor Mr. Henry—"

"Aha!" Trevor's eyes glinted in savage triumph. " 'Poor' Mr. Henry! In your heart, Clarissa, you know he is not your equal, and never can be. Eustace Henry is no fit match for you."

"He will not care for that! He is too noble, too unworldly a man to care for that."

"I don't mean your birth," said Trevor impatiently. "I mean your natures. You would be bored and unhappy with a man who worships you! I know you, Clarissa."

His eyes raked her features mockingly, but he was brought up short by a sudden revelation. I'faith, it was true. *He knew her.*

The advice he was giving her was sound; had his motives been entirely disinterested he would have given her the same advice. The insight shocked him. He felt connected to this girl on some deep, instinctive, primitive level. He could not remember ever feeling such a thing before. "I know you," he whispered again, and wonder dawned in Clarissa's eyes as she saw his expression change.

His voice became low and urgent, husky with sudden emotion. "Don't do it, Clarissa. Don't chain yourself to a man you cannot love. You would regret it to your dying day."

She looked uncertain now, and dropped her eyes in confusion. "You are very persuasive," she said hesitantly. "But you cannot predict the future, after all. And we are speaking of hypotheticals. Mr. Henry may never propose marriage to me. Or if he does, by then I may have learned to . . . to care for him."

Trevor snorted derisively. Clarissa lifted her chin, defiant again. "I like him very well! Many people marry with less."

"But a *lifetime,* Clarissa! A lifetime of Eustace Henry! Is that the price of respectability?"

She set her jaw, but he thought he saw despair and desperation in her resolve. "If it is, I must pay it."

His eyes gleamed with sudden humor. "Clarissa, I am going to give you a little business advice. Never pay a high price for a commodity you can obtain cheaply elsewhere."

She tilted her head, puzzled. "What do you mean?"

"I can give you respectability," he said softly. "And you won't have to marry a moonling. I'll make you a present of it."

Her voice was nearly inaudible. "How can you?"

Trevor shifted his arms to hold her more gently. "Here is my offer, Clarissa. Place it alongside Eustace Henry's and weigh them carefully against each other."

He paused, gazing intently at the perfect face turned up to his. Her expression was attentive—wary, but no longer hostile. He spoke softly, choosing his words as carefully as he knew how.

"I would like for you to stay with me here, at Morecroft Cottage, as the lady of the house. I meant what I said about tearing out the pink; we will remove every trace of Rosie's presence and I will give you carte blanche to redo that room however you choose. Money will be no object. You may have whatever you wish, both in furnishings and decoration. My servants will be your servants. If you wish, you may order the meals and run the house; if you don't care for housekeeping, there is no need to bestir yourself. Everything shall be exactly as you choose, Clarissa."

Her face had gone still and shuttered. He could no longer read her expression. He continued, more urgently. "You may go to London to shop for your clothes and personal effects. Hire the most expensive modiste you can find, and order whatever takes your fancy. Fill that wardrobe upstairs with frocks and hats and boots and silk stockings, everything of the finest. Then buy another wardrobe if you like, and fill it as well! Hire an abigail to take care of it all. Spend whatever it takes, to have what you want."

She still did not react. Trevor plunged recklessly on. "Does London life appeal to you? We'll go there whenever you say the word. I'll put you up at one of the finest hotels. I'll show you a London you've never seen! You may have a box at the opera. We'll attend every theater in town. I'll take you to Vauxhall. We'll dance and drink champagne and watch the fireworks. Would you like a horse? I'll make you a present of Daisy. Or if you don't care for her, I'll find you another. I'll buy you a team if you like! What would you like?"

Realizing he was rambling, he stopped abruptly. Why didn't she say something? His eyes searched her face desperately, but she neither moved nor spoke. It was like holding a lifeless doll. "If something else occurs to you, name it! Be my queen, Clarissa, and I will be yours to command."

Now she spoke, tonelessly. "For how long?"

He smiled in relief. "Why, for however long the arrangement suits us both."

Animation returned to her features, but not as he had hoped. That was not temptation he saw shimmering in her eyes, but cold fury. "And what becomes of me then?"

"When?"

"Afterward. After you are *done* with me." Her voice shook with loathing.

But he had foreseen this question. He grinned triumphantly at her. "Why then, Clarissa—I make you respectable."

Her brows snapped together. Trevor raised an imperious hand to ward off interruption. "At whatever point our alliance

ends, I will buy you a house. You may have a cottage in some
rural village, or a town house in Bath, or whatever you please.
Wherever you please. No one need know how you came by it.
You can call it a legacy from your great-aunt Mildred for all I
care. It will be yours, outright. No strings attached. Say yes,
Clarissa, and no matter what your future holds, from this day
forward you will always have a roof over your head. You shall
have that bargain in writing, my dear. Up front."

That had thrown her. He had chosen his bait well, for once.
Clarissa had never had a home of her own. Why, the idea had
struck her so hard she almost flinched. He saw her eyes close
in momentary pain.

"A house," she whispered. "My own house." Then, slowly,
her eyes opened to his. She had donned that blank, shuttered
expression again. "And what else?"

Surprise doused him like cold water, making him feel
strangely vulnerable. Then cynicism came to his rescue. He
ought to have known. All women were mercenary creatures at
heart. He had thought Clarissa different. He had been wrong,
that's all.

Odd that it should sting so much.

His lip curled. "Of course you may keep whatever presents
I bestow on you while you are under my protection."

"Very well. Clothing and knickknacks. What else?"

Trevor's sneer became more pronounced. "Doubtless there
will be some jewelry among your souvenirs."

"Jewels," she repeated, as if adding the item to a mental inventory. "And what else?"

Confound the wench! She was going to drive a hard bargain. Well, no matter, he reminded himself grimly. He was
prepared to offer her more.

Trevor's jaw tensed angrily. He had wanted this to be a gift,
and it had given him pleasure to picture her receiving it with
surprise and gratitude. But if she insisted on making it part of
the formal arrangement, so be it.

"Five hundred pounds a year. For life. No strings attached."

Ah. He had startled her at last. For a split second, her eyes
widened in shock, and her mouth opened in a soundless O. He
rushed back into speech, pressing his advantage. "You may
have that in writing as well. Today. And by 'no strings attached,' I mean the income is yours, yours alone, to do with

as you will. What does a governess earn? Thirty pounds a year? Forty? If you wish to hire yourself out as a governess and live on your wages, you may do so. Invest the five hundred, or give it to charity, or throw it in the Thames! It's yours. And if you marry, you may spend it on your children or . . ." He hesitated, but only fractionally. "Or share it with your husband. It's none of my affair."

He felt a tremor run through her. "Five hundred a year," she said in that same colorless tone. Then she seemed to recover. A muscle jumped in her jaw. "But my fortunes would be forever linked to yours," she uttered coolly. "What if you suffer losses in the future? What if your businesses fail?"

Anger licked through him. Damn her bluntness. He had never had to spell matters out like this before, but leave it to Clarissa to dispense with delicacy.

"I will set money aside now, Clarissa, while I am still relatively plump in the pocket!" he said sarcastically. "Sufficient funds will be safely invested in the three-per-cents. They will be held in trust for you during your lifetime, and the income will be paid to you quarterly."

"During my lifetime," she repeated, her head tilted consideringly. "But nothing to leave to my children."

"Perhaps you could bring yourself to set a little of your income aside from time to time!" he suggested through his teeth. "No, Clarissa, I am afraid I must reserve the principal to revert to my own estate."

Her eyes lifted again to his, fathomless, fathomless depths of blue. "What if," she inquired softly, "the children are yours?"

For a moment, Trevor forgot to breathe. Once, long ago, one of his schoolboy friends had surprised him during a heated argument by suddenly planting him a facer. Clarissa's statement had very much the same effect. He instantly went numb with mingled shock and chagrin. Why had he not been expecting that? It was so obvious. He ought to have been prepared. Of course she might, despite all precautions, conceive a child.

A vivid image of Clarissa, her belly swelling sweetly with his son or daughter, suddenly superimposed itself on the slender girl he saw before him. He was as unprepared for the emotion this triggered as he had been for her mention of its possibility. He swallowed past the lump that had suddenly formed in his throat.

"In that case . . ." he said hoarsely, then stopped and cleared his throat. "In that case, of course, additional arrangements will be made."

He still could not read her expression. She gazed at him, as enigmatic as the Sphinx.

"Then that is your offer. That is the sum total of your offer. Is it not?"

Flummoxed, he nodded. Hang it all, it was a generous offer! Nothing Eustace Henry could offer her would compare to it! Even an innocent like Clarissa Feeney must realize that.

"Let me go, Trevor. I have heard you out."

He stared at her. "What?"

"You said you would let me go, once I had listened to you. I have done so. Let me go."

Unbelieving, he dropped his hands to his sides. She stepped away from him as calmly as if he no longer existed, rang for a servant, and bent to pick up the backgammon pieces. He was left staring down at the top of her coiled black braids; her face was no longer accessible. These were not the circumstances under which he wished to receive his answer.

Seething, he began to vent some of his emotions in pacing the room. One of the dailies arrived in response to Clarissa's summons, and he continued to prowl restlessly back and forth while Miss Feeney directed the wench to take her package up to her bedchamber. After the door had closed behind the departing servant, Trevor felt he could bear the suspense no longer.

"Give me an answer!" he barked.

She was standing before the fire again, folding the backgammon board and placing it, the last piece, into its box. She settled the lid on the box with an air of finality. Then, and only then, did she glance at Trevor. Her expression was as remote and forbidding as an Alpine summit. And as cold.

"I answered you the day we met."

He advanced on her swiftly, mad with anger and frustrated desire. "Has nothing altered since that day? Nothing I have done, nothing I have said, has had any impact on you whatsoever?"

He seized her face in his hands and tilted her chin up, forcing her to meet his eyes. Now he was close enough to see the torment she was hiding behind her set expression. "Aha!" he whispered. "You are tempted."

Her skin was like warm silk beneath his fingers. He could feel the pulse beating in her throat, strong and rapid. But she was utterly still, motionless in his grip, a silent reproof to his ferocity. Her voice, though quiet, was very clear. And what she said was, "No."

She was strong. She was admirably strong. But there was something between them that might prove stronger yet. A slow smile curved the edges of Trevor's mouth. He waited, feeling her pulse quicken, knowing it was a reaction to his nearness. Color rose in her cheeks, and she dropped her eyes to conceal what they might show him. Too late.

"Liar," he whispered.

And bent to touch his mouth to hers.

Chapter 21

Oh, it wasn't fair. It wasn't fair for a simple touch to do this to her. As long as he kept his distance, Clarissa felt safe on this dangerous ground, clinging to her solid determination like a shipwrecked sailor to a solid rock. But when his lips touched hers, treacherous emotions surged up like a riptide, sweeping her away, buffeting her, pulling her under.

Now, resistless, she clung to him instead. Reason evaporated, pride vanished, all thought stopped.

His mouth, tender and demanding, was moving against hers, coaxing her. She felt her knees go weak as a powerful, bone-deep longing flooded her. Trevor's arms tightened around her, and she clung closer, shaking. She felt joyous and light and fierce and needy. What was it? Dear God in Heaven, what was this terrible, wonderful feeling?

He muttered some choked exclamation and pulled her tighter, even tighter. His kiss became fierce, urgent. Then her arms were sliding round his neck as if of their own volition and her head fell back, giving him access to her throat while she gasped, panting for air. His lips traveled down her neck and she shivered with terror and delight.

"Clarissa," he whispered, and his mouth captured hers again. She felt him bend, felt his arm sliding under her knees as he lifted her like a baby and carried her to the nearest chair.

She buried her face in his shoulder and moaned. He sat, holding her as tenderly in his lap as if she were a child, and she suddenly realized she was weeping. Those were tears salting her lips.

Trevor's arms closed round her possessively. He cradled her head against his shoulder with one strong hand. "God help me!" he said hoarsely. "I want you so much I can scarcely speak."

I want you, too, she thought miserably. What a dreadful discovery. What a calamitous turn of events. Why hadn't anyone told her that women could feel passion? She hadn't bargained for this. It was difficult enough to tell him no, caring for him the way she did, without this hot rush of desire clouding her judgment.

He fumbled in his waistcoat and pulled out a handkerchief. She silently took it from him and passed it over her face, trying to collect her shattered thoughts. It wasn't possible to move, even if she had wanted to; he was resting his chin on the top of her head. She supposed it was perverse to cling to him for comfort, since he was the source of her misery. But cling she did.

"I cannot stay here," she said finally. Her voice was small and sad. He immediately moved to free her so she could get up from his lap, but although she sat up, she shook her head. "I mean, I cannot stay in your house."

A brief silence fell. She glanced at him, but when his eyes caught hers, she felt like she was drowning again. She had to look away.

"You still mean to refuse me." It was a statement, not a question.

She nodded, twisting his handkerchief nervously. "Of course."

Clarissa felt his muscles bunch and tense beneath her, and braced herself for his anger. It didn't come. He pushed her off his lap, but not roughly. She stood miserably by the chair while he strode to the fireplace. His back was to her. He placed one foot on the fender and leaned a hand against the mantelpiece, staring down into the flames.

Finally he spoke. "Very well," he said quietly. "You win."

She hadn't realized she was holding her breath until he spoke. But she was so surprised by his words, the air rushed out of her in a soundless whoosh.

He turned to face her, his harsh features drawn into lines of defeat. "I am not imagining the bond that links us, Clarissa. I know now that you feel it, too. And still you deny me. Since that is the case, I have done all that I can do. I am not a man who chases after lost causes."

He straightened, dropping his hands back to his side to address her formally. "It will give rise to gossip if you leave Morecroft Cottage now." A faint, ironic smile curled his lips. "I see no point in saving your virtue if we simultaneously ruin your reputation. I think the best course is for you to remain, in the guise of my ward. You need not fear that I will force my company on you; I will no longer attempt to manage my affairs from here. I will either vacate the house entirely and remove to London, or drive to the City every day. Either way, you will not be burdened with my presence overmuch."

Misery filled Clarissa's eyes and paralyzed her speech. All she could do was nod dumbly, twisting his handkerchief. His generosity made her feel small and mean and wretched. And Trevor was going to distance himself from her. She knew he had to, of course. It was for the best. It was what she wanted.

No, it wasn't what she wanted. But that made it all the more necessary. The depth of her unhappiness told its own tale. She had grown far too attached to him. She saw his shoulders move as he sighed, and thought her heart would break. It took every ounce of willpower she possessed to keep from running to him and telling him she didn't mean it, that she would stay on whatever terms he desired, that she—

That she loved him.

Oh, madness! Clarissa closed her eyes in pain. She must never tell him that. Was it true? She didn't know. She was so confused. Perhaps what she felt for Trevor was friendship, and her loneliness had magnified it into something more, something it was never meant to be.

But he was speaking again. "I suppose it will worry you to feel beholden to me, but that cannot be helped. Comfort yourself with the knowledge that you did not place yourself in this awkward situation. I put you there, and it is my duty now to make matters as comfortable for you as I can."

What did he mean? It was hard to think while being buffeted by so many feelings. Now the faint smile had returned to his features, and he pulled something out of his pocket. It was her handkerchief, the one she tied up her money with. He tossed it to her and she caught it, bewildered.

"The groom's boy gave it to me when I took your package from him," Trevor explained. Then he held his hand out. She walked numbly over to him and handed him his own handkerchief. "Thank you," he said, and pocketed it.

"It's a little damp," she said apologetically, speaking with difficulty past the constriction in her throat.

"That's what a handkerchief is for," he said quietly.

His nearness made her feel faint with longing. She dared not move, and fixed her gaze on the topmost button of his waistcoat. After the briefest of pauses, he stepped away from her and bowed.

"I hope we may remain friends," he said. His voice sounded hoarse and strained.

"Always," she whispered.

He bowed again, and was gone.

The weeks that followed were wretched ones for Clarissa. Trevor kept his word that she would not be burdened with his presence; she scarcely saw him. He left the house early in the morning, while she was still supposed to be abed. Unbeknownst to him, however, she woke early to keep a daily vigil at her bedroom window. She would throw a quilt round her shoulders, press her cheek against the cold glass, and wait there in her nightgown to see him off, whispering a prayer for his safe return. She was ashamed of this weakness, but somehow she couldn't help it. Her heart would ache as she watched his carriage disappear down the lane. He always returned late in the day, tired and uncommunicative, and often would give her no more than a curt nod on his way up to bed.

She missed him terribly.

Sometimes she wondered if he was forcing himself to keep his distance from her. Once or twice he stopped to converse with her on his way up the stairs, almost as if compelled against his better judgment. There was a sort of hunger in his eyes—

they devoured her, as if he were starving for her as much as she
starved for him. But he always mastered himself after a few
minutes and left her, saying he was tired, or had pressing business. It was naturally impossible to trail after him, or to call him
back. One had one's pride, after all.

She soon discovered what he had meant by warning her that
she would feel beholden to him. Bess announced, beaming with
pride and excitement, that Mr. Whitlatch had told her she was
to be Miss Feeney's personal maid. This came as a surprise to
Miss Feeney, but she was very glad of Bess's help in designing
and making up gowns from the fabric she had purchased. Bess
definitely had a genius for this sort of work, and long before
Clarissa believed it was possible, she had a beautiful new
wardrobe as tasteful and well-fitting as it was fashionable.

This was well enough, but then the gifts began to arrive.
While Mr. Whitlatch was off in London, package after package
was delivered to the house, and every one of them was addressed to Miss Feeney. Shawls of Norwich silk, slippers of
Moroccan leather, hats and bonnets too lovely to resist, bolts of
rich silks with yards of trimmings, cloaks and frocks and gloves
and boots and reticules! When they first began to appear,
Clarissa was scandalized, and laid in wait for Trevor that
evening to tax him with it the instant he walked through the
door. But he gave her to understand, in no uncertain terms, that
so long as everyone believed her to be his ward, his ward she
must be. He would not allow her to go about in public looking
like a poor relation. He said it shamed him.

This aspect of the situation had not occurred to Clarissa. The
argument effectively silenced her. It would be a shocking thing,
after all his kindness to her, if Mr. Whitlatch was unfairly criti-
cized for failing to provide for his "ward." He was quite right
that a guardian was expected to clothe his ward in a manner befitting her station. But he had also been right in expecting that
she would feel oppressed by his generosity. Every kindness he
showed her, every gift he forced her to accept, weighed more
and more heavily upon her.

There was nothing she could do to repay him. The only thing
that might suffice, she had refused to give. There was nothing
to do but accept the gifts, the wonderful, gorgeous, perfect gifts,
and wish it were possible to enjoy them. It wasn't, of course.
Bess would tear them eagerly open, oohing and aahing at each

new proof of Mr. Whitlatch's good taste and eye for beauty.
And Clarissa would listlessly agree, feeling more crushed by
every parcel that arrived.

It should have helped, knowing that she looked so well in
the new clothes. It was gratifying, she supposed, that the girl
gazing mournfully back at her from the looking glass was un-
deniably beautiful. And for once in her life, she valued being
attractive. It was important, after expending so much effort on
it, to succeed in attracting someone. Her future depended
upon it.

And it did seem to be working. Eustace Henry was reduced
to speechless idiocy in her presence. This was tiresome, of
course, but surely he would overcome that eventually. In the
meantime, it was rather an advantage. She could do no wrong.
He was so dazzled by her, he hardly seemed to notice when she
was sad and silent, or cross with him from time to time.

During their rare snatches of conversation these days, Trevor
no longer mentioned the employment opportunities he was still,
supposedly, seeking for her. And Clarissa ceased to ask him
about it. It appeared more and more likely that she would, one
day, defy the odds stacked against her and marry.

She was being courted. Actually *courted,* and by a young
man who obviously adored her, a young man who was everything she had dreamed of—educated, kindhearted, respectable,
and even passably good-looking! If such a man proposed marriage to her, the secret wish of her heart would come true. She
could scarcely believe she was on the cusp of realizing a dream
she had longed for, but had never seriously believed would
come to her. It was so amazing, she found it difficult to picture
living with Mr. Henry.

That must be why she viewed the prospect with so little enthusiasm. These ought to be the most exciting days of her life.
Yet, somehow, this astonishing stroke of good fortune was failing to thrill her. She told herself over and over how lucky she
was. She was able to summon gratitude, but try as she might,
joy eluded her.

Still, she was feeling so lonely for Trevor that she always
greeted Mr. Henry with pleasure. It was a relief to have company to distract her. She assented to each and every expedition
he proposed, because it was also a relief to get out of the house.
Left to her own devices, she had a lamentable tendency these

days to mope. Thank God she was not left to her own devices
often. Mr. Henry arrived punctually at two o'clock every afternoon.

Chapter 22

"Miss Feeney, you possess such keen sensibilities! Such elegance of mind!" Eustace Henry exclaimed, pushing
back the lock of hair that had fallen, inevitably, across his forehead.

Clarissa, with difficulty, repressed a sigh. "I only said what I
suppose a dozen others must have said."

They were exploring a very scrubby and uninteresting patch
of ground that Eustace had assured her was a Roman ruin. It did
not strike Clarissa as a particularly good example, and since she
did not wish to hurt Mr. Henry's feelings by sharing her opinion with him, she had simply remarked, in a general sort of
way, how difficult it was to imagine Romans in Britain. It was
her comment on the hardships one would face, moving to this
island from a warm and sunny clime, that had excited Eustace's
admiration. But everything she did or said seemed to excite Eustace's admiration.

"You do not realize how your comments betray the inner
workings of your soul," Mr. Henry assured her feverishly. "You
are always concerned with others' welfare, others' feelings!
Even the Romans, who are no longer here to benefit from your
solicitude. You cannot imagine how charmingly it strikes an ob-
server."

"Thank you," she said, as quellingly as she could. Uttering
any sort of disclaimer usually caused him to expand upon his
theme, so she dared not chide him for his absurdity. Instead, she
walked a little farther along the narrow footpath and tried to
think of some topic that her companion could not twist into a
paean to her virtues. Eustace instantly rushed to her side and attempted to assist her, as if she were incapable of negotiating the
rough ground without his guidance.

It was bitterly cold today. The terrain around Islington had turned bleak and dun-colored during the past fortnight, as if the land itself were turning up its collar against the oncoming winter. She supposed she might form a different impression of the ruined villa at another time of year, or with a different escort. A picture of Trevor at her side intruded, and she found herself imagining the outrageous comments he would make, and how they would have laughed so hard that they would never feel the cold. It was impossible to be bored in Trevor's company. This time, she did not succeed in repressing her sigh.

Mr. Henry, observing this sign of discontent, rushed into anxious speech. "It looks quite different in spring, but I thought you should see it without all the grasses and flowers in the way. It's easier to see the outline of the walls at this time of year."

Clarissa eyed the surrounding hillocks doubtfully. "Is it?"

"Oh, yes! Only fancy, we are standing in the very spot where some Roman matron spun her cloth or stirred her pots!" Eustace waved energetically at a row of what appeared to Clarissa to be ordinary rocks. His eyes shone with enthusiasm. "It makes one think, doesn't it?"

"Yes, indeed," said Clarissa politely. It certainly made her think. It made her think she was mad to allow Mr. Henry to drag her all over the countryside on these expeditions to nowhere. So far he had shown her the Sadler's Wells Theatre, which might have been interesting had it not been closed for the winter, the local waterworks, a tile kiln, and every scenic overlook within ten miles. It was very kind of him to take her out so frequently in his father's gig, and it certainly was preferable to languishing about the house and waiting for Trevor to return from London. Still, she feared that being seen so often in Eustace's company was giving rise to gossip in the village. He had become extremely particular in his attentions, without ever coming to the point.

For the next forty minutes or more, Mr. Henry stumped vigorously over the uneven ground, gesturing, exclaiming, and discoursing with real excitement, and a fair amount of knowledge, on the Roman occupation of Britain. Clarissa listened in tolerant amusement. It was impossible not to sympathize with his eagerness. He really seemed to have made a study of it, poor boy, and clearly he had few opportunities to indulge his pet subject.

"You ought to go to Rome yourself one day," she told him, smiling.

"By Jove, don't I wish I could!" Eustace exclaimed with genuine feeling. "And Athens, as well! And Egypt! What I wouldn't give—" but he stopped short, his face reddening. "I beg your pardon; I daresay it isn't very interesting to a female."

"I own, I had rather see Venice," Clarissa admitted. "I'm afraid I don't know much about antiquities."

She was soon sorry she had said that. A kind of glow came over Mr. Henry, and he launched into a jumbled recitation containing so many facts and dates and exotic names that Clarissa became completely bewildered. Eyes shining, face flushed, and hair flopping repeatedly into his face, Eustace was the picture of schoolboy intensity. But they were standing on a barren outcropping in a windswept field on a very cold day. Clarissa, lacking the warmth that his hobbyhorse gave Eustace, eventually began to shiver as she listened. She comforted herself with the thought that at least in extolling the perfections of the ancient world, he had given the subject of Miss Feeney's perfections a rest.

A blast of icy air whistled across the turf, so cold she thought it could almost lift the skin off her face. Her teeth began to chatter. Clarissa, rendered desperate, interrupted her companion. "M-Mr. Henry! I beg your pardon, but m-might we remove ourselves from the wind a t-trifle?"

His face fell, almost ludicrously, from dreamy-eyed rapture into an expression of dismay. "Good God! I have kept you standing in the cold! Oh, Miss Feeney, I am a villain! I don't know what I deserve! Oh, pray, take my arm—take my coat—allow me to assist you!"

He was simultaneously chafing her hands and struggling out of his greatcoat, and Clarissa could not help laughing as she tried to pull her hands away.

"No, really—this is quite unnecessary! Mr. Henry, don't be absurd. I will b-be fine directly I am back in the c-carriage! Oh, for the love of heaven!" This, as he lost his balance and toppled over onto the rocky ground, inadvertently pulling Clarissa down as well.

Mr. Henry, half in and half out of his coat, and extremely red in the face, managed to sit up, seize her hand, and embark on a lengthy apology. She listened with what patience she could muster to his bitter animadversions on his own clumsiness, his stupidity, his unworthiness to serve as her escort, et cetera, and when she felt she could bear no more, she interrupted him again.

"Thank you; that will do! You did not knock me down on purpose, after all. Only help me to rise, and I will gladly forget this extremely embarrassing incident."

She had instinctively spoken in a schoolteacher's tone, and was instantly sorry for it. But Eustace obeyed her, just as her charges had always done. "You are too good . . . too kind," he uttered in a choked voice. He started to remove his coat again, but seemed to think better of the impulse, and instead offered her merely his arm on the way back to the carriage. By the time he had assisted her into the gig and silently tucked a lap robe round her, his expression had become morose. He untied the horse, clambered up beside her on the box, and gloomily started them down the lane.

"I know you think me nothing but a boy, and a silly boy at that," he said bitterly. "Whenever I am with you, I seem to behave like a perfect gudgeon."

It was quite true, but Clarissa was touched by his evident distress. He really was a very nice young man. She was ashamed of herself for treating him like a child; she had no business doing so. "Nonsense, Mr. Henry," she said gently, and smiled at him. "It was a stupid accident, but it might have happened to anyone. Pray do not think of it again."

He turned to her, his enormous brown eyes filled with despair. "I will never be worthy of you, however hard I try."

Clarissa was so startled by this sudden assertion, she could think of nothing to reply. She stared at him, wondering if she had heard him aright. Was this the moment at last?

Mr. Henry appeared to be in the grip of strong emotion. His eyes searched hers hungrily, and he raked the lock of hair off his forehead with one impatient hand. "I know my case is hopeless. But if I had any chance of winning you, I would do anything! Anything!"

This was the moment. He was going to propose marriage to her. This was what she had schemed for, hoped for, dreamed of. And yet the strangest sensation of panic raced through Clarissa. She was conscious of a strong, irrational impulse to jump out of the gig and run away.

She found herself stalling, stammering, "Mr. Henry, pray . . . pray do not put yourself in a taking. You and I are friends, are we not?"

Eustace's expressive eyes burned like liquid coals in his suddenly pale face, and two spots of color flamed high on his cheeks. The intensity of his emotion was painful to behold. "Friends! It will—it will *kill* me—to always remain your friend!"

Clarissa then sat in stunned silence, wondering what on earth was the matter with her, while Eustace relieved his pent-up feelings in a flood of heated eloquence. In addition to his highminded worship of the ground she trod, he told her of his circumstances, of his hopes of securing a post as clerk to a local solicitor, of how there would not be much money at first but how very diligently he meant to work, of where they might live and how they might contrive.

He had dropped the reins long ago, and now caught her hands in a deathlike grip. Somehow he even managed to get down on one knee in the confines of the narrow box. Clarissa was painfully aware of the spectacle they would present to any chance-met stranger, with Mr. Henry kneeling, oblivious to the world, in the driver's side of the gig as his father's horse ambled placidly along between the shafts! But Eustace was misconstruing her sudden blush and disjointed exclamations. He was taking her confusion as encouragement.

"Miss Feeney . . . Clarissa!" breathed Mr. Henry, his eyes shining with hope. "Only say the word, and I will wait forever!"

Clarissa stammered something incoherent. The last thing in the world she wanted to do was hurt the sensitive feelings of a shy, dreamy-eyed boy who believed himself to be in love with her. And of course she didn't want him to wait forever. She either wanted to marry him and be done with it, or refuse him and be done with it. Until this moment, she had had every intention of accepting him with alacrity. Now her tongue seemed to cleave to the roof of her mouth and she stared helplessly at him, completely flummoxed.

"This . . . this is so sudden," she said feebly. The remark sounded absurd to her own ears, but Eustace's eyes lit with delirious joy.

"You do not say no!" he exclaimed. "Oh, dear Miss Feeney,

that is all I ask! You have not refused me! Oh, that is more than I had hoped for!"

Clarissa became aware that a farmer's cart was rounding the corner ahead of them. She blushed furiously, tugging urgently at Eustace's hands. "Mr. Henry, pray—!" she gasped. "There is someone coming!"

He struggled back onto the box beside her, his face as flushed as hers, but beaming. She dared not raise her eyes for fear of reading sly knowledge in the unknown farmer's face. Scarlet-cheeked, she stared at her toes.

Mr. Henry seemed to think she was behaving with maidenly decorum. He picked up the reins with an elaborate air of uncon-cern and pretended to drive, although the vicar's cob required no directions to take them back toward the village and was, at any rate, an animal unreceptive to suggestion.

"I suppose I ought to tell you," he said shyly, "that I am not precisely of age yet."

Oh, dear. Clarissa hardly knew whether to feel glad or sorry. There was no hope whatsoever of the vicar and his wife con-senting to their only son's engagement—at least not to her. Mrs. Henry's animosity toward this penniless, unknown girl was so thinly veiled that Clarissa felt deeply uncomfortable around her, even while attending church.

She cleared her throat. "Then perhaps we should not be hav-ing this discussion," she suggested faintly.

Mr. Henry raked the hair off his forehead again. "You are so noble!" he exclaimed fervently. "I suppose I ought to have waited—I *meant* to wait—but I could not contain myself any longer! And besides, I shall attain my majority in another week or so."

"Oh!"

His shy smile returned. "Yes, that is what I meant to explain to you. I shall turn one-and-twenty on Christmas Eve."

"H-how nice." It was an idiotic thing to say, but Mr. Henry did not seem to notice. His cowlike eyes were filled with adora-tion.

"I know I should have spoken with your guardian before ad-dressing you, to be quite correct, but I—" He gulped. "I hardly liked to do so. I mean, there seemed no point in it, unless . . ."

It occurred to her how extremely formidable Mr. Whitlatch must appear to a sensitive lad like Eustace Henry, and despite the extremity of the moment she almost had to bite back a smile. "No," she agreed. "I understand perfectly."

The farmer's cart had passed, and Mr. Henry's hand fumbled for hers once again. "But now . . . may I speak to him? Oh, please, Miss Feeney—Clarissa—say yes!"

She stole a nervous glance at him. The poor boy looked so eager, so vulnerable, his eyes shining with hope and anxiety. It was written all over his transparent face that this moment was the pinnacle of his life. How could she turn him down?

Clarissa steeled herself by thinking what it would mean to spend her life alone. She remembered how dreadful it was for a lady to live unprotected. She thought of washing dishes for pennies, or spending her life dusting other people's furniture and making other people's beds. She reminded herself that she liked Mr. Henry, and if she married him, none of those fates would befall her. He would be a kind and faithful husband. And she might have children.

She forced a wavering smile. "Yes," she said. "Of course."

Chapter 23

What a damnable evening! What a stupid, senseless, insipid, crashing *bore* of an evening!

Trevor flung himself with savage carelessness onto his sister's chaise longue. The springs whined in protest, but no ominous cracking sound emerged. Scowling, he ripped at the starched cravat that had been choking him for the past four hours.

The door to the morning room flew open with an inelegant bang and Augusta marched in, candle held high. "I knew I would find you here," she said severely. "Really, Trevor! You are quite impossible!"

"This is the only comfortable room in the house."

"It's the room where my guests are least likely to appear!"

"Yes! That's a large part of its charm."

"*Well!*" Augusta flounced over to a chair opposite her brother and plopped into it, slamming the candle onto a nearby table

with a fine disregard for flying wax. "Of all the ungrateful remarks I ever heard, that one bears the palm! Why the *dickens*
did you badger me into inviting all these high-toned people to
dinner? When I think of the time I wasted, and the care I took,
and the money I spent—"

"Never mind that! Give the bills to me."

"Why, so I will! But pray do not hoax yourself into believing
that makes all right, for it doesn't! Trevor, there isn't enough
money in the world to buy your way into the *ton.* You can't, you
simply *can't,* adopt the manners of a barbarian and expect the
aristocracy to welcome you into its midst! What on earth is the
matter with you?"

"Nothing! I have never been any good at parties."

"Yes, but I never saw anything to equal your behavior
tonight! Whatever possessed you to utter that crack about Miss
Marsden's hair? I was ready to *sink!*"

Having freed himself from his cravat, Trevor tossed it aside
and crossed his arms belligerently. "I have never understood
why women torture their hair into curls!" he announced.
"*Curls,* for God's sake! What's so confounded attractive about
a halo of frizz?"

"I daresay the poor girl had burnt it a trifle with the irons.
Most unhandsome of you to point it out to the entire company!"

Trevor hunched one shoulder pettishly. "I made amends. I
took her in to dinner on my arm, didn't I?"

Augusta clapped one hand to her forehead and collapsed
back into her chair with a moan. "Pray do not remind me! What
a disaster!"

"Why? What was wrong with that? I thought I showed extraordinary civility."

"Yes, but only to Miss Marsden! She had no claim to be led
in to dinner by you. And by doing so, you slighted Lady Winnifred!"

Trevor gave a shout of laughter. "Good! She needed it."

Augusta glared at her unrepentant brother. "Lady Winnifred's manners are not conciliatory, but she did me a great
favor in accepting my invitation."

"Rubbish!" he said flippantly. "You did her a great favor in
issuing it. And why the devil shouldn't her manners be conciliatory? Her family's ready to sell her to the highest bidder!"

Augusta gave a little shriek of vexation. "I declare, I could *shake* you! Isn't that the very type of female you specifically asked me to find? An aristocrat, you said, who was willing to make a *mésalliance*!"

Damn. That's exactly what he had said. Nonplussed, Trevor rose and began prowling restlessly round the room. "Well, find me another!" he barked.

"I will have to!" snapped Augusta. "You did everything imaginable to cause Lady Winnifred to regret her condescension. I daresay she will never set foot in my house again."

Trevor raked his hands through his hair. "Fiend seize it! What should I do? Must I go downstairs and apologize?"

"Everyone has gone. Thank Heaven! It would be just like you, to rush downstairs with your hair askew and your cravat torn off!"

He halted in his pacing and favored Augusta with a crooked grin. "They might have ascribed my shocking manners to drink, and viewed me a little more charitably."

Augusta's lips twitched. "Hm! If you think Society will embrace a drunkard more willingly than a churl, by all means, start the rumor! But my hope is that we can pass you off as an entertaining eccentric."

Trevor pursed his lips thoughtfully. "Not bad!" he approved. "I might easily pass for that."

Augusta uttered a little peal of laughter. "Trevor, that is what you *are*!"

"Am I?" Unmoved, he dropped back onto the chaise longue and gave a prodigious yawn. "Good. The *haut ton* is full of eccentrics. Lord, what a fatiguing way to spend an evening! Are all well-bred women so dull?"

She opened her eyes at him. "Did you think them all dull? Hannah Chesteron is thought to be quite witty. I thought you liked her. You laughed at several of her remarks."

"I laughed at that Harlequin we saw at St. Ives, but I wouldn't want to marry him."

"My word! How difficult you are! Were none of the ladies to your taste? Lady Winnifred is an elegant creature. Not that that will matter now, since the only notice you took of her was to stare her out of countenance before walking off with Miss Marsden."

He snorted. "Faugh! Lady Winnifred is a self-important

snob. Miss Hamilton has no chin, Miss Marsden is a frizzy-haired zero—and what was the redhead's name again?"

"Fairchild."

"Hah! She may have been a fair child, but she's grown into a hideous girl! Why did you invite her?"

Augusta's eyes flashed. "I invited her, you obstinate booberkin, because she is connected to nearly every important family in England! I thought you wanted to advance yourself. For Heaven's sake, make up your mind! Are you seeking a bride, or aren't you?"

The bluntness of her question was like a dash of cold water. A sudden vision of himself drearily attending dinner party after dinner party in monotonous succession, and winding up at the altar with some faceless, simpering nonentity rose up in all its nauseating horror. An involuntary shudder wracked Trevor Whitlatch.

Augusta saw the shudder, and her brother's sudden expression of bleak dismay. She sat up, her jaw dropping, "Oh!" she exclaimed. "You are no more seeking a bride than I am! You *wretch*! If you only knew the trouble I've gone to—"

He raised one hand hastily, as if to ward her off. "Now, Gussie, don't fly out at me! I appreciate everything you've done. And I do mean to marry one day."

"One day soon?" He did not immediately reply, and Augusta's eyes narrowed in sudden suspicion. "Trevor, do you have some high-flyer in keeping?"

"No, I do not!" He left the chaise longue with violent haste, and began pacing the room again. "And a lady shouldn't mention such things!" he added, as an afterthought.

"Fiddle! If that is not it, what is it? Oh!" She jumped up, seizing her brother's sleeve as he went by. "Is it the *schoolteacher*?"

Trevor stared down at her, rattled. "What?"

"You told me—a month ago, or more—that you had some creature in your keeping. A schoolteacher, she told you she was." As Trevor appeared frozen in place, she shook his sleeve impatiently. "Surely you remember! You tried to palm her off onto me. Tried to wheedle me into hiring her as a nursemaid or some such. You sounded vastly taken with her, I thought, and whenever you are in one of your fits of admiration there's no doing anything with you! I have always believed that if I could only catch you between infatuations, I might succeed in marrying you off! But I haven't, have I? You're still enamored of the nursemaid chit."

He flushed darkly, and pulled his sleeve out of her insistent grasp. "No such thing!" he muttered.

"Well, if she's not your mistress, who is? For I can't think of any other reason why none of these women would appeal to you!"

"Oh, for God's sake! I've changed my mind, that's all. For the time being! There's nothing mysterious about it. What difference does it make, whether I make my bows this Season or the next? I'm going to bed!"

He slammed out of the room and tore upstairs as if the devil were chasing him. Once alone, he surveyed his sister's guest chamber gloomily. His own gear was stacked neatly on a bench near the bed, but the floor was crowded with boxes and parcels, all bearing the stamp of Bond Street shops. Earlier today, as happened far too often lately, he had found himself unable to concentrate on his work and had soon given up. Instead, he had spent the day like a man possessed, compulsively prowling through shop after shop, poring over merchandise and buying, buying, buying. These were today's purchases. Silk chosen to match the blue of Clarissa's eyes, a hat that would look well perched on glossy black hair, a velvet pelisse to keep a girl rosy and warm, dainty dancing slippers—had he ever seen her dance?

He passed a hand over his eyes, shaken. Gussie was right, of course. Marriage was unthinkable, out of the question. Until he recovered from this mania, it would be impossible to court the ladies of the *ton*. He was no stranger to infatuation, but this was like nothing he had ever experienced. Every woman he met, he unconsciously compared to Clarissa. And they all fell short.

He remembered Clarissa as he had last seen her, standing forlornly in the hall at Morecroft Cottage. He could hardly bear to spend three minutes in her company anymore; the overwhelming urge to sweep her into his arms was more than a man could stand. So he had kept his distance, standing by the door, yanking his gloves on while he told her curtly that he would not return until the morrow. She had looked absolutely stricken. Recalling it now, standing in a London bedchamber in the wee hours of the morning, he swore, long and softly. It was all he could do to keep from calling for his curricle and racing home to comfort her!

In the morning, he promised himself. Even if he could only spend a few minutes with her, at least he would see her. Tomorrow. Vague specters of important tasks he had neglected, orders he needed to issue, and decisions he needed to make flitted briefly through his mind. He dismissed them impatiently. His business could wait. The staff could carry on without him. That's what he paid them for! Whatever silly mistakes they made, he could correct later.

He swiftly removed his clothing, tossing it all on the floor, then pulled on a nightshirt and threw himself into bed, where he glared at the ceiling and thought ugly thoughts about Eustace Henry. Trevor was convinced he had been in a fair way to winning, until the entrance of Eustace Henry. His carte blanche was a generous offer; anyone could see that it was preferable to employment as a governess! But the unworldly Mr. Henry might be prepared to offer Clarissa the one thing Mr. Whitlatch was not—marriage. And an offer of marriage, to a girl like Clarissa, would outshine mere riches.

Trevor punched his pillow and cursed under his breath. He could almost feel the crisis coming.

Sure enough, the very next afternoon he found himself face-to-face with Clarissa's youthful admirer. They were closeted in Trevor's study, and the moment of truth had arrived. But Trevor would see Eustace in hell rather than make it easy for him! So he waited, silent, his face a mask.

It was really rather fascinating, watching Mr. Henry's color fluctuate. His youthful countenance flushed scarlet, then paled, then blushed again. "I . . . I suppose you will have guessed my errand, sir," he finally managed to utter.

"Yes," said Trevor. His tone was not encouraging. His fingers absently turned a quill pen, end over end, gently tapping the blotter on the desk before him.

Mr. Henry appeared to be suffering the agonies of the damned. The room was cool, but sweat dewed his brow. He was perched on the extreme edge of his chair, as if poised for instant flight. And Mr. Whitlatch supposed that Eustace would be extremely sorry, later, when he perceived how he had mangled his

hat. In the uncomfortable silence that had fallen, he was twisting it convulsively in his hands.

Now Mr. Henry launched into a breathless recitation of his
circumstances. As if that mattered! Trevor waited, his expression growing more and more sour, as Eustace rattled off every
conceivable point in his favor, every hope he had for his boring
little future. Trevor soon felt he could not listen to another sentence of it, and interrupted. He still had one card to play, and
was impatient to see if it took the trick.

"Never mind all that! I am sure your prospects are excellent,
Mr. Henry. I congratulate you! But what is your point?"

"My—my point, sir?" Eustace gulped, and stared at his iras-
cible host with the eyes of a startled fawn. "Why, I—I wish
to—I wish to marry your ward!"

"But you haven't asked me what *her* circumstances are!"

Mr. Henry goggled at him in unfeigned astonishment. It had
obviously not occurred to this unworldly idiot that Clarissa's
circumstances mattered one whit.

"Well, sir, I . . . I had not thought about that. One hardly
takes such a thing into consideration, does one?"

Trevor felt a stab of irritation. "You don't care what her
prospects may be?"

The light of fanaticism suddenly burned in Mr. Henry's eyes.
He drew himself up proudly. "No, sir, I do not! It would not
matter to me if Miss Feeney were the veriest pauper!"

"Well, she is," said Mr. Whitlatch bluntly. He had the satisfaction of seeing the air abruptly leave Eustace's sails. Mr.
Henry blinked foolishly at him for a moment, then flushed scarlet again. He looked both chagrined and apprehensive, and
Trevor guessed at once that Eustace's parents had already im-
pressed upon their heir that they did not share his noble uncon-
cern regarding his prospective bride's finances.

A short bark of laughter escaped Trevor. "Just so!" he said
cordially. "Clarissa has no dowry, so you will have to support
her from the outset. But I daresay your parents will be delighted
to house you both at the vicarage."

Mr. Henry paled, and further crushed his hat. Trevor watched
in unholy amusement as Eustace pondered these distressing tid-
ings. His visitor rose shakily and crossed to the narrow window,
where he stared, unseeing, through the panes of glass.

By God, he might trump Eustace's ace yet. He kept his voice

deceptively bland. "She has no dowry because she has no family. It is a fortunate circumstance that you care nothing for such things. Most men would consider Miss Feeney completely unmarriageable."

Trevor waited expectantly. Eustace's gaze did return to him, but he appeared somewhat dazed.

"Wh-what? Unmarriageable? Why?"

Trevor smiled politely. "Oh, didn't you know? Her parents weren't married."

He watched with interest as this bombshell dropped on poor Mr. Henry. Eustace's shock was palpable. His jaw slackened, and he blanched to the color of new cheese. Trevor could almost find it within himself to feel sorry for the luckless Mr. Henry. One could hardly blame Clarissa for failing to confide this tidbit of information to her suitor, but really, such news was bound to come as something of a facer to an idealistic lad.

Trevor transferred his gaze to the quill in his hand and began pulling it rhythmically through his fingers. "Or, perhaps I should say, her father was married. But not to her mother."

Mr. Henry uttered a strangled sound that might have been, "Good God!"

Something like glee was building in Trevor. He could almost feel Clarissa, pushed out of range by the attentions of this upstart puppy, coming within his sights again.

He coughed, grinned, and spread his hands deprecatingly. "So you see, many men—perhaps most men—would turn their eyes elsewhere when seeking a bride."

Mr. Henry sat, with suspicious suddenness, on a spindle-legged chair by the window. Trevor hoped the poor sod wasn't going to faint. The mangled hat slid from Eustace's nerveless fingers and dropped, unnoticed, on the floor. He voiced something between a moan and a sob, and buried his face in his hands.

Trevor donned a demeanor suitable for a kindly uncle, and tried to inject a little sympathy into his voice. "Come now, it isn't as bad as that. You haven't taken any irretrievable step. Why don't you go home and think about it calmly for a day or two? One mustn't make a decision like this hastily. Talk it over with your parents! Then, if you're still of the same mind in, say, a month from now—"

"I shall always be of the same mind!" uttered Mr. Henry. His voice, although passionate, was muffled in his hands. He appeared to be choking on tears. "But they will never let me do it! Not now! I shan't be able to have her at the vicarage—I shall have to wait until—oh, the devil!"

He raised a haggard face and gazed bleakly at his host. "It doesn't matter," said Eustace in tones of desperation. "Nothing matters. Nothing but her."

Despite himself, Trevor found the lad's devotion oddly touching. A sentimental young man in the throes of his first calf-love was a rare and fragile thing. Was he ever that young? wondered Trevor. It seemed unlikely.

"Sir," Eustace asked abruptly, "have you ever been in love?"

Trevor's brows flew upward, then snapped fiercely down to hood his eyes. "No," he said shortly. "I can't say that I have."

Obsession, maybe. Lately he was uncomfortably aware that he knew what it was to be obsessed. Thoughts of Clarissa hounded him day and night, making life a living hell. The only relief he experienced came when he gave in to his obsession, dropped whatever else he was doing, and headed for Bond Street.

Now Mr. Henry's countenance blazed with emotion, transforming him. He no longer appeared nervous or gawky. He looked exalted, strong and eager. "I tell you, sir, that once in a man's lifetime there appears a girl who is—The One!"

Trevor stared blankly at him. "The one what?"

Mr. Henry rose to his feet, completing the ruination of his hat by inadvertently trampling it. He clasped his hands ardently before him. "Miss Feeney is everything, simply *everything*, I ever dreamed of! So charming, so modest, so womanly, so—so *sweet*!"

Trevor's lips twisted wryly. "And so pretty!" he suggested.

But irony was lost on Mr. Henry. "Yes!" he agreed rapturously. He returned to stand before Mr. Whitlatch, and gazed with limpid eyes at his forbidding face. "Miss Feeney possesses every virtue. Worldly concerns simply cannot intrude in such a case."

Trevor snorted impatiently, but Mr. Henry continued, his voice soft with conviction. "Her price is far above rubies."

Trevor suddenly stilled. His dark eyes widened, startled. "What?"

Eustace offered him a shy, slightly apologetic smile. "It's out of Scripture, you know, sir. The Book of Proverbs."

"What is?"

"The verse, of course." Mr. Henry appeared mildly surprised by Mr. Whitlatch's sudden theological digression, but quoted dutifully. " 'Who can find a virtuous woman? For her price is far above rubies.' "

Rubies. What an odd coincidence. Trevor felt an unsettling shiver of gooseflesh.

But Mr. Henry, in the grip of his own fervor, continued to speak. "If only they knew her, I feel quite sure my parents would come to love her as I do."

"Really? How awkward!"

Mr. Whitlatch's sarcasm was, again, wasted on Eustace Henry. The cowlike eyes lost none of their glow. "So I had a . . . a sort of an idea, you know, that I might invite Miss Feeney to a dinner my mother is planning for Christmas Eve. And you, too, sir, of course!" he added hastily.

Mr. Whitlatch bowed ironically. "I am glad to see you are not entirely lost to propriety, Mr. Henry."

"No, sir, certainly not!" Mr. Henry appeared shocked at the very idea. "I would like to keep everything perfectly on the up-and-up, you know. But it so happens I will attain my majority on that date. And . . . and I would very much like to announce—" He gulped, his cheeks turning scarlet.

Seeing that Eustace was foundering in a morass of delicate emotion, Trevor politely finished his sentence for him. "Your betrothal?"

"Yes, sir," said Mr. Henry gratefully.

Trevor leaned back in his chair, frowning blackly. If he were a different sort of man, he thought resentfully, he would put a stop to this nonsense. If he were a different sort of man, he would boot this moonling out of his study and tell him not to come back until he'd grown some sense. That ought to send him away for the next decade or so.

Damn the fellow. He was everything Clarissa had described as her ideal. What was it she had told him not so long ago? She dreamed of a kind man. A reader of books. A vicar's son! Well, here he stood, as if conjured out of her very imaginings. It availed Trevor nothing to scowl and growl and sneer. He had lost, and this milk-faced bleater had won.

He made one last-ditch effort. "You seem very certain."

"Yes, sir."

"And yet you have only known Clarissa a short time."

The fanatical light returned to Eustace's eyes. "The instant I saw Miss Feeney—within five minutes of making her acquaintance—I *knew*!"

Trevor's lip curled sardonically. He understood the effect Clarissa had on an unwary male. None better! But an older, wiser man would never mistake that impact for undying love. An older, wiser man would keep his wits about him. Consider the consequences. Look before he leapt.

And give Clarissa up to a man who was young and foolish.

Rage and pain suddenly stabbed at Trevor's heart. He knew it was idiotic to envy Eustace Henry his youth and inexperience, but for an instant he wished, almost savagely, that he himself cared nothing for Clarissa's birth.

He rubbed his eyes wearily. "Very well, Mr. Henry. If Miss Feeney wishes to accept your offer, I will raise no objection."

Chapter 24

On the morning of December 23rd, the sky darkened ominously. Shortly after midday, it began to spit snow. Sporadically at first, then thicker and thicker, the flakes fell. By nightfall the world was blanketed in white.

Clarissa rose on the morning of the 24th and pulled back the curtains of her bedroom window. It's an omen, she thought despairingly. Snow had evidently fallen steadily through the night, and an arctic wind was blowing, tossing drifts against the walls of the cottage and the stable yard across from her window.

The snow stopped halfway through the morning, and the sun struggled to show itself. Clarissa began to think the sky would clear, but then the clouds closed in again, and the snow turned sleety. Mr. Whitlatch announced that they must leave early for the vicarage; if they tarried, the roads might prove completely impassable. Clarissa listlessly agreed, and went upstairs to change her clothes. It was difficult to look forward to the Christmas Eve dinner at the vicarage with any degree of pleasure. She had seldom felt less inclined for merriment.

Bess helped her don the jonquil silk, which she had never before worn. The gown was elegant, yet chaste. It was also very becoming. Clarissa hoped, rather apathetically, it would do justice to the occasion. Bess seemed much more excited about Clarissa's invitation to the vicarage than Clarissa was. The entire staff must be expecting the announcement of her engagement to Eustace. It was impossible to keep such things secret.

In honor of Christmas, she decided to wear an evening cloak of cherry-red velvet. It was a gift from Mr. Whitlatch. Of course. Clarissa stroked the soft folds lovingly for a moment before slipping on her gloves, and sighed. For a girl who was about to achieve a lifelong dream, she felt unaccountably depressed.

Trevor was waiting for her in the hall. She had never seen him so impeccably dressed. He must have had assistance, something he usually scorned. No man could wedge himself into such form-fitting apparel without the aid of a valet. He looked massive, gorgeous, and extremely intimidating. Her heart sank with hurt when he scarcely glanced at her but held his hand out silently, his expression remote and impassive. She took his arm, her gloved hand trembling slightly.

Simmons stepped out of the shadows and held open the front door. A blast of icy wind slapped her. She halted, shivering, and cast an imploring glance at Mr. Whitlatch. "Perhaps we ought not to go."

A spasm of emotion crossed Trevor's features. "We must!" he barked, as if goaded. "Let's get it over with."

Dawson was directly outside, peering gloomily at them over the folds of a gigantic muffler. He was well wrapped against the cold, and held the head of an enormous and powerful carriage horse. Clarissa had seen this animal before. She knew it for a placid beast. That the horse seemed nervous, tossing his head and blowing, caused her to shrink back again.

"But what if this weather continues? We will not be able to get home tonight."

"We'll get home," said Trevor grimly.

It sounded like a vow. He was evidently looking forward to this evening with even less enthusiasm than she. Clarissa said nothing more, but allowed him to lead her to the closed carriage and help her in. Hot bricks and lap robes were waiting in the narrow confines of the coach, but the vehicle itself was old, small and ill-made. Dawson shut the door on them with difficulty. Cold wind whistled and whined through cracks around the door and, it seemed, from beneath her feet. Clarissa looked round her dubiously.

"Is this conveyance yours, sir? I do not recall seeing it before."

"No, it isn't."

She waited expectantly, but apparently that was all he was going to say. She pulled the lap robe a little higher, crossed her arms for warmth, and turned to stare pointedly out the window. If Trevor wished to sulk, let him sulk!

Their progress was slow. Silence stretched between Clarissa and Trevor, and she soon felt tears burning the back of her throat. What had become of the friendship she had treasured? Not so many days ago, she and Trevor had conversed with affection and shared easy laughter. The man who sat across from her, so distant and forbidding, seemed a complete stranger.

Her bleak musings were interrupted by the coach coming to a halt. Trevor muttered some smothered oath, and they both turned their eyes to the door. Dawson's brisk knock soon sounded, and the door opened. His eyes were apologetic over the top of the muffler.

"Well, what is it?" Trevor barked.

"Beg pardon, sir, but there's a tree down."

"A tree? Why the devil are we stopping for a tree?"

"It's lying across the road, sir. Shall we turn round and try the cart track? We can't go forward here, that's for certain."

A muscle jumped in Trevor's jaw. "Damn. Isn't the cart track likely to be worse?"

"Well, sir, it might," said Dawson cautiously. "But it's hard to see how. I wouldn't take a coach down it in clear weather, for the ruts and all, but one lane's as good as another on a day like this. And it runs through the fields, sir, so there won't be trees down at any rate."

"Very well, we'll try it."

Clarissa's eyes dilated with alarm. She tugged on Trevor's sleeve. "Oh, sir, *pray* do not! What if we get stuck there, out of sight of the road? What will we do?"

He shook off her hand impatiently. "Let's go," he snapped. "And shut the door, for God's sake! There's snow blowing in."

On the third slam, Dawson succeeded in closing the door. There followed an alarming series of jolts and slides while he struggled to turn the coach in the icy lane. Clarissa clutched the seat in fright.

"He'll ditch us!" she gasped.

Trevor shrugged. "I daresay. Dawson is an excellent groom, but an indifferent driver."

"Oh, this is madness! Why are we even making the attempt? Pray ask him to take us home!"

"We are going to the *vicarage,*" said Trevor, with such barely suppressed violence that Clarissa almost jumped. "We are going to have a pleasant dinner, after which our host's son will announce that you have accepted his offer of marriage. Exclamations of delight will fill the room, we will raise our glasses in a toast to you and Mr. Henry, and I daresay dancing will follow. I mean to smile, and drink your health, and shake that sheep-faced blighter's hand. And then I mean to go home with all possible speed and get royally drunk."

Clarissa pressed her shaking palms together. "Why do you say such things to me? I don't know what upsets me more— your constant disparagement of Mr. Henry, or the prospect of returning to Morecroft Cottage with a man who plans to get drunk!"

"It is not a habit of mine," he replied, still speaking through gritted teeth. "But there are occasions in life that call for it!"

A protesting neigh sounded outside the coach, which began, in fits and starts, to back. Then came a muffled shout of exasperation or alarm. It seemed to proceed from the vicinity of the neigh, which indicated that Dawson had gone to the horse's head. The vehicle executed a swift backward glide, jolted to an abrupt stop, then tipped slightly to one side, forcing its occupants to brace themselves against the off-side wall. It stayed that way for an ominous length of time. Just as Trevor appeared ready to climb out of the door himself to discover what was toward, the coach gave a creaking shudder and righted itself. Presently another knock came, this one not so brisk and not, apparently, on the door.

"What now?" shouted Trevor.

The door did not open. Dawson's voice, sounding much harassed and a trifle distant, called, "Sorry, sir, but you're stuck fast in a snowbank—and the traces have broken!"

Trevor covered his eyes with one hand and groaned.

Clarissa looked anxiously at him. "What does it mean?"

"It means, among other things, that we won't arrive at the vicarage anytime soon! But I am not so easily defeated." He raised his voice to a shout. "Dawson! I'm coming out to help."

"No, sir, no point in't! For one thing, you're not dressed for the weather, and for another, there's nothing to be done. A shovel's what we need, and mayhap another horse or two. I'll take Dobbin and fetch help from the village. We're almost there now, sir, so it won't take long."

Trevor glanced ruefully down at his finery. He seemed to debate with himself for a minute, then surrender to the inevitable. "Very well, Dawson, be as quick as you can."

They waited in awkward silence while Dawson ponderously unhitched Dobbin and called a reassuring farewell. The horse's hooves made no sound as they departed, so thick was the snow on the ground.

Solitude then closed in on the occupants of the stranded coach, wrapping them in a dark blanket of cold and isolation. Clarissa had never felt more alone than sitting here so close to Trevor. This stiff and unnatural muteness, where once there had been effortless camaraderie, formed the loudest and most miserable silence she had ever known.

And she was freezing in her silk gown and thin slippers. Her nose and toes were completely numb. She reached up and cupped her hands around her face, breathing into her gloved palms.

"What are you doing?"

"My nose is cold."

The silence fell again. Trevor had crossed his arms across his chest and was frowning at the window. Since it was covered in frost or steam, there was nothing to see. Clarissa realized he was simply looking anywhere but at her, and thought her heart would break.

Seconds ticked by, then minutes. It grew colder and colder. Clarissa tried pulling her cloak more tightly around her, but when the satin lining touched her skin it was like ice. A violent shiver seized her.

A shattering oath split the air. She looked up, startled, and saw Trevor's face gone suddenly haggard. He reached across the space between them and pulled her roughly into his arms.

Clarissa uttered a faint protest, but he overruled it, dragging her onto his lap. "You'll catch your death of cold. Do you think I want that on my conscience? Come here and be still."

She was ashamed of her own weakness, but could not resist snuggling gratefully against him. Whatever his reasons, it was heavenly to feel his arms around her again. She was glad to have such an excellent excuse. He tucked both lap robes around them with swift efficiency and cradled her close, sharing his warmth with her.

Quiet descended again, but now the silence was electric. Words, unspoken, vibrated in the air around them. Her head pressed against Trevor's broad chest, Clarissa closed her eyes and listened to his breath going gradually more ragged, to his heart pounding. She waited in a kind of trance for whatever would come next. It was not possible for a silence this charged, this eloquent, to continue unbroken.

So connected were they, she felt his words gathering, felt them run through him before he spoke.

"Clarissa," he whispered hoarsely. "Kiss me good-bye."

Aching, wondering, she raised her head and looked into his eyes. They were filled with torment. She reached up with the languid movement of a sleepwalker to touch his face with one hand. So dear, she thought. So dear to me.

"Good-bye," she whispered.

A rush of emotion shook her to the core of her being. No further thought was possible. She tilted her chin, arched her neck, and touched her lips to his. They clung there sweetly, light as breath. He kissed her back, his movements as soft, as delicate as hers, the essence of tenderness. Their farewell kiss was full of longing, sweet and dangerous.

It was impossible to tell how the kiss changed, whose impulse was stronger, or who began it. Clarissa sobbed and Trevor groaned, and each swept the other into a fierce embrace.

His hands slipped inside her cloak and slid around her waist, his palms hot and intimate against the thin silk of her gown. Shaking, she pressed herself closer against him, then instinctively shifted to give his hands more access. They immediately ran hungrily up and around her, in a primitive dance of greed and possession that made her senses swim. Her hands fluttered frantically against him, clutching his shoulders, his arms, his back. She could not hold him tightly enough. She wanted to feel every part of him at once. Maddened, she moaned and struggled against him, arching her back.

The coach door suddenly banged open, flooding the interior with daylight and a blast of cold air. For one frenzied moment, Clarissa did not even notice. Then the shock of their discovery struck her like a blow. She tore her mouth away from Trevor's and blinked dazedly at the horrified faces framed in the open doorway.

"Well!" uttered the vicar in a voice of outrage.

Clarissa gave a strangled sort of scream, and buried her face in Trevor's shoulder. It was an instinctive, unreasoning, attempt to hide. Had there been as much as a rabbit burrow handy, she felt she would have tried to crawl into it. Dear Heaven! If only it were possible to disappear!

Trevor's arms tightened protectively round her. He neither shrank nor cried out. His voice sounded over her head, and she marveled, terrified, at its utter lack of contrition. "Well?" he said coldly.

The vicar's voice throbbed with revulsion. "What is the meaning of this—this *spectacle*?"

"It did not become a spectacle, Reverend, until an audience arrived. Kindly remove yourself from that doorway!"

Clarissa gasped, and emerged from the depths of Trevor's greatcoat to stare disbelievingly at him. His dark eyes, fixed on the vicar, were blazing with anger and contempt. She would never have dared to speak so to a man of the cloth! For Trevor to *bark* at the vicar, after being caught in such grievous wrong-doing, and with Clarissa still actually in his arms, was the most amazing display of impertinence she had ever witnessed! And yet it was so like him. So exactly like him. To her dismay, she felt a foolish smile wavering across her face.

Mr. Whitlatch's gimlet gaze was transferring to Dawson. "And what the devil do you mean by sneaking up on me? Why did you bring the vicar along, of all people?"

Dawson, unlike the Reverend Mr. Henry, seemed properly cowed by Trevor's fury. "Sir, I never!" he gasped. "I never sneaked! 'Twas the snow, sir! And the vicarage was the first house I come to—and the vicar already mounted, and all—so I brung him!"

The vicar swelled with righteous wrath. "Do not seek to shift the blame for this regrettable incident onto the shoulders of your servant, sir! I spy the hand of Providence at work!"

Trevor seemed startled. "Providence?"

"Yes, sir, Providence! Providence, I say! It was ordained that Dawson should come upon me, and bring me to this spot, to witness what might otherwise have gone undetected!" The vicar's voice had taken on the ringing tones of the pulpit, and his face was scarlet with anger. "I have heard rumors, sir, of your past—tales of your conduct with females—tales that I would blush to repeat! I refrained, in Christian charity, from judging this girl, of whom nothing was known, but I suspected from the start that she was more to you than a *ward*! Verily is it written that 'wickedness proceedeth from the wicked!'"

Mr. Henry took a deep breath, preparatory to further remarks, but Trevor interrupted him. "Yes, very well! And I am 'the wicked,' I suppose! This is all quite elevating, but let us come down from the heights for a moment! Stand aside while Miss Feeney and I descend from the coach. You cannot shout at us in comfort while your face is at the level of our knees."

Some of the air went out of the vicar, but he continued to splutter indignantly as he backed off from the coach. Dawson, still appearing chastened from incurring Mr. Whitlatch's displeasure, hurriedly tossed aside the shovel he was gripping, pulled the step down, and reached to assist his employer to alight. But Clarissa hung back, her eyes wide with panic. She clutched rather desperately at Trevor's sleeve. Preparing to descend, he glanced down at her and offered a reassuring smile. He even patted the terrified hand that clung to his sleeve. "Come, Clarissa! The vicar cannot eat you."

She could not find words to express her shame and distress, so shook her head at him mutely. It seemed impossible to exit the coach and face Mr. Henry!

Trevor's hand tightened over hers and a swift frown darkened his features. "Come! I won't allow anyone to upset you."

A strange little laugh, almost of hysteria, escaped her. As if she could feel any worse than she did now! But Trevor climbed out of the coach and held his hand out to her with such calm authority, she took it. He lifted her effortlessly from the interior of the vehicle and set her neatly in the snow, where she somehow managed to stand. She placed one trembling hand on the door frame for support, feeling almost faint from embarrassment. But Trevor was beside her, lending her strength. She lifted her chin and willed her knees to stop shaking.

But it was even worse than she had guessed. In addition to Dawson and Mr. Henry, three slack-jawed yokels stood by, one leading a horse and another carrying two shovels. Their eyes were almost starting from their heads with curiosity and salacious enjoyment. It was clear that nothing so interesting had happened in the village for many a day.

Clarissa wondered, in a detached sort of way, if it were really possible to die of shame. She was inclined to believe it was simply a figure of speech. Had it been possible to die of shame, she would even now be lying lifeless in the snow.

Ignoring everyone else, Trevor turned to face the vicar, his demeanor conveying courteous deference. He started to bow, and opened his mouth to begin what Clarissa devoutly hoped would be a more conciliatory speech than he had yet offered. However, no words escaped his lips. The vicar bore down on them grimly, his aspect as fierce and unyielding as an avenging angel.

"Do not dare to mock me, Mr. Whitlatch! Do not dare! I stand before you, sir, as the spiritual leader whom God has sent to this parish! I demand your respect, sir! I go further: I command it!"

Mr. Whitlatch froze, his lips compressing into a thin line. He seemed to struggle with his temper for a moment, but, to Clarissa's relief, conquered his irritation and finished his bow. "I do not dispute your calling, vicar. I would be loath to show disrespect to a man of God."

Mr. Henry, gaining strength, pulled himself up to his full height and extended his arm, pointing accusingly at Mr. Whitlatch. "It is well! But I stand before you as something more than a humble vicar, sirrah! I stand before you as the father of the unfortunate lad whom you sought to dupe!"

Trevor's black brows snapped together. "You are laboring under a misapprehension! Nobody sought to dupe Eustace."

In his rage, the vicar's voice became shrill. "My boy believed this wretched female to be as innocent as he!"

"She *is* innocent!"

"She is your *doxy!*"

The ugly word seemed to echo in the stillness. For a moment,

everyone in the clearing ceased to breathe. They all stood paralyzed by the enormity of the vicar's epithet.

Then Trevor Whitlatch's right arm shot out from his shoulder
and his fist connected neatly with the vicar's jaw.

Chapter 25

The Reverend Mr. Henry dropped like a stone.

Almost immediately, the red haze of anger cleared from
Trevor's eyes. He stood over Mr. Henry, looking down at what
he had wrought. The vicar lay sprawled on his back in the snow,
seemingly stunned. Contrition stirred, but then he remembered
what the man had said and his face hardened. He would not
apologize. It was a shocking thing, no doubt, to strike a vicar,
but the biggest injury had probably been dealt to the man's
pride. And it had been the swiftest and most effective way to
deprive Mr. Henry of speech. He could hardly regret that.

"Help him up, Dawson," Trevor said shortly, and turned
away.

His eyes fell upon Clarissa. She was clinging gracefully to
the coach's door frame, but any impression of ease that her pose
might have conveyed was belied by her face. Shock had driven
all the color from her cheeks and widened her eyes into twin
pools of anguish. He had never seen anyone who looked more
in need of a stiff jolt of brandy.

Trevor crossed to Clarissa in two swift strides and put a sus-
taining arm around her. She did not move. Her eyes were still
fixed, dazed with horror, upon her prospective father-in-law
lying prostrate in the snow.

"I'm sorry, Clarissa. Fiend seize it! I shouldn't have done
that, least of all in your presence. I don't know what came over
me. Clarissa? Are you all right?"

Behind him, Dawson and the village boys were pulling the
vicar to his feet and dusting him off. Clarissa's eyes turned
slowly, painfully, to Trevor's. He saw the bewilderment in their
depths, and the shame. She did not appear to have heard him at
all.

She was trying to speak. He leaned in to catch her words.

"Did you hear what he called me?" she whispered pathetically.

Trevor suddenly longed to deck the vicar again. He put his other arm around Clarissa and held her close. She was shaking, whether from cold or shock, and as soon as his arms went round her, she clutched him like a drowning person. She also began to cry, in great, wrenching, sobs that he thought would tear his heart in two.

Bloody hell. He had ruined her life.

Aching to console her and not knowing how, he held her and patted her, murmuring foolish things into her hair. He tried to tuck her cloak around her, but, like most female clothing, it was an impractical garment. The slippery lining defeated every attempt to gather it. Her sobs did not subside. He finally lifted her bodily off the ground and tipped her into the coach. She landed on the floor, but it didn't matter. At least she was out of the snow.

Trevor turned to issue orders to Dawson, and discovered him tenderly tying up the vicar's jaw with a scarf. His mouth twisted wryly. If the facer hadn't succeeded in shutting Mr. Henry up, Dawson's bandage surely would. The village boys stood idly by; they had obviously been watching him comfort Clarissa. Well, let them look! He was past caring.

"Dawson, for God's sake, take these men away! And see the vicar home, would you? You can come back for us with a couple of saddle horses."

A few quick orders and the thing was done. The vicar, still livid but now rendered mercifully speechless, was bundled back onto his horse. Trevor summoned sufficient civility to bow and beg his pardon, but his apology was purely perfunctory. Dawson led the vicar's animal, and the village lads trailed reluctantly off in the party's wake. Trevor, having commandeered the extra blankets they had brought, returned to the still stranded coach. He tossed in the blankets, climbed in, and shut the door behind him before daring to look at Clarissa.

She had ceased weeping, at any rate. She had dragged herself onto the seat and was huddled against the wall of the coach, a woebegone and pathetic figure wrapped incongruously in red velvet. Trevor handed her a blanket. He then dropped onto the seat across from her and buried his face in his hands.

"I seem to spend most of my time apologizing to you for one thing or another," he said almost inaudibly. "I promise you, Clarissa, I'll put things right somehow."

"How?" she whispered.

He straightened himself with an effort. It was very hard to meet her eyes. He knew damned well there was no way to remedy this particular disaster. But hope was the least he could give her.

"It all arose from a misunderstanding. When the vicar recovers his temper, he'll see that. Why, I never would have struck him if he hadn't insulted you! He'll come to his senses and realize he must have been mistaken. And once the vicar acknowledges his error—"

"There was no error." It was the whisper of despair. Her eyes were blurred with tears. And even in this extremity, she was the loveliest sight he had ever seen.

Trevor clasped his hands tightly to keep himself from reaching for her. "There is no reason in the world why you shouldn't marry Eustace Henry. I will go to the vicar and crawl, if I have to, to make him see that." Anger welled within him as he recalled the vicar's self-righteous stupidity. The memory made him punch his fist into the seat beside him, and he winced as his sore knuckles protested. "Hell and the devil confound it! How dare he think for a *moment* that you aren't good enough for his precious son? He ought to thank God, fasting, that you're willing to marry so far beneath you!"

Clarissa gave a shaky little laugh, and he was glad to see a tiny smile warm her perfect features. "Thank you, Trevor. But it won't do."

He frowned. "Yes, by God, it will. That nincompoop! That Pharisee! He thinks his idiot son has fallen for nothing but a pretty face. Well, that may be, but what does it matter? There's so much more to you, Clarissa, than a pretty face! I envy him the discovery." Trevor's voice suddenly cracked. He looked away, startled by his own vehemence, and struggled to get a grip on his emotions.

He felt the light brush of her hand on his knee and glanced down to see it resting there, like a white bird that would fly if he moved. He did not move.

Clarissa's voice was very quiet. "If you manage to convince

Mr. Henry that I will be a fit wife for his son, then Eustace will renew his offer of marriage."

"Yes," said Trevor with an effort.

"But I cannot accept his offer."

Trevor looked up, startled. Clarissa's eyes met his, clear and steady. She looked perfectly calm, if a trifle sad. The tiny smile reappeared fleetingly. "I cannot accept his offer," she repeated.

"Why not?" he asked roughly. "What's to stop you?"

Her eyes were so beautiful. A man could drown in those blue depths. She removed her hand from his knee and leaned back against the squabs, regarding him gravely.

"I am very fond of Eustace, but I do not love him. He deserves better than that."

Trevor moved impatiently. "Rubbish! Eustace Henry, to deserve better than *you*? That's a loud one! Why, he's a nothing, a zero, a complete nonentity! You deserve better than *him*! You, with your beauty, and your fire, and your wit, and your sweetness—dear God!" His voice was cracking again. "There's not a man on the planet who is good enough for you."

And suddenly she was in his arms, laughing and crying at once, and covering his face with kisses. "Oh, Trevor, I do love you so!" she said.

The words shot through him like a lightning strike. He held her away from him and stared. She was smiling at him, with a look that took his breath away. "You love me?" he repeated stupidly.

She nodded mistily. Then sadness tore at the edges of her smile, turning it ragged, and dimmed the glow in her eyes. Her expression was that of a martyr—a willing martyr, but a martyr nonetheless. "I cannot marry Eustace Henry. I am in love with you."

Wordlessly, he folded his arms around her and pulled her close. Victory. Victory at last. Triumph surged through him, and fierce joy, and an odd twinge of guilt. Guilt?

"Are you sure?" he asked hoarsely.

She nodded against his chest. And then she said, haltingly, in a sad little whisper, the words he had thought he would never hear her say. "I would rather be your mistress than another man's wife."

Trevor let his breath go in a long sigh. Yes. This was wonderful. It was a pity she could not give herself to him unre-

servedly, but no matter. Victory was sweet—almost as sweet as
the girl in his arms.

But nothing was as sweet as Clarissa. Nothing as rare. Nothing as precious. He knew what it was costing her to offer herself to him, and felt humbled by the enormity of her sacrifice.
Humbled and ashamed.

Trevor closed his eyes and pressed his cheek against the top
of her head, breathing in the fragrance of her and fighting back
a lump in his throat. He finally had what he thought he had
wanted, and it was proving to be Dead Sea fruit. If he accepted
Clarissa's offer, she would never be a respectable woman again.
Not in her own eyes—nor in the world's eyes, for that matter,
and he had just experienced a sample of what that would mean.
His knuckles still stung from his reaction to it.

A surge of fierce protectiveness shook him to the core of his
being. No whoreson vicar was going to insult his darling girl.
Never again.

"Marry me," he murmured. The words were out before he
could stop them. His eyes flew open, startled. Good God! Had
he actually said what he feared he had just said? Or had he only
thought the words, in a moment of weakness?

Oh, Lord, he must have said it. Clarissa had pulled back and
was staring at him in shock. "Wh-what did you say?" she asked
faintly.

Her hair, her beautiful, touchable hair, was tumbling down.
There were tearstains on her cheeks. Her cloak was all awry,
and most of her was hopelessly tangled in the blanket. She
looked ridiculous. She looked gorgeous. He felt an idiotic smile
spreading across his features.

Well, what the hell.

Trevor slid onto one knee in the broken-down coach and
grinned recklessly at the unmarriageable girl before him.
"Clarissa, will you marry me?"

He had become used to her extraordinary beauty, but nothing
could prepare a man for the sight of Clarissa Feeney transfig-
ured with joy. Before his very eyes, she transformed into a creature so dazzling that if he had been able to think at all, he would
have congratulated himself on escaping with his vision intact.

"Oh! Oh! Oh!" was all she said for some appreciable time,
but she said it repeatedly. It was only after he had kissed her
thoroughly that she was able to reply sensibly.

"Trevor!" she gasped, clutching his lapels. "Are you sure?"

"Perfectly."

Her eyes searched his anxiously. "But . . . do you love me?"

"To distraction!"

"But you told me you wanted to marry a titled lady."

His eyes gleamed, and his arms tightened across her back. "You will be Mrs. Whitlatch before the year is out, and that will be title enough for the present."

Her starry-eyed glow returned. "There is no title I would rather have. But—"

"But?"

Her forehead puckered again. "I don't like to think of you abandoning your social ambitions, just to marry me."

He grinned. "Very well, I won't. By this time next year, you will be Lady Whitlatch. The crown owes me a favor or two."

"How lovely! But—" She blushed guiltily, and bit her lip.

"Yes?"

"Oh—poor Eustace! What will become of Eustace?"

Trevor cupped Clarissa's face in his hands and addressed her with great firmness. "Eustace Henry will fancy himself heartbroken for perhaps a month. Two, at the outside. To repair his spirits, his parents will send him to visit a favorite uncle, where he will promptly fall in love with the sister of one of his cousin's friends. And, my darling, you have not yet answered me."

A ripple of laughter escaped Clarissa. She curled contentedly on his lap, playing with his fingers. "Then yes, Trevor," she said, shyly but happily. "I will marry you."

Epilogue

Shortly after the New Year, Fred Bates received a letter in the morning post. This is how it read:

Dover, 4th January

Bates—

You'll be glad to hear I took your advice. Found respectable employment for C. & removed her from Morecroft Cottage. You may send felicitations to us c/o Pensione Bella Vista, Venice, Italy. Returning to England in April.

Wish me happy, old man.

W.

P.S. Still consider it my duty to avenge you. Have formulated new scheme that will completely ruin La G.

I plan to make her a grandmother.

The Wily Wastrel by **April Kihlstrom**

Juliet Galsworth was surely unmarriageable—imagine a lady interested in fixing mechanical things. But then James Langford came to visit, revealing the fine mind of an inventor behind his rakish exterior. Shared interests turned to shared passion. But would dangerous secrets close to James's heart jeopardize their newfound love?

0-451-19820-4/$4.99

The Magic Jack-O'-Lantern by **Sandra Heath**

A heartbroken—and invisible—brownie hitches a ride with an angelic heiress...and brings his mischievous brand of Halloween chaos to high society. The problem is, the pompous Sir Dominic Fortune does not believe in such superstitions...until the magic of love makes his heart glow brighter than a jack-o'-lantern.

0-451-19840-9/$4.99

To order call: 1-800-788-6262